CHASE

THE SENATOR'S DAUGHTER

KAT BEAUPRÉ

DEDICATION

In Loving Memory Of Kathy Hall.

Table of Contents

Chapter 1

In the summer of 1995, Lieutenant Jack Chase was home on leave in Virginia as the state faced its worst flooding disaster on record. Two opposing weather fronts converged over the Appalachian Mountains, and for the next four days, the superstorm dumped several feet of rain. By the end of the first day, Tuesday, June 27th, many western rivers toppled their banks, emptying a deluge of water across Greene and Madison Counties. Homeowners could only watch in horror while overflowing rivers washed away houses and farms. Entire lengths of roads and bridges were eroded by the power of the currents as though Mother Nature took a giant eraser and rubbed them out. The TV weatherman claimed half the state had washed away and the other half would follow the next day. Jack stepped outside and noted the water draining from the house but did not see signs of erosion to the foundation. He wiped the rain from his eyes and took his waterlogged body back inside. Upstairs, he packed his uniforms and civilian clothes to report back to duty the next day. That night, another foot of rain fell, causing vast swathes of mountain forest to slide down the western slopes of the Appalachian Mountains, choking the valley rivers with uprooted trees, giant rocks, and billions of tons of mud.

The following morning, residents that remained woke up to a scene not unlike Armageddon, forcing many to regret staying in their homes when leaving was still an option. That Wednesday morning, some could only watch as the mud and trees filled their houses before their walls burst. Many lost their homes, which had been in the family for several generations. The TV meteorologist called for another 36 hours of heavy rains, leaving many with few options, knowing crying won't do any good. Jack Chase stood in the kitchen watching the local news, looking out the window as several inches of water covered the ground. Soon, his mind began devising a plan to help. He was the firstborn, a natural leader, and a born fighter for others less fortunate, and Jack exemplified the young, solid Marine Corps officer. He was a fortunate man from a wealthy family, home on leave, and ready to save the town of his childhood.

As he looked out the kitchen window that morning, lightning flashed across the dull grey sky, revealing silhouettes of trees and hills hidden in thick, low clouds. He went to the rear door of the mudroom and opened it. The door swung outward, letting in a loud roaring sound from the tons of rain pelting the trees and bushes while thunder rolled in the hills behind. The clouds looked like smoke as they lay on the ground, blocking out the sun and giving the day a premature twilight. The brick steps that led to the garage lay underneath several inches of standing water. The raindrops were undiscernible; they flowed steadily like a giant waterfall. When the door closed, the butler leaned his head around the corner from the kitchen with a look of surprise, his mouth half agape, as Jack stood in the middle of the floor, adjusting his sock. He plunged his foot into his rubber farm boot and reached for a set of car keys hanging on the wall.

The older man approached a moment later, holding a raincoat under his elbow and a Stetson hat in his hand. He said, "Jack, the roads are impassable, so where do you think you are going?" He spoke in a professional demeanor, with a slight Irish accent. His voice carried his words in a matter-of-fact yet respectful tone. Jack smiled as he turned and looked into Mr. Digby's soft green eyes. The older man rubbed his clean-shaven chin and continued pleading with the always insatiable Jack. "If your daddy hears about this, he will surely have my job. Please, Jack, I've known you since you were a pup, and never once did you listen. Just look at it out there, my god. Just this one time, will ya think before ya jump?"

Jack scoffed and shrugged. "Relax, I'm just taking some sandbags for the farmers; no further than Madison Hills, I promise."

The butler said, "Don't ya think they should stay here when we need them, sir?"

"If the water level gets that high, we'll need an ark." Mr. Digby's eyes looked out the window with a slight nod. Jack stood up and said, "The town can use these more than us."

"But your father— "

With a gentle pat on Mr. Digby's back, Jack smiled and said, "My father worries too much about some things."

Jack lifted back the curtain as several more flashes of lightning crossed the window. Looking out, Mr. Digby said, "Your father gave strict orders, so at least take a coat and hat."

Jack placed the hat on with the brim just at his brow and climbed into the dark green rain parka.

Mr. Digby scratched his head and said, "Jack, this house has been in your family for many generations, since the time when James Madison was the president. I know how badly you want to help those in need, but... Oh, very well, just promise not to go getting yourself killed doing something foolish." Jack patted the man's shoulder with a smile. Mr. Digby nodded and said, "Aye, sir." Jack grabbed his Cannon camera bag, added a new telephoto long lens, zipped the bag, and closed the door behind him.

Outside, he looked up as a lightning bolt crackled overhead and squinted when rain showered into his eyes. Thunder crashed, and large raindrops mixed with hail pelted him. He paused, stooping and shrugging his shoulders, letting his hat brim drain the water in front while his rubber boots waded through the water to the garage. The garage had six standard-size bays, with a seventh bay housing an RV. Mr. Chase called it the family land yacht. Jack ran through a waterfall from the overflowing gutter and stopped at the third bay. His silhouette cut a fine profile, punching in the access code and waiting for the garage door as it opened. He had an athletic frame and stood just under six feet erect like a pine tree. Inside the bay, he walked to a row of pallets stacked with empty sandbags. He hopped onto the forklift, lined the forks to the pallet, and lifted the first one over the bed of his old cream-colored 62' Chevy pickup, careful not to damage the car in bay two. Nudging the levers to the left, and lowered the pallet onto the bed, sinking the truck's rear a few inches. In the second bay was his father's old Corvette Stingray, a 63 dark blue with a split rear window—the one his father took his mother in for their first date.

Jack climbed onto the truck's bench seat and shut the door with a clang. Deftly, his left hand reached for the choke on the red-colored metal dashboard while the other slid the key into the ignition. He pulled out the choke, pumped the gas pedal, and turned the key. The cold engine sputtered, so his foot pumped the gas pedal until the engine smoothed to a steady idle. The gear shift was on the steering column, with three forward gears and reverse. He pushed the lever up, eased out the clutch, let off the brake, and rolled out of the garage, splashing through heavy standing water on the brick driveway. He switched his wipers to high speed and leaned forward to see the road through the heavy, pelting rain as the windshield started to fog up from his body heat. The town was just five miles away, but by the time he approached the main road, there were road barriers and flashing lights on orange warning signs that read, BRIDGE OUT AHEAD. The old truck veered around the barriers. Ahead, he could see the road partially washed away on the edges, forcing him to drive around large rocks and parts of trees in the oncoming lane. He kept the engine RPM up through the foot deep of water while holding his speed slow so the water did not splash into the ignition system and stall the engine.

In Madison Hills, he stopped at Giffords Gas, and while his tank was filling, he surveyed the scene of destruction while leaving the engine running. The town was next to the Rapidan River, whose banks had overflowed, covering much of the town. When the gas pump stopped, he wadded inside to pay. He paused inside the door; the familiar smells in that old wood and brick building raised the corners of his mouth into a smile. His eyes wandered over the shelves' rows that held many of his childhood memories. As kids, he and his friends collected bottles and cans for change and rode their bikes to Giffords to buy gumballs, ice cream, and candy bars. In the last two days, the rains removed half of the town. Several homes he used to play at were gone, taken by the river, and replaced with piles of debris and fallen trees. The same river he used to fish in, and just below the old bridge is where he learned to swim. In high school, he and Betty went skinny dipping under the full moon and drank his first beer. Floods on rivers were common and manageable, but this was his first experience with real devastation. He caught a glimpse of himself in a convex mirror, now a grown man, he wondered what it would be like to be in a war. He saw an older man standing at the counter, the shop owner, Mr. Gifford. That man never did like him or his friends, but his wife was always nice.

Mr. Gifford asked, "Just where do you think you're off to in this weather? Most roads are closed, you know."

Jack handed a twenty for the gas, saying, "Bringing down some sandbags."

The man snorted while shaking his melon-sized head, his large carcass leaning over the counter while raising his finger to make his point at Jack's fool-hearted actions. Perhaps sometime in the man's childhood, he failed at a dream or endeavor, and then forever after that, he followed the herd carrying a grudge. For some people, failure is a potent deterrent to pursuing personal goals. Now, after a lifetime of under-achieving, the man with a grey beard criticized Jack's willingness to help. He wagged his finger as a neighbor, lecturing a little boy caught doing something stupid. He said, "Never did understand your death wish, Jack. It seems crazy to willingly go out in this kind of weather; you could get swept away in the blink of an eye. Only a fool would do such a stupid thing."

On the other hand, Jack's father believed that failure was the opportunity to learn, and when one knew enough about something it would lead to success. At that moment in the store, seeing the clerk wagging his finger reminded Jack of the time when he was a little boy watching a Roadrunner and Coyote cartoon. He chuckled when the coyote flew passed the Roadrunner in a bat suit and fell off a cliff with the whistling sound of doom followed by the cratering thud. Little Jack rolled on the floor with laughter as his hands imitated both cartoon characters with his little hand splatting on the floor.

His father said, "Do you know why the Coyote never catches the Roadrunner?"

Jack, being a small boy, shook his head, his little mind never gave it a thought. His father said, "Because he has that," He pointed to the TV as Wiley Coyote: Genius, flipped through the pages for a new plan in the Acme catalog. "If he were to pick just one of those plans, such as the rocket skates, and perfect it, he'd surely catch the roadrunner. Always practice, practice, practice. And always stick to your plan."

Over the years, this philosophy has worked for Jack; someday, he would instill it in his kids, hopefully boys. His father taught him that the road to success is paved with failure, so embrace your failures; it's one step closer to success, and what parent doesn't want their kids to turn out?

Jack smiled at the clerk and said, "Thanks for staying open." He nodded and touched his hat to the lady. His boots made a solid thud with every step, and his jeans accentuated his athletic figure. As if an added accent, the bell gave out a bright ring behind him when the door closed.

The wife, still smiling, said, "No, it's no death wish. That's a real man. The girl that marries him will be real lucky."

"Whose that?"

"No one yet, but I know she won't be from here."

Jack drove the old truck through a foot of water and stopped two miles down the road, or what remained of it, next to a group of volunteers placing sandbags against the rising river. The two pallets of bags he brought should cover a quarter mile for about two more feet of water height. He and three others unloaded the pallets of bags and he returned to the truck for his camera bag. Leaning into the cab, he unzipped his parka, tossed the camera strap over his neck, switched it to auto mode, and zipped his parka over it and stuffed the telephoto lens in his pocket.

A familiar woman's voice called out from behind, she had to yell over the river's roar. She said, "I see you're back home, Jack. I'd like for you to meet my niece, Elizabeth." Jack turned around, and the lady smiled and pointed to an SUV about fifty yards away. The older woman said in a perky voice bordering on pleading, "She's very nice. She's from Utah and not used to our climate, but she goes to school at Georgetown. Won't you meet her, Jack? Oh, and don't worry, she's not a Mormon."

He smiled and looked down the road to the parked SUV with its flashers on and saw her sitting wearing a red parka with its hood over her head. "Sure, just give me a few minutes here." He walked over to the workers laying sandbags, picked up a bag, turned his torso, laid it on the growing sandbag wall, and grabbed the next. After several minutes of sweating in the rain, he snapped pictures of giant boulders and trees rolling down the river, with workers in the foreground pointing to them. Across the river came a loud crashing sound. He switched to the telephoto long lens and snapped pictures as a large tree barreled through the old Morgan place, washing it downstream. A collective sigh came from the onlookers.

The foreman told Jack, "Without these bags you brought, we would have to give up. Thanks." They worked quickly to build a wall above the overflowed river to control water erosion. Their sandbag wall grew in length and height. But would it hold against the new rain forecast?

A yell came from up the river near the old bridge wash-out. Jack looked through the crowd and heard a boy shouting, he pointed in the river. A little black dog swam about two hundred yards away, caught in the current, trying to keep its nose above water. The boy's older brother held his hand, as he leaned over the water as far as his arms would stretch, grabbing for the little dog as it floated past. His brother and he stretched more, but then his grip slipped. The river swallowed him, and he bobbed as he flowed away. One person said someone should call for help, and another pointed to the boy. Working further downstream, Jack saw the bobbing body nearing and knew that calling for help does not save people; it only recovers bodies. He handed his camera, dove into the muddy torrent, and swam with all his might after the boy while the current pulled them farther downstream.

Though his raincoat slowed him, his quick actions helped him to grab the boy's ankle above his shoe. Jack scooped the torso into his armpit with his other arm, leaving his arm from the elbow down, free for paddling. He reached the other arm around the boy's shoulder, giving him two arms and two legs for swimming. He stroked and kicked his hardest, angling toward the near shore using while avoiding floating trees and rocks. Two hundred yards later, he reached out, grabbed the sandbag wall, and climbed onto it. The boy had stopped moving moments earlier. He placed the body on the wall and pumped the river out of his lungs. Cold, wet, and exhausted, he helped the boy to his feet, and looking up he saw a crowd rushing towards them.

After several congratulations and thanks, Jack's body started shaking uncontrollably with hypothermia. He returned to his truck along with Mike, his old school friend, who returned his camera, saying, "I took a few pics of you diving in after that boy, and I hope you don't mind." He fist bumped with Jack and chuckled, "Dude, that was awesome."

The niece, Elizabeth, left the warmth of her aunt's SUV, adjusting the hood on her raincoat, she walked along the bank fifty yards to Jack's truck, and slowed when he began stripping off his wet clothes. Standing naked above the waist, he leaned into the truck, pulled on an olive-green t-shirt. Then, he put on a gray hooded sweatshirt and a ball cap before adding his parka. Mike watched the young woman approaching, "Hey, Bro, I got to go help these guys, but next time you come back, let's hang out."

Elizabeth approached the truck smiling, and with a wave, she said, "Hello, I'm Elizabeth. My aunt came over earlier. Wow, that was scary, but you saved that boy."

Jack looked into her eyes, and his chills stopped, then his body felt warm. He lost all sense of time. His ears were full of river water, and he heard himself say mutedly, "Hi, Elizabeth, I'm Jack." He swallowed and said, "I usually don't do things like… this—."

She cut in and said, "—What, save little drowning boys or meet local women's nieces?"

They laughed, and he said, "Guilty, ya for sure, small town's gossip so much that it's best not to go there. But, to show I have an open mind in your instance, let's get a picture of our first meeting." He handed his camera to Mike and put his arm around Elizabeth. After clicking the aperture, he asked her, "So, Elizabeth from Utah, what are you doing for dinner tonight?"

She laughed and said sarcastically, "Oh, it's probably not a good idea to be dating one of the local boys. I have heard stories and know the type. Besides, you're crazy, doing dangerous things; besides, you easily could easily have drowned."

Jack said, "I think that when it's your time, it's your time."

She said, "Even if I were to go out with you, all the restaurants would be closed. But we are having fried chicken and potato salad. Why don't you follow us instead?"

"Your aunt makes the best-fried chicken in the county." He gazed at her face; her parka hood covered most of her head, and her wet bangs covered so much of her eyes that it was difficult to know they were sapphire blue with a hint of violet. He noted that her wet hair looked chestnut brown with a reddish sheen, and she stood several inches lower, a perfect height for slow dancing and kissing. Though her bulky parka concealed much of her physique, he supposed, coming from the mountains of SLC, she more than likely stayed in shape, possibly hiked and skied. Reid was her last name.

Was she from the same Reid family that ran a nationwide logistics business? From the corner of his eye, he noted an image approaching; it was her aunt. He said, "Looks like your aunt is ready to go, and I should run home and change first."

Elizabeth agreed, so when her aunt approached, he asked Elizabeth, "Were you just out here on a visit and came to see the great flood?"

She cocked her head to the side and her lips curved up in a grin. She said, "Not really. I'm going to law school at Georgetown, and since classes are over for the summer, I'm visiting before I go home to Salt Lake City next week for the summer." Jack felt her aunt's eyes watching his face with every word Elizabeth spoke.

Her aunt tugged his arm, pleading, "Jack, now you must come by for dinner. Now I won't hear a word otherwise…"

"Sure, I'd love to if it's not an intrusion."

The aunt chuckled and then pointed to the side. "Looks like you have an interview to give before you can get out of those wet clothes."

A newspaper reporter, along with her cameraman, combed the crowd, asking for details of the near drowning. The crowd retold the tale, he saw the photographer take the boys picture and Jack climbed in and started the truck. As he let the clutch out, Elizabeth opened the passenger door and climbed onto the bench seat wearing a big smile. "Sorry, I hope you don't mind me coming with you, but my aunt wants to be sure you come for dinner."

Jack smiled and turned the truck around and headed back home. His eyes glanced over to her and he asked himself, 'Can this girl be the one?'

When they neared his family's land, she scooted next to him. She said, "I was getting a chill, but you're so warm." He pulled her closer still. She asked, "Are you as crazy as they say you are? Risking your own life to help others is one thing, but doing stupid things for no reason is another story." She leaned her head on his chest and put her hand in his.

He laughed with her. After a long silence, in a quiet voice, he said, "As an officer, I have a duty to protect my troops. In one of our war history classes, I learned about a great warrior named Crazy Horse. In battle, he was unbeatable, and witnesses on both sides said that after a fight, he would shake hundreds of bullets from his clothes. He was fearless, knowing the gods protected him."

She scoffed, "Graveyards are full of men who thought they were bulletproof."

Jack pulled her wet hair away from her eyes and said, "When it's our time to go, then we go, but until the good Lord calls my number, I'm giving life all I have."

"How about me? Will you protect me, too, Jack Chase?" His chest heaved. She reached up and held his face in her hand. He nodded yes. Her blue eyes grew brighter, and she snuggled back onto his chest. "That's good."

His foot slipped off the clutch as he downshifted, and they laughed. He pulled into the driveway and set the brakes. Looking deep into her eyes, he said, "You're not like the other girls."

She held his hands and said, "Well, I focus on school."

"That's it. You are a serious person, Elizabeth, and not one to be taken lightly. Some of them can be annoying because of their immature self-centeredness. Honestly, I find it boring." He turned off the motor and looked at the rain pelting the fogged-up windshield. "We'll have to make a run for it in this rain."

"Do we have to? This feels so good right now."

He pulled his hood up and tossed the truck's door open and said, "I'll introduce you to Digby."

Chapter 2

At the start of the fall semester, Jack married an expecting Elizabeth and began his classes at Georgetown for the Marine Corps. That following spring, Elizabeth gave birth to Ryan, the first of their two boys. After receiving his master's degree during the peacetime in the nineties, Jack's company made several trips overseas, participating in various joint ally exercises. Most of those trips meant Elizabeth and the boys we're on their own for a week or two. Fourteen months after Ryan was born Cody arrived along with Elizabeth's law degree. She and Jack worked hard to balance their professional careers while raising their two young boys. Their mom held each up to the bathroom mirror and pointed to all their common characteristics. They had dark- blonde hair, but Cody's was lighter, blue eyes, though again Cody's were bluer and both were big for their age. Often, she'd tell them how smart they were. The boys excelled in school, and the Chase family seemed blessed.

While Elizabeth doted over the boys' upbringing, Jack taught them to be responsible young men, taking them to ball games, fishing, and church on Sundays. Jack and Elizabeth spent all of their free time with their sons, and those boys were the favorites of the neighborhood kids and their teachers. They lived in officer housing at Quantico, Virginia, near Jack's family home at Madison Mills, where they spent half their holidays. Though Mr. Digby was getting on in his years, he still helped and doted with excitement when the boys visited. The Chase family estate was a large three hundred acres of horse ranch where they raised thoroughbreds. In the summer and every other Christmas, they visited Elizabeth's family home in the mountains near Salt Lake City, where they learned to ski, fish, and hike. Everyone looked forward to the holidays. Before 9/11, they shared the assumption, like many Americans, that terrible things only happened to bad people and that, somehow, their lives were shielded from the darker side of life.

Then came a morning in September that left Americans shocked and thirsting for revenge. After 9/11, Jack received new orders to report to Camp Lejeune, North Carolina, where his unit would receive training for the upcoming war against Saddam Hussien. When he shipped out with his unit, they promoted him to captain, and Elizabeth took a job in Wilmington working as a junior attorney for the DA's office. In school, their sons, excelled at everything they did, and their classmates admired them. However, the ongoing Iraq war changed life for Mr. and Mrs. Chase. From an outsider's point of view, everything appears the same, but for Elizabeth and Jack, something has changed at the core of their relationship. Fate was busy germinating a seed that would someday disrupt everything in their world. Elizabeth's hard work brought her career opportunities, and Jack thrived as a fighting unit leader overseas. After time and a promotion to major, Jack decided to stay the military and make it a career. They each seemed satisfied and Elizabeth and the boys supported his career decision, and the boys remained honor students. The family missed Jack Chase and video conferenced regularly. All looked forward to Jack's return on leave from the war. They had several plans for the two-week leave but had to postpone it indefinitely. The following year, the boys grew bigger, while Jack spent most of it on the front line in Iraq, so Elizabeth focused her energies on her career now that the boys were big enough to care for themselves more. At the office she was encouraged to run for public office, which appealed to her, but had to be put on hold until after her new pregnancy.

The following summer, Elizabeth gave birth this time it was a little girl that she named Emma, in honor of her grandmother, Emma Reid who had dark hair and hazel eyes. She was a tiny baby with dark hair and large dark eyes. Everyone knew her as a happy baby who never cried at night. That winter, Elizabeth took the kids to SLC for Christmas while Jack stayed and fought in Iraq during the big push to capture Saddam. The following summer, when Jack returned home on leave, Ryan and Cody were supposed to go fishing with him, but he drank too much and spent more time with his Marine buddies than his family. Elizabeth reasoned to the boys that it was from combat fatigue, but he was a war hero. While Jack was at home his uniforms adorned the coat rack, the backs of chairs and in the master closet. His sons admired him and spent hours looking at his uniforms and ribbons asking him to tell and retell the stories how he earned each medal. After that, they begged him to take them shooting.

In 2009, Emma turned seven and started second grade. By this time, Ryan and Cody were in high school and stars on the football and baseball teams. Emma's mom bragged about Ryan and Cody to the other moms while shopping. Little Emma listened to every word, though she heard the stories a hundred times, and dreamed someday people would praise her accomplishments. She heard stories about how awesome her brothers were at kickball in the second grade and how they always scored the winning run in the big game. Emma concluded she would grow up just like her big brothers and her mom would boast of her super awesomeness.

Unlike her brothers, the tallness gene eluded little Emma, but it didn't stop her from having a big dream. In the second grade, she told her family and everybody in her class her dream of kicking the winning score in the big kickball championship, just like her big brothers did. Dreams aside, Emma loved kicking a ball and running around the bases. Kickball is like baseball but does not use baseballs, gloves, or bats; instead, it uses a big, bouncy, pinkish-red schoolyard ball kids can kick or throw; the same ball used for dodgeball. Emma learned two essential points about playing kickball from Cody: it's easy to understand, and a big play can make even a little kid popular. She remembered that the neighbor kids practically worshipped them. Now a second grader, naïve little Emma couldn't wait for kickball season, which coincided with baseball season—at last, her day had come.

That spring, when the recess bell rang, Emma was always the first kid to run to the gym box and grab her favorite yard ball. She would tuck the ball under her little arm and race across the classroom through the outside door straight for the ball field. Somedays, the teacher barely got the door opened in time. Emma's little legs moved so quickly that her feet hardly kept up. Those were her favorite childhood memories. Like all kids, she imagined herself as a great player. While the other little girls liked to scream and run from the boys, Emma wanted to win the big one and be a hero, just like Ryan and Cody.

One May morning, in the last week of the school year, her teacher, Ms. Radcliffe, said, "I have a special announcement. All of you have been working very hard this year, so tomorrow, we will play Mrs. Bogensberger's class in a kickball game at lunchtime. Eat fast, and let's meet at the field for practice." The cheers echoed in the hallway. Emma's first thought conjured up an image of her family at the game, cheering her team on and maybe the press would interview her after the game. She imagined her picture on the front page.

After school, when Emma's mom got home from work, she ran to the door jumping all around and asked, "Mom, can we go to the store, please? I want to get a pair of boots like Cyndi's. Please, Mom?"

"Honey, I have a lot of work to do to prepare for this case. Get one of your brothers to drive you and grab Domino's for dinner."

"OK, Mom, but can you tell Ryan for me 'cause he never listens to me?"

That night, while the Chase family ate pizza, Emma's cheese topping plopped onto her lap while she stared at her new boots. Her mom scolded her, and Emma went to clean the mess. When she got up from the table, she asked Cody, "How do you like my new boots?"

He glanced down and said, "Hmm, I thought you said you wanted boots; those things look like they were bought at the hardware store. They're just green rubber and look like frogs," he laughed and reached for a couple more slices, stacked them on top of each other and stuffed them into his mouth in one swallow.

After dinner, Emma skipped down the hall to her room and tried on all her socks to get the perfect snugness. Next, she swung her feet, kicking at the air, running up and down the hallway for several minutes. Spinning and laughing, she ran into her mom. "Emma, stop running in the house and take those boots off. Show some respect, young lady."

"Yes, Mom. Hey, can you come to my kickball game tomorrow?"

"I'm sorry, hon, but momma has a lot of work to do."

"They just don't understand," Emma told herself, "But they'll see." Her excitement kept her awake that night as she lay in bed, hugging her little green frog boots.

Her class played the other second-grade class at lunch recess the next day. Miss. Radcliffe's team took the field first, and Emma was between first and second bases. The other team scored a couple of runs since Tommy, one of Miss Radcliffe's outfielders, was sleeping in the outfield, and the ball bounced behind him. The following two batters kicked the ball right to the pitcher for easy outs. Then, her class was up to bat, and their first batter, a big kid for his age, walloped a kick over everyone's head, making it look easy. Then they scored one more run, and Emma stepped into the batter's box with two outs. She kicked her boots at the ground, digging in with her plant foot. The catcher laughed, "Hey, check out the dorky frog boots."

Emma exclaimed, "Ha, frogs might be small, but they can jump really far."

The pitcher was a lefty, so when he delivered the ball, his arm swung in a wide arc like a sidewinder rattler. The ball bounced with a reverse spin that rolled right into her plant foot, preventing her from stepping into her swing. It did not go as she had dreamed, and she kicked the ball right at the first baseman and was out number three. Emma stood looking at the pitcher momentarily, unable to think or speak. The pitcher and catcher laughed as she hung her head. One bad play in baseball, deflates the player, but everything changes with one good swing at bat. When she again could think, she sulked back to the sideline, wanting to cry. Her brothers should have taught her that baseball is a game of winning and losing. In every pitch and every swing, there's a winner and a loser.

Miss Radcliffe meant for the game to be a classroom rivalry to learn about fair play and teamwork. While most kids tried their best, they jeered and cheered, just having fun being little kids. Both teachers often reminded the kids, "Be a good sportsman, cheer on your teammates, and do your best, but winning isn't everything." Emma's brothers taught her that winning isn't everything, it's the only thing and win at any cost or you are weak.

Near the end of recess, with a tied game, Emma's teacher blew her whistle. She said, "We have time for just one more kicker before the bell rings." All the kids raised their hands to be next up. She pointed at Emma. "That's no fair," cried Jimmy, "She's your favorite." He frowned at Ms. Radcliffe, scrunching his face as if he drank vinegar.

Ignoring Jimmy's opposition, she turned to the other kids and said, "Most of you have been on base twice, and some have gotten to home plate. Let's play fair and give others a chance, too. Emma hasn't been on base yet."

Jimmy pointed to Emma and yelled, "But she will blow it! Now, there goes our chance to win." He threw his hat on the ground and kicked at it, but his foot missed, and the other kids laughed.

Emma dusted off her new boots, stepped into the batter's box, stared at the pitcher, and took a deep breath. The pitcher yelled to the field, "weak batter, move in." The team filled the infield diamond. Emma looked out at the empty outfield. Next, she looked at the runners on bases; her class had kids on the first and third bases. "Come on, Emma, kick me home," yelled the boy on third base. She lined up towards the pitcher, stepped off three paces back, and kicked her toe into the ground. As Emma swung her leg, the pitcher rolled a fastball that hit a rock in front of her, causing it to veer to the left. The other team yelled, "STRIKE ONE," and laughed.

"This is going to be so easy," said the pitcher.

Her face remained expressionless. She paced three steps back from the box, kicked the toe into the ground, bent her knees, and leaned forward with her eyes glued to the pitcher's hand.

"Hey, Em. You're a loser," laughed the pitcher.

She yelled back, "The only reason you're the pitcher is because of your mom. Come on, roll one right here," she pointed down to her toe. "I dare you."

The catcher gestured towards the side of the field. "Hey, look over there, it's your dad."

Emma turned to look, and her eye caught the moving ball as it rolled past. "No, fair. I wasn't ready. That's cheating."

Her teacher, playing the ref, said, "Strike two, Emma, make this one count."

Emma stood still, facing the pitcher, her hands clenched into fists. This time, he rolled a curve ball around her. Her classmates laughed at him. Emma stepped off three steps, bent her knees, and kicked her back foot into the dirt. He rolled the next pitch right down the alley. It was the pitch Emma had hoped for. When the ball was halfway to the plate, she began her steps. She leaned forward, planted her left foot, and, keeping her head down, she kept her eyes focused on the middle of the ball. Her right foot swung and hit the ball the hardest ever. The ball flew off of her foot. WHAM! She looked up as the ball flew over the second baseman's head like a bullet. The other team screamed at the outfielders to hurry. The ball bounced safely deep into the outfield since the other team was inside the baseline.

Emma screamed and jumped up and down, and her team waved their arms like windmills, yelling, "RUN EMMA, RUN!" She ran the bases, then stopped at home plate, jumped up as high as she could, and stomped her feet on home plate. Now a victor, she stood up with her arms stretched to the heavens while her class mobbed her. For Emma, this was the best school day ever. Standing on home plate, she wiped off her little rubber froggy boots. As her class cheered, she couldn't wait to get home and tell her mom. That night at home, her mother and brothers were at a high school game, missing dinner. Over another Domino's pizza dinner, she told her dad about the game and how she scored the winning kick. He nodded twice, grabbed a plate with five slices then shuffled off to his study, shut the door, and drank with Jim Beam. For little Emma, many years would pass before she won at anything again.

***

Her dad received new orders a month later, and the Chase family moved again. But at her mom's insistence, her and the kids moved back to her hometown, Salt Lake City, Utah. Emma spent her days playing alone that summer since she didn't know the other kids. Later that summer, her dad was put on severance, the Corps. was sending him home after eight years of combat in Iraq and Afghanistan. Major Chase spent most of his days and nights drinking whiskey and sat alone snarling at shadows and yelling in his sleep. Emma closed her door daily after breakfast, turned on music, and colored or read. One day, just before the fourth of July, while playing with her dolls in the front yard, she met another girl walking her dog. The girl approached Emma and said, "Hello, are you going into the third grade?"

Emma stood up and studied the red-haired girl, and she said, "Yes." Her neck craned as she looked up at the taller girl. Rachel stood four inches higher, her blue eyes sparkled in the sun, and two front teeth were missing when she smiled.

Emma asked, "What's your name?"

"I'm Rachel, and you must be Emma."

After a minute, Emma asked, "Will you be my friend?"

Rachel giggled into her hands. She held her gaze on Emma's face, and her smile grew even bigger. "OK."

Life at home for Emma dragged on that summer. Her parents fought too much, and her brothers were too busy, so Emma often went to Rachel's house to play. She learned about the new school, her new teacher, and which boys were cute. Rachel had no siblings, and for her, Emma was like her little sister.

Emma couldn't wait for school to start. One day, she asked, "Does your class play kickball?"

"What? I've never heard of it. What's that?"

While Emma explained the game, Rachel shook her head and said, "It sounds fun, but we use those balls to play dodgeball or tag. One time, playing dodgeball, I threw it so hard that I hit Marcus in the face, and his nose started to bleed." They giggled. "I'll show you where he lives, it's just a couple of blocks over in that ugly green house."

* * *

That fall, Emma started the third grade. At recess, she'd eat lunch and play outside, but one day, she didn't feel well and stayed behind in the classroom. The teacher took her to the nurse's office. After the nurse checked her out, she waited in the nurse's office for her dad to pick her up since her mom was at work. When he entered, she sunk farther into the chair, turning red as an apple. His breath smelled of alcohol, his appearance was scruffy, and his clothes were unkept. She lowered her head and stood behind the nurse. After that incident, she never said she didn't feel well, no matter what. She loved her dad, but since his discharge or leave or whatever it was, he had nothing to do and wasn't his usual self. Later, when she asked her mom about his behavior, all her mom said was that she didn't understand either. At home, Emma did her best to cope with being alone. Her oldest brother Ryan was a senior in High School, far too busy being popular, and Cody was a junior. Worse, her mom was too busy running for an open congress seat, and her dad just cleaned his guns and drank. Everyone was too busy for little Emma. Rachel replaced her own family.

After the scene in the nurse's office, Emma didn't have the same enthusiasm for recess and began waiting at her seat until the other kids left before she went outside. Sometimes, she stood alone off to the side. On her father's bad days or after one of her parents' knockdown blowout fights, she'd stay at the back of the schoolyard looking out the rusty cyclone fence. Alone and away from the others, she would press her little round face against the rusty chain-link and stare at the backwoods. On those extra sad days, she wore her lucky green froggy boots. Instead of sitting at the front of the class, she moved to the window side at the back. While the teacher talked, she would gaze, lost in a daydream, looking out the window at the Wasatch Mountains.

One day, Eric moved his seat behind her to look out the window. As they looked at the new snow on the peaks, he told her why he moved to that seat. He said, "As soon as the new snow covers the mountains, it's elk hunting season. Would you like to go?"

Emma realized she was no hunter nor interested in killing any animals. After that, she sulked while the teacher lectured. She nodded off, dreaming of climbing over that tall fence in the back and seeing a beautiful and fun land where she felt happy and safe. That afternoon when the bell rang, she waited at her desk until the other kids left. When the room was quiet, Emma crept out the back door and walked to the rusty cyclone fence at the back, dragging her boots and looking back to see if anyone followed. Sure that she was unobserved, she walked the three hundred feet and stopped.

Though the fence stood a full ten feet, it towered at least thirty feet in her mind. Her little fingers felt the corroded cyclone wire, and she looked up to the top. She pulled downward, and it held her weight, so she wrapped her fingers around the wire. Next, her right boot came up and tucked into the mesh. After a deep breath, her little hand grabbed up higher. She kept climbing higher and higher, always looking up at the top. Past the midpoint, she placed her boot toe, reached above as far as her short arm could go, and grabbed hold as tight as she could grip. She reached up with her left arm and grabbed hold. Then higher, after she caught her breath, she went for the top, but her left boot slipped off. Emma didn't want to get in trouble, but now she worried she would fall and break her neck. Then, her family would for sure make fun of her.

As her hands clung to the wire, they weakened. She tried to get her foot onto a hold. Her hands and feet trembled, and then the fence started shaking. She hung exhausted and unable to get her footing. The more she tried, the more they slipped off from shaking.

At last, she got the left boot's toe barely set on the wire, but her foot shook, and it was about to slide off. She looked up at the top, and then the fence shook harder. She panicked, her breathing turned into sobs, and then she made the big mistake of looking down. The ground swirled, making her dizzy; it looked far below. Her little hands were wet with fear and losing their grip. Tears streamed down her little face. One girl came to the fence. "Emma, come down, or I'm telling, and you'll be in big trouble."

Emma's voice was weak. "Help me, please. I'm going to fall. Hurry."

Little Emma never again tried to climb that, or any other fence. As she grew into a young lady, she avoided risky actions. Instead, she focused on safe endeavors, like the praises of being a good student. She graduated High School with top honors winning praise from the Chase grandparents. After which, she chose to attend BYU and stay close to home. When she completed her junior year of college, her future looked certain. Emma knew she would follow her mom and next go to law school. Stay on the ground and leave the climbing to fool-hearted crazy risk-takers.

Chapter 3

In May 2024, Emma completed her third year of college at BYU in Provo, Utah. Above Provo, the still, snow-covered Wasatch Mountains shimmered in the clear blue alpine air. The lofty peaks shimmed in the morning sun and retained their white caps deep into the summer months. One of the tallest peaks rising above the campus is Provo Peak. Every year, the Phys-Ed Department held its annual Provo Peak Trail Challenge to celebrate the end of the spring quarter. Since her freshman year, Emma joined the herd, walking, running, and scrambling up the jagged ridge to the summit of Provo Peak. Students jeered each other while others cheered for their friends. For Emma, it reminded her of those days playing kickball. Her friend Rachel said that Emma obsessed about beating Brandon that year, but Emma overlooked her comments.

Earlier that Christmas, one of her friends gave her a Garmin watch. After learning to use it, she started hiking the peak weekly and timing her hikes and runs. Next, she evaluated her shoes and boots and improved her diet. When the race day arrived, she stood in the middle of the pack but drifted into the front with the faster runners at the start. A month earlier, she had determined to get a better result she would need to start near the leaders. It was a sizzling summer morning, and puffy clouds drifted overhead while birds sang in the forest. She shook her arms and legs, jumped and rotated her neck, and then crouched with her knees bent for the starting gun.

The pistol fired with a loud bang, and onlookers cheered the tight group of runners as they sprinted like a mob into the woods. She sped her fastest through the flatter first part, trying to stay up with the real contenders. When they entered the woods, the trail angle kicked up and narrowed with patches of rocks and fallen trees. Their shoes danced over the awkward boulders and cobles while less agile ones stumbled or tripped. After another mile, the trail rose at a steeper angle before switching back and forth through a forest of tall fir trees. As the cross-country team surg ahead, she slowed down and jog-walked on the twenty percent slopes, her Garmin said she was just a little faster than her personal best time. She was ahead of her personal best time by a few minutes. Her friend, Brandon, helped coach her and told her she could expect to go harder than in her training during the race. He was right; though she was at her limit, she knew not to give in to the pain. When she got to the creek crossing, everyone leaped from rock to rock to avoid wading the stream. She did her best to follow another girl's feet, watching as they darted over the rocks just a step behind giving her no time to process but only to act. Her Hoka trail shoes kept their grip to the weird angles of the rocks. She never stopped or slowed and made it across without a misstep to her own surprise.

The course went through a patch of melted snow for another mile higher on the mountain. When the girl in front of her skidded, she slid into her, knocking both of them down. After they untangled their legs, she checked her watch and was still three minutes ahead of her best time. Around another switchback lay a big fallen tree. She climbed under the trunk as a man leaped over it without breaking his stride. She looked up and recognized the blue shorts and red Bonzai t-shirt. It was Brandon. DANG, IT. When she got to her feet, she put her head down and ran her fastest to catch up. After half a mile at maximum effort, she was right behind him but out of breath. He slowed for the next obstacle and she caught her breath again. They tromped and slipped through another muddy section, causing her to fall backward off a slippery rock like slipping on ice. It hurt when she landed but she rolled onto her front and leaped up to stay with Brandon. His shoes sprayed mud on her face as she followed through the mud. She wiped her eyes and kept running as the trail led towards the backbone ridge above the tree line.

The jagged backbone ridge loomed for hundreds of feet above, and most runners scrambled up the low-angle rock face avoiding it until it joined at the upper section of the ridge. Emma opted for the backbone ridge. During her practice, she found a route along the ridge where there were hand and footholds. It was a quarter mile scramble along steep, exposed rock with no ropes but the view was fantastic soaring a mile above Provo. Sticking with her plan, she cut to the left and rose higher to get on the ridge route. It was slower than the face direct route but seemed to her, safer. Emma slipped that winter and slid several feet before stopping by grabbing hold of a small tree. After that hike she learned about Hoka shoes, and like her little green froggy boots they became a form of security. While other girls wore heels, Emma often wore her green Hoka shoes. She once told Rachel, 'If a man doesn't like them then he's no man for me.'

Not relenting to her fears, she veered u a little trail to the narrow bare rock edge, above was only blue sky and the other side dropped down a cliff for a thousand feet. Using her hands and feet, she grabbed hand holds and placed her feet flat on the ridge's grippy granite. Her foot placed she reached above and grabbed the edge of a large broken rock and pulled herself higher and made another foot placement. Always looking up for the next hand hold and always moving she climbed up to a crow's nest on the ridge. A flat spot that she stood and took in the view to the valley. Below she saw the trail runners scampering up the face, ahead of her she knew the ridge grew sharper but with good foot and hand holds. After a few more minutes of climbing, she scrambled to the top of the ridge and saw the trail as it switched back to the right. Below, she spotted Brandon moving steadily up the face route making good time. She stood up and ran over the next rocky section along the top of the ridge, jumping from boulder to boulder, ignoring the hazards, he looked up as she moved ahead. She knew it was a risky, but brilliant move. Her smaller frame and lower center of gravity gave her an advantage on the knife edge over his larger, huskier frame.

Close to the summit, the ridge merged into the trail. Less than a mile from the finish, the trail again flattened out. At that point, his larger more powerful frame and faster speed gave him the advantage. She grunted and breathed in gasps, forcing her legs to keep running in the thin air. He turned his head as she joined the trail, just two feet behind, with the finish line was nearing. He stopped and climbed over a large fallen tree while Emma dove under the trunk and pushed herself ahead.

Brandon pushed himself passed Emma and nearly printed away on the flatter section below the top, but Emma put her head down and forced her legs to run quicker. The gap closed and they sprinted for the finish line, passing, both three more runners. Emma grunted, leaning forward, stretching her legs, and widening her stride. She moved to the left seeing the cross-country team and the coach clapping at the finish line yelling encouragement, and waving towels. They lunged for the finish line. From the corner of her eye, she saw him gasping and out of breath with drool and snot flowing down his haggard muddy face. He grunted and looked across and stumbled on a loose rock. He put his hands in front as his body crashed on the trail, but Emma never changed her stride. Exhausted, muddy, and sweaty, she crossed the finish line at full speed and hit her stopwatch. She kept walking across the summit and stopped at the lookout view sign. With her hands on her hips, she tried to catch her breath. Her Garmin showed she had a new PR, finishing by nine minutes, but for Emma, the best part was the view of Brandon behind her after the finish line. It took months of hard work and good coaching, to beat Brandon was a great accomplishment for a non-athlete. It felt good, maybe as good as making the winning kick in kickball back in the second grade.

Brandon stopped at the viewpoint and looked down at his bleeding knees. He wiped the sweat from his face and checked his elapsed time on his watch. Out of breath, he nodded to Emma, "Congratulations, good run. You had me even if I didn't fall."

Emma smiled and said, "Thanks. I gave it all I had I wanted to make my coach proud." "Wow, what a view. I'm so amazed Emma, sheesh, you was a good student."

Brandon shook his head and deeply breathed, "Geez, I never knew you had it in you." He shook her hand and patted her on the shoulder. Next year I'll be ready for you."

***

That night, the BYU students celebrated the completion of another school year: Frat and sorority houses filled with students celebrating their accomplishments. At Delta Chi Rho, students crammed inside, dancing and laughing, surrounded by booming music. Out back, more hung out in the pool, splashing and diving. Emma and Rachel adjusted their chairs to view the patio roof better.

Daredevil fools dove from the roof doing funny stunts like Keystone Cops. They climbed up the side of the building, like the cliffs of Acapulco, to the patio roof and then pushed each other off while their audience laughed. A large football lineman leaped and landed with a flop near their seats, spraying water high into the evening air and dousing them.

Emma shrieked, grabbed her beach towel, and shuffled out the side gate in her flip-flops. She dried herself and plopped on the stairs, wrapping her towel around her shoulders. A gray and black husky dog approached the bottom of the stairs, wagging its curled tail. Emma held her hand out and whistled, "Come here, sweety." The dog barked and wagged its tail. "Come here, boy." The dog bounded up and nuzzled her. She stroked its thick gray and black hair above its eyes, then scratched behind an ear. The dog nuzzled her hand to keep petting, then laid its head in her lap and sighed. Behind her, the sliding door slid open, letting out the rowdy noises layered with smoke and beer; she cringed at the foul odors. Her shoulders and neck scrunched under her towel, and she rubbed her eyes. The dog lifted its head and watched the other person approach.

Rachel said in a cheery, lighthearted voice, "There you are. You had me worried. I thought you were doing another one of your disappearing acts. What are you doing? The party is back there. Come on, Em." Her body hovered over Emma, her hands on her hips.

Emma's head looked down at her feet. "I'm drying off.

"Well, we should get back in there. You're missing out on all the fun."

"This morning before the run, I heard a song at a coffee shop, but it was nothing like what I had heard before. The words gave a haunting warning, and the music was mesmerizing; it was like I was traveling through time and space." Emma's voice trailed off while her fingers played with the dog's fur, yet her eyes looked out into the distance. She did not turn around.

After a moment, Rachel came down the steps in front of Emma. She bent her knees, picked up Emma's hands, and smiled. In a gentle voice, like the one used when speaking to children, Rachel said, "Yeah, that's cool, and I'd love to talk about it more, but come on, Em, everyone's here."

Her brows furrowed as her voice pleaded, but Emma did not respond. Rachel looked at her friend sitting in the evening air, a large towel wrapped around her, wet hair hung over her back in long curls. She looked back at the party. "Come on, Em —."

Emma sang-spoke, "Kicking around in your hometown, waiting for someone to show you the way —."

Rachel shrugged, "OK, that sounds weird if you ask me. What's so special about it?"

"It made me think of when we were kids. We always used to say, 'when I grow up,' remember that I wanted to be a Zookeeper and you wanted to —."

"And I wanted to be a rich millionaire and travel the world, and I still do. Next year, we graduate." Rachel huffed. She rose, her red hair shined under the porch lights, and her lanky figure grew into a tall voluptuous body. She could have come from a model shoot.

Emma stood up, and though her friend was standing a step lower, their noses touched.

Emma shrugged her shoulders, her face scrunched up, and she said, "We graduate, and then what?"

"What do you mean?"

"OK, you become rich, but that's not all… so what else will you —." Her phone vibrated and chirped.

Rachel cooed, "Ooh, a late-night text. Is it from that cute boy?"

Emma shook her head, "It's my mother. URGH, if she'd just — ."

Rachel exclaimed, "Oh, my god, you are so lucky to have such a great mom. Now, come on before they forget about us in there."

Emma said, "Forget you? I doubt it." She giggled, then looked over her shoulder at the patio door. "Fine, let's do this." She forced the edges of her mouth into a smile and gyrated her hips with a giggle. They rocked and swayed their hips and shoulders and raised their arms to the beat as they entered the party, squeezing between the crowd. One girl asked Emma, "OK, we are having this major discussion and need your help, so where is the greatest place for spring break?"

One boy yelled, "Tell her, Emma, it's Daytona—." No, it's not," yelled another. "It's Cancun."

Emma said, "who cares? As long as it's not Cleveland."

Rachel turned around, and her eyes grew large and focused on the stairs. The staircase descended into the living room. Several kids sat and lay on the stairs, hanging out. A shirtless young man tromped down in his boxers, wearing a tie printed with images of various sexual positions on his head, like a bandana. Rachel exclaimed, "Talk about an entrance. Wow, Cammy, baby."

The young man slid across the floor in his socks, spun around, and called, "Hey dudes, who's hungry? I had some extra money on my parent's debit card." He slid across the Pergo floor in the foyer, spun around, snapped his fingers, thrust his pelvis Elvis-style, and pointed to the door.

The doorbell rang, and someone called, "Hey bro, it's the pizza dude."

Cameron bowed and raised his hand, then ran the gauntlet of hands high-fiving. He slapped hands behind his back, over his head, and with one girl, they tickled the palms. He spun around, pointed to the door, and said, "Big John, care to do the honors with me?"

His friend opened the door and let the dude with boxes of pizza in. The pizza dude carried the stack to the table. Cam and Big John counted the pizza boxes and checked the toppings. After the last box, Cam pointed to the boxes and said, "Hey man, where's my meat lovers with extra cheese, bro? Where is it, man?"

The pizza dude wiped his upper lip and pushed his glasses up as he fished out the order- from his pocket. His eyes moved up and down the order twice as he looked at it. With a cough, he apologized and explained that the order didn't include meat lovers with extra cheese, only the meat lovers and the pepperoni ones. He stood motionless, looking across at Cameron. Someone cut the music off then the crowd murmured in almost silence.

Big John scratched at his beard and said, "Cam bro, sorry, I thought I added it."

Cameron turned to his best friend, "You did. If mistakes were made, it was by this low life that can barely masturbate." He picked up a red plastic solo cup of beer and took a big drink. The pizza dude shuffled his feet and stuffed his hands deep into his pants pockets. He looked at the people in the room, and his eyes stopped on the tall, red-haired diva, Rachel; he smiled. His voice stuttered and almost broke.

He asked, "d, d, does, does that mean… does it mean that… Uh, damned, I delivered all these; you owe me a tip!"

"You want a tip?" Cameron took a sip, reached his arm out, and turned the cup upside down, pouring beer over the kid's head. "Next time, make sure you get the order right if you want a tip, asshole. Now get out of my house."

Big John shoved the kid out the door and shut it. The party cheered, then Big John and Cam high-fived and bowed to the music beat.

Rachel hugged Big John, "That was amazing. You guys are great."

A picture fell off the wall, and the front door shuddered when it slammed. Rachel turned around, "Em?"

Emma stood out at the street corner as the night breeze gave her goosebumps. She pulled the towel tighter around her neck and shoulders. Behind the door opened and closed. Emma looked up at the clear night sky. The stars glowed in the high mountain air.

"Hey, you gonna go back in?" asked a male voice, "or you gonna call it a night?"

"Hey Martin, what are you doing out here? Thought you were chasing that girl?"

"Brittany," he said. Oh, she's not really into me. I guess I'm too boring. You look sort of good, Em. Anyway, I just wanted to ensure you're, OK?"

She turned around and hugged him, "Thank you for caring. I'm fine, but sometimes, it seems I'm living an alternative life. I mean, what if none of this is real? What if I'm in the third grade dreaming and wake up to my real life." She looked at his imperfect profile under the streetlights. Even in the dark, his looks made her feel comfortable and safe. He stood at an average height and had black hair, a scruffy goatee-ish beard, and thick, messy black hair, wearing a Hawaiian shirt and flip-flops. She stopped noticing any of his imperfections years ago. To her, he was Martin, like family.

"Yeah, Em, I'm that way a lot, too. It's weird how everything can flip." He held her hands, looked her in the eyes, and said, "We've been friends a while. I remember this awkward little girl when you moved to the hood." They laughed. "Hey Em, remember the first time we drank a beer?"

Emma giggled, "Oh, geez, and how about when we snuck that pack of cigarettes from your dad? Geez, I could use one right now."

"So, out with it. What's really bothering you?"

"Well, is this what I'm going to be doing for the rest of my life?"

"Repeating your junior year of college forever? Trapped as a forty-year-old still going to school with the same dumb-ass friends in the same town, yeah, that would be terrifying. Sure, it's fun now, but as Einstein would say, it's all relative."

Emma nodded and crossed her arms. She said, "Brr, I'm getting cold."

He put his arms around her shoulders and hugged her. She turned around, put her fingers around his neck, and kissed his cheek.

"Come in before you freeze into a popsicle." He said.

"Geez, one more year of this and then law school with more of it with future attorneys. God, it's so complicated. How am I going to finish?"

Martin nodded, "Yeah, sometimes I wish I would have been a welder or a plumber. My cousin is one, we're the same age he's out there working making good money and I'm here mooching free pizza. He said they do well, and he seems happy."

"Everyone in there just seems to try to impress each other. The only reason Rachel is my friend is that she is so impressed with my mother. My oldest brother is an officer in the Marines, and Cody's an attorney—"

"Yeah, they are just like your parents."

"Well, I realize that I don't want to be an attorney; I feel so trapped." She wrinkled her nose and lips like a bunny, and Martin chuckled as he slipped his arms around her, pulling her closer to his chest. He held her in silence. "Hmm, this is nice," she said faintly. "I guess there it is, now that I've said it."

"Em, that's way too deep tonight for my little brain. I wouldn't know what you should do about anything. Hell, I'm still thrilled with drinking beer and watching porn without getting in trouble." Thy chuckled. He said, "Hey, want me to give you a ride home?" He smiled and winked, but Emma shook her head. "Oh, hey, congrats on beating Brandon, so nice job, girl. Bet that shocked him."

Emma laughed then stood on top of the curb leaned out and kissed him. "You're cute in your own nerdy way. We had some fun times, but—"

"But?" He shrugged, relaxed his shoulders, raised his eyebrows, and gave a curious smile.

After a moment's hesitation, she said, "But," her voice trailed off, "I have to go do this fundraiser early with my mom tomorrow. Sorry, but it's election year again."

Martin hugged her and kissed her on the head, "Call me anytime, babe." He leaned to her ear and whispered, "I know you'll be back someday. Hey, I guess this means I should give Brittany another shot." He pranced back up the stairs and grabbed the door. He called back to her, "wish me luck. Woo."

Emma swayed and giggled, "Tell you what, if I'm still around this weekend, let's hang out. See ya."

He stopped and turned around; she stuck out her tongue, and he smiled. "Sounds good, Em." He slid in the door and disappeared with a whoosh. Emma laughed, then crossed the street, humming an old tune. 'I love rock and roll. Put another dime in the jukebox, baby.'

Chapter 4

The next day, Emma stood off stage at the Hyatt Hotel's Grand Auditorium, looking at the full house. Sure, her mom has had to be at rally events in the past, but this one looked to be making some sort of statement to the press and the voters. Maybe this election her mom was worried about her Democratic opponent. Her feet shuffled in place while she looked at her phone. She stood in the wings off to the left, across from the podium. Loud popular music played over the PA system, and the walls echoed and reverberated. Rachel yelled over the noise, "It's like a concert. This is so cool, Em." A man wearing a tuxedo passed by, stopping at the center-stage.

At the podium, he said, "Hello, Utah. Welcome, brothers and sisters, welcome to our Republican Patriots." The crowd cheered and stomped. Sporting a smile and joining in the applause, he said, "I would like to extend my heartfelt welcome to the individuals of the genuine American party, the party that stands for the best qualities of America." He paused while the people clapped and waved their arms high overhead. He exclaimed, "You are the keepers of faith in God's country." The crowd roared. When the applause dwindled, he raised his deeper voice and said, "I give you Utah's OWNnn, Senator, Elizabeth, Reid, CHAASSSe." His voice sounded like the announcers at the WWE wrestling matches. The senator waved her hands as she stepped up to the podium. She smiled and waved to her adoring fan base. The music and the applause erupted as bright digital lights flashed across the room to the music's beat., changing from bright white to red and blue. Behind the podium hung a giant screen that showed an animated eagle soaring in front of an American flag waving in an imaginary wind. She waved and waved, stepped to the podium, and adjusted the microphone while flags waved and confetti fluttered from above. Senator Chase wore a blue power suit with white trim. She parted her shoulder length, straight hair on her right side and combed it to the side behind her ears. For a senator, she looked young and healthy. Emma noticed she looked taller on the stage than her five-foot, four-inch frame. She and Rachel watched the giant screen with her mom in front of the American flag screen. Her mind rendered up one word: hypocrisy. Rachel looked more animated than the night before at the big frat party. When her mom began speaking even, Emma shut her brain off and listened to the words spoken in her mom's speech.

"Thank you all for taking time from your busy morning to come here and to support the good work we have started. Yes, thank you, sir, mam. It's good to see you, Utah." She pointed to specific large donors in the crowd and applauded. "How are we doing, Utah? Ah, yes, do we have the greatest state? Yes, we sure do, and today, I am not here to give the usual political speeches but to talk about critical issues within our community. Though we have reduced crime since we took control from those ungodly Democrats, we have much more work to do. It's not perfect yet and this fall I need everyone to vote. Those liberals want to defund our police and we know what that will mean. We want to give our police and prosecutors more funding to get tougher, enforce the laws on our books, and bring God back into our schools and get that liberal filth from our public libraries and schools." The audience applauded and the screen behind her showed animated confetti with the police arresting Democrats. "There is an additional problem; those blue states, like California, made such a mess of things that we're seeing a rise in homelessness and crime right here in our beautiful state." The crowd booed. "Yes, they screwed it up so bad that now vagrants are coming here. I guess they thought they could come here and squat on our sidewalks and take up our resources. Many are illegal foreigners, stealing from our businesses, assaulting innocent people, raping innocent girls and using drugs in our city. Now, we must clean up after those liberals once again to make it safe for our families so they can once again attend church services."

Emma looked at the wall of people swaying and clapping in unison to the blaring pop music that shook the floor and the walls while dress shoes and high heels stomped with the beat. Rachel grabbed Emma, "This is the greatest thing I have ever seen. Oh, my god." The moment swept Rachel along like a tsunami, she waved, clapped screamed and stomped along while uploading selfies.

Her mom leaned into the microphone, "I'd like to introduce my own Utahans. You all know my two sons, Ryan and Cody. I promise they will continue our fight when we pass the torch. Here they are, along with their little sister Emma." The two men, one in uniform, pushed past Emma, waving to the crowd and giving their mom a huge hug to an even greater applause.

Rachel said, "Go on, Em, we're all waiting for you." She shoved Emma, then clapped with the beat. The music and cheering continued; Senator Chase waved as if to each person in the auditorium. With her sons on each side, Emma stood outside of Cody. Emma's petite five feet all but vanished behind Cody's six-foot-four frame. Their mom posed for the cameras with her hands on her son's shoulders, she smiled as wide as the Grand Canyon. Emma looked at the hundreds of exhilarated faces while lights and lasers flashed and changed colors to the throbbing beat. The crowd chanted six more years to the beat.

The Senator stepped back to the microphone when the music subsided again, and once all eyes were back on her, she changed to a somber tone. She said, "Sadly, not with us anymore, but here in spirit, a true war hero, an officer who brought freedom under the American flag for so many millions of people in Iraq and Afghanistan, a great man who made many sacrifices, the departed, Major Chase of the United States Marine Corps, my husband. Can I get a Hoo-rah? As we all know, someone brutally assaulted my husband while he was on leave from the war at our own home, a place of sanctuary and peace. A burglar stabbed him multiple times. Today a liberal crooked judge released the evil man who did this from prison. Join with my family, let's all stand up for justice and the safety for our families. Who here among you stands with me?" We can't do this fight alone, but I promise we will fight them with all our strength. But we need your support, generosity, and love as decent God-fearing human beings so give to a worthy cause, or this could happen to anyone else. With Jesus' help we shall win this fight God bless all of us.

Emily looked about the room; the people cheered and clapped harder, and their shoes stomped louder. The floor shook as if the Earth was splitting apart. Even though she knew her mom was full of shit, Emma clapped and cheered with the tidal wave of emotion that swirled around the auditorium. Emma shook her head and thought, 'Mom does this same speech daily, and yet the money pours in.'

After another electrifying rally, Emma stood at the auditorium exit in the lobby of the Hyatt Hotel. She spent the next hour shaking hands and smiling for pictures with many of the senator's supporters until her smile muscles were too sore. She worked one side of the room, her brothers another, and her mom stood in the center. Emma looked over her shoulder while listening to benefactors say how nice was to have her mom there for them. She took a long breath when she saw a large crowd gathering waiting their turn. After a long hour of smiling too much, she gave one last toothy smile for the cameras and excused herself to join her mother. "Excuse me, congressman, may I cut in and borrow my mother for a moment?"

Her mom kept smiling as they stepped away, "Oh, Emma, have you thought about your birthday?"

"No, Mom, I haven't, but I am sure you've made all the arrangements."

"Well, dear, it's not every day that a girl turns twenty-one. I may have a few suggestions, so meet me in the limo. David here will escort you." Her mom lowered her voice and looked around. She said, "We can't be too safe with security in this part of town."

"That's what we need to talk about, Mom. I don't want a big deal; I'm fine." She looked down at her phone screen to see who was calling.

Her mom leaned into Emma's ear, smiling like a Cheshire cat, while her hand seized the phone. She lowered her voice, "Why can't you be more like your brothers? Sometimes, I can't believe that you're my child. You act like it's all about you, but there's so much to learn about life. Now grow up." Emma's mom could have been a ventriloquist, her smile never left her face the whole conversation.

Emma shook her head and put her hands in front, "I wish I were never born." She snatched her phone but dropped it. As she picked it up, her mom's phone rang. Her mom said, "Do you have it? Then call me when you do, but for now, get busy." Emma looked up at her mom's expression. It could have been good, bad, or even the end of the world, but her mom's facial expression revealed nothing and her eyes remained big and happy. Emma looked around; her mom shook hands, smiling with her adoring supporters. After years of her mom's rallies, she knew that her mom could get pretty keyed up with too much caffeine at these events, and who knew what else. Any time for an honest conversation with her mom would have to wait till the smoke and dust settled. Besides, Emma loved her life and knew she didn't mean to hurt her feelings. She knew her mom must be correct, and after re-thinking she did feel bad for talking like a spoiled little girl so after they were alone in the limo, she'd apologize. Her mom stood with her brothers for the cameras again, they all looked to be enjoying their time together so much Emma began to cry. Her family was hugging laughing and tasing ach other like best friends.

Emma went to the Lady's Room wiping her tears. "Rach, where are you? Rach, oh, there you are. Let me borrow your car, and you can ride home with my mom. Where are you parked?"

Rachel stood still. "Uh, it's in the parking garage Aisle D, and the keys—" Emma finished, "are in the gas tank door." They giggled. "Thanks, Rach, I owe you."

"Where are you going, Em? When will you be back?"

"I don't know, and I don't know. See ya later. I need some air. Trust me, I'm fine." They giggled, and she said, "I'll see you tonight. Love you."

Chapter 5

Emma left the auditorium side door to the parking garage entrance, outside the heat radiating off the sun-exposed concrete wall, filled her lungs with hot air like a dry sauna booth. She felt her skin begin to sweat under the direct sunlight. Walking in high heels with a backpack draped over one shoulder fatigued her legs and before she made it to the garage her legs started shaking. Inside the garage her phone chirped, the sound echoed off the concrete walls. She glanced down, 'Ugh, mom,' she half said. Car doors shut, engines started, and tires squealed around the tight corners in the parking garage. While Emma read the text, a large, black SUV screeched around the corner, catching her off guard. It sped towards the exit; its hulking large size took up most of the aisle. She jumped away and pulled herself tight against the side of a concrete post, her heart pounding. When it passed, its mirror whipped the air next to her head. She gasped out of breath.

"Geez" She exclaimed.

After a moment she caught her breath and spotted Rachel's white Audi. She pushed on the gas door, popped it open, and lifted the key. Chirp-chirp, the car's lights flashed when her thumb hit the unlock button. She tossed her phone into the center console, pushed the start button, put it in reverse, then stopped and adjusted her rear mirror. Her phone chirped again, and she glanced at another text message from her mom. 'Urgh.' and continued backward. Her eyes glanced into the sideview mirror. She screamed, hit the brakes, opened her door, and ran to the back of the car.

On the ground behind lay a businessman not moving. He could have been at the rally moments ago. Her eyes moved up and down the body. Was he still alive? Was he breathing? She watched his chest, but it was too hard to tell if he was breathing. Her hands shot up to her temples. She almost screamed, but instead, she ran for the car. "I need to get help." She opened the car door and grabbed her phone to call her mom. At her side, another car trying to pull out honked, and she jumped in to move her car out of their way. Too excited, her foot hit the gas, and the tires squealed. She hit the brakes and stopped where another car was backing from its parking spot. She reached for her phone, but it had slid off the console onto the passenger floor. She hit the horn and yelled to herself. A rear car blocked her from going backward, and the way forward was blocked by a gray-haired lady backing up slower than a snail. Now, to get back to the man, she needed to exit the garage and re-enter. She honked the horn and the old lady creeped forward. Once there was enough gap, she drove around her car, raced for the exit and grabbed for her phone. Her right hand gripped it tight while she turned onto Temple Street. She saw a green light up ahead and hit the gas to make it while trying to call her mom to get help for the man. She would make an illegal U-turn at the light and return to the garage. Everything became a white blur when her body slammed against the side window. The airbags exploded from the dashboard in less than a millisecond. Glass filled the interior, letting in the hot midday summer heat, and she gasped to breathe.

Emma pushed and shoved on her door, but the airbags gave her no room. She reached for her seatbelt. She tried and tried, and finally heard a click. Struggling to get out of the car she slid under the airbag while looking for her phone. With her right arm, she reached, but it was too far away. She caught her breath, and after a moment, the airbags started deflating. Her hand snatched the phone sending a wave of relief to her overly tense muscles. With the phone inches from her eyes, she tried to call 911 but the touchscreen had shattered and didn't work. She yelled, threw it, and pushed at the jammed door, but it didn't budge. She leaned her shoulder, rocked back, then shoved the jammed door open, and clambered onto the middle of the intersection.

Clambering onto her feet, Emma began to run across the street to the sidewalk in her high heels. Her face began to sweat while dodging the oncoming traffic. After avoiding a pickup that was driving around the accident, she leaped onto the sidewalk, ran inside a Café, and into the bathroom. She splashed her face and arms with cold water and removed her dress. Underneath her dress, she wore a tank top and shorts. She let her hair down and sat on the toilet with a cold towel on her neck. There came a noise behind the bathroom door. She sat still and lifted her feet off the stall floor. Under the stall, a pair of men's shoes stopped at the stalls, and she sat motionless, holding her breath. After a long moment, the shoes returned and opened the bathroom door. Emma leaned over to see a pair of black Puma gym shoes. She held her breath and remained motionless for another minute. Her lungs began to hyperventilate. She needed to breathe fully, 'But what if the man returns?' She needed some water to drink. Finally, she left the stall and wiped her face and neck before looking for a seat in the cafe.

Emma chose a booth facing the door near the emergency exit and asked for ice water as she slid onto the bench seat while searching through her little wallet. She had keys to a car that did not work, a broken cell phone, one debit card to an almost empty bank account, and a few dollars in cash. Looking up, she noticed the room décor. On every wall hung stuffed game animals. Her eyes studied the animals above the reception as six workmen followed the waitress across the floor near her booth. A young man with striking good looks smiled as he helped move a couple of tables. She turned away and noticed the head of a deer looking at her. It had an odd expression, one of remorse, like "Why? Why me? I was having a good life, then you had to bring the gun. Are you some crazed, sadistic person? Why did you do it, why me?'

She turned her head away, but then her eyes drew to the tables as the men sat down. One of the workers went to the jukebox. A sad song started playing, one of longing and despair by Patsy Cline: 'I fall to pieces.' Emma turned around and saw the young man at the jukebox. He stood below that mounted deer that was looking at her. He turned and smiled; she smiled back. For the first time that day she smiled for real, but she grew nervous when he approached her.

"Hi, I'm Roy," he said with an irresistible big grin.

"Hello, Roy." His hair was dark almost black, his eyes looked hazel in the low light and when h smiled his teeth looked perfect, in fact she did not see any defects to his physique.

"Would you like to dance?"

"Where, here? I am fine, but thank you. I should really be going." Her eyes watched the waitress set a glass of water down. Ignoring the conversation, the waitress blurted out, "Excuse me, deary, can I get you anything else?" Emma shook her head no. "How about you, cowboy? What can I get for you?"

"Just this pretty girl's number, hon." He chuckled with the waitress, but his eyes remained locked with Emma's; they were playful and vibrant. His smile grew as he looked at her, and so did hers. Roy stood over five feet nine and was muscular with light eyes and dark hair. She liked his hair and wanted to feel it on her fingers. When he looked only at her, she felt warm and lost her previous concerns and worries. That face and that hair took over her mind. His demeanor looked gentle. And just like Patsy was singing, Emma fell to pieces.

Emma nodded yes with a giggle. She said, "No… Uh… I need to get going, well uh…."

He held his hand out, and after a pause, she placed hers on his, and his eyes grew larger.

She said, "OK, but just one dance."

He spun her around, two-stepping her into the center of the floor. Their bodies merged, and he held her waist in his arm while his other hand held hers. She held his face in her hands, and its smooth-shaven, perfect complexion had no flaws to distract her senses away from his lovely face. When he leaned her back, she ran her fingers through that thick black hair and melted. His arms felt strong as he held her after the music stopped. Then he said, "I promised just one dance. Come, meet my brother and my cousins." He escorted her to their table and brought up another seat.

He said, "This is my brother, and down there is Chico. That's my cousins Miguel and Luis. This is another cousin, Juan. We've been friends since we were little."

"Hello, everyone. What's your brother's name?"

"Francisco, but we call him Kiko."

Francisco turned and nodded to her, "What did you say your name is?"

Emma looked up at the TV over the bar just as the local noon news covered a story about her mom's rally. "Uh…" she looked back at Francisco, "I'm Emma, nice to meet everybody." She clasped the car key in her hand. "What kind of work do you guys do?"

Francisco said, "We work for the railroad, and after lunch, we're leaving."

"Where are you guys going?"

Roy laughed, "Everywhere, Emma."

A new song started with a piano intro; the singer had the voice of an angel. He sang about being free to face the life ahead. Emma turned and looked at the jukebox. Francisco leaned towards her and asked, "Do you know what this song is about?"

Her eyebrows scrunched together; her mouth puckered as she turned her head upward. "Uh, not sure, but it's so beautiful, and his voice is unusual. Is he English?" She smiled and swayed to the piano with her eyes closed. She said, "Tell me about it." Francisco stood five feet six and was built with stocky brown skin and big warm, dark eyes. He talked differently than the others. Perhaps more education, he just spoke in a typical quiet voice. She could tell he was not there to dance or impress her. She liked him and felt an instant trust.

He said, "There was a time when this musician was ready to give up; he had tried for years, but the band's records never made it to the next level. Instead, they became known as the support act for the headliners. This song was about his despair. He wanted to fly away and leave his life because he felt he was letting his family down. Anyway, his new bandmate, also a good songwriter, told him to try again. He hoped they could put all that despair into a song but not worry about the outcome this time. He rewrote this song, 'Come Sail Away,' Follow your dreams by embarking on a journey into the unknown by car, boat, or maybe by spaceship. Have faith and seek your pot of gold. It became a huge hit, and his life changed forever."

Emma sat still, looking forward at his face. She let out a sigh and smiled. "Have you ever done something like that yourself?"

"Well, here we are in Salt Lake, listening to this song, and yesterday it was California. Maybe tomorrow will be Colorado."

"So, you are Francisco, and you are his brother, why do you have such different names?"

Roy leaned into the conversation and pointed to his brother. He said, "That's because we have the same mom, but Francisco's dad is a burnout. He might even have invented wake and bake." He laughed and jabbed his brother.

"That's not very nice, you should apologize."

"Me? No-no-no, my dad was a hard-working man, and he married our mom and moved here to the US, where I was born. Kiko is from Mexico. I'm not going to apologize to him for his old man being a piece of shit.".

Emma's mouth was agape, and she sat back with her arms crossed, "It's been nice meeting you guys, but I should be…" then something caught her eyes from the bar TV. It was Senator Chase waving to the crowd. Francisco turned to see what she was reacting to, and then he watched her face. He asked, "How about you? What's your father like?"

"I don't know. He died when I was young. Mom said a burglar killed him when he was home on leave, but I don't remember."

Francisco said, "Sorry, but no kid should grow up without a dad."

Emma watched him reach into his jeans pocket as he set four quarters on the table. She looked at them, "Funny, but I don't use cash nor carry any change. How old are you?"

He laughed, "24. Here's to the past. Take these and go play G-25; it's for your loss."

"But I've never done that. How do I…?"

Francisco rose with a smile, "Bring the quarters, and I'll show you." She went to the Wurlitzer jukebox.

He said, "This is one that's old school all the way,"

"What do you mean?" she asked.

"See the records on the carousel, this plays real 45s. Put the money in here, and now push the buttons, that's it, G now the 25." The record dropped, and the needle glided on the top of the record.

"There, just like the old days, isn't that nice?" the singer sang, "Yesterday."

Emma leaned her back against the Wurlitzer, "This song is so beautiful; who is it by?"

"It's by the Beatles, or more precisely, Paul McCartney of the Beatles. He dreamed that he went away forever, and the whole song played in his head when he woke. Since it came to him before breakfast, he called it scrambled eggs. He realized our time is limited and to make the most of every moment."

"I can't imagine."

Roy said, "Waiting for life to begin, so typical of gringos."

Emma said, "With my dad in the military, we traveled all over, but that's not the same, and with my mom's career, I never get to be myself. I've never done anything I've wanted to do."

Francisco said, "I hear that a lot these days. Let me ask you, that woman on the news, who is she?"

"She's Elizabeth Chase, I'm sure you've never heard of her if you're not from here. What do you do when you are not a jukebox savant?"

Her eyes noted movement and the flash of something shiny by the door. She said, "Dance with me." She wrapped her arms around his torso. The scent of jasmine flowers wafted over his senses. She held him tight and buried her face in his work vest. He rocked left and right to the sad, slow beat of the song.

"You can come up now; he's gone."

Emma's arms dropped to her side, "Sorry, I guess I got lost in the song."

"Or maybe you wanted to avoid the cops. It's OK, you're among friends."

"Can I trust you?"

"Sure, what's up?"

"In the parking garage at the Hyatt was a man, or a man's body, I think. I don't know how it got there, but when I was backing up the car, I almost hit a man lying on the ground. I've never seen a dead body, but it looked as if he just died from a sudden heart attack."

"Why didn't you call 911?"

"I panicked, because to get back to that spot I had to drive out of the garage and re-enter. That's when a car ran the red- light and hit me. I tried to call 911, but my phone's screen is broken, so I ran in here for help. I think I was followed, but I don't know by who. Can you go back and take a look? It was on aisle D. Oh, it's on the first floor."

"But are you sure you did not run him over?"

"Positive, please? I literally forgot what I came in here for when Roy asked me to dance. Guess all the stress messed up my thinking."

"OK, I'll be right back. Roy, do you want to go check something with me?"

"Naw, I'm good. Hey Miguel, give me some more quarters. I see they have El Rey."

The waitress came back with the bill and asked, "Is there anything else you hombres will be needing?"

"No, my brother will pay for it. He will be right back."

"Suite yourself, sweety. Here ya go." She left the bill on their table.

Francisco returned and plopped down next to Emma; he took a big drink from his iced tea and then wiped his brow. She asked, "Well, did you see it? What do you think?"

"Uh, I'm not sure if you are delusional or just plain crazy, but there's no body lying there."

"Yes, there was. Because I saw it, right behind the car, aisle D."

"I looked, but there was nobody. Maybe the stress you've been under with finals and studying has played with your mind; relax, it'll be OK. Here's one of our favorite songs from the homeland."

The men at the table cheered and sang to the next song from a famous Mariachi singer. They clapped with their arms on each other's shoulders, swaying to the happy beat of a forlorn song. The men sang their lungs out along with the music. The owner marched out from the kitchen, yelling at the men, "I told you guys before none of that Mexican music in my place," he pulled the plug, and the music stopped. "Now get out, or I'll throw your asses out." He waved his fist at their table.

The men stopped their singing. Chico shook his head. No sir. When Chico stood up, his chair fell over. He went to the plug to plug it back in. The owner, a large, burly older man, grabbed Chico's shoulder and shoved him away from the Wurlitzer. "No, now leave, all you damn Mexicans, get out and don't come back."

Chico swung at the man and caught him on the side of the head. The larger man grabbed Chico, threw him against the wall, and smashed him in the front of his face. Blood streamed down Chico's nose and lips. Francisco ran across the room and grabbed the larger man off of him. Two friends put their arms around Chico. He smiled and said, "Vamanos muchachos." After they went out the side door, Chico returned and yelled, "El Rey."

Chapter 6

Behind the back of the café Emma said, "Wait, where are you going?" She ran after them as they turned to go down an alley.

She said, "Roy, wait."

He turned around on the sidewalk. She shook her head and said, "Where are you heading?"

"We are going all over. Are you coming? I have to go, or I'll miss the train again."

Emma paused and looked up the street, "I need to think it's so fast," she took a deep breath, "Are you going through Colorado?"

"Colorado? Sure, we are going there. Why?"

Emma shrugged and said, "Oh, not sure why." After one more look at SLC, she nodded yes, "Please, take me with you. I need to get away because nothing is making sense. Let's go sail away."

Francisco said, "No, we can't take you. It'll just bring us trouble."

Roy said, "Come on, Kiko, let's bring the girl."

"No. What can she do, besides go to school? We need workers, not prima donnas. Enough talk, let's go, Roy."

Roy asked Emma, "What can you do?"

"I don't know, uh… Oh, I took a chef class, so I guess I can cook."

Roy said, "Try to keep up." He called to Francisco, "Hey, Rubin went home this week, and she can cook."

Francisco turned around; it's a bad idea. Are you going to be responsible for her?"

"Sure, what's the big deal, Kiko?"

"Because I'm the boss, it's my ass, and I'd like to keep my job. Remember, Mom is counting on it."

Emma stubbled in her heels and stopped to adjust the strap, then ran to catch up with Francisco and Roy. She said, "Please, I won't be any trouble. I can help."

"I got this, bro," argued Roy to his brother.

He grabbed Emma's hand as they turned onto University Drive. The group cut through an alley near 300 Road between the city and the freeway. Emma's heels broke down, she grunted when Roy tugged on her hand.

She yelled over the noise, "How much further is it?" she swiped her hair from her eyes and looked around as they turned the next corner.

Roy pointed in front at the railroad tracks. He yelled out, "It's over there." He pointed across five sets of rail tracks.

Emma stopped running and asked, "Where are you going?"

Across the tracks idled a yellow train. The driver honked the horn and waved from the window. A crewman threw the door open to a passenger car and waved. Francisco followed the crew into the door of the unusual-looking yellow train. A white company pickup truck idled behind the train on the tracks.

Emma said, "That's a strange-looking train."

"It's a rail grinder to fix the rails, you'll see." Said Roy.

Emma stopped to look the train over. "I don't know… Is it safe to do this?"

"Come on, before they leave without us."

Emma slowed for a step and looked at Roy, then back at the city skyline as he ran up the ladder. He stood on a patio. Behind him was a sliding door with a large window in it. A loud hissing sound came from under the patio. Emma jumped back. After a moment, she followed him up the ladder and shut the door. The train blew its loud horn, the train made a series of clunk sounds when the engineer released the brakes. and then she heard wheels squeak when the four train engines added power. The train chugged on the sidetrack towards the mainline heading south. Interstate 15 lay right next to the tracks with a clear view over to the city center. In the middle of the day the rail grinder rolled onto the mainline unnoticed leaving behind no trace. Though none of them knew it, Emma's mom already had a task force searching for her daughter. Officers checked motorists within a three-mile radius of the Hyatt Center. By nightfall they expanded their search to include roads and freeways.

Emma leaned against the rail that wrapped around a patio looking at the city scene as it faded behind shopping malls and apartment buildings. The train increased its speed making her body sway and though they were moving it felt fun. Up above was another beautiful summer day with a clear blue sky dotted with small airplanes and crows flying in flocks. She took a deep breath and smiled, 'freedom,' she whispered to herself.

Roy said, "Follow me, this is the dining car. Don't worry about my brother, sometimes he gets that way. Come." He twisted the handle on a metal sliding door and pushed the door back along its tracks, then stepped to his side like a gentleman and bowed as Emma passed inside the train. Her first steps made her body wobble so she held her hands onto the doorway while the train jostled along the tracks.

"I don't know about this Roy, its hard to walk, the train knocks me to the left and right."

He said, "You'll get used to that real quick. Andele."

Chapter 7

The crew dining car had a kitchen and dining room on the rear half that Emma entered, with staterooms, and a closet for dry goods on the other side. The walls were Union Pacific yellow with white ceilings and fluorescent lights. The crew sat at tables; each table sat below its own window. The men wore reflective orange long-sleeve shirts and orange safety vests. Roy slid the door shut. The coolness and quiet surprised Emma. The men stopped talking, and then Francisco picked up a clipboard and crossed to the tables where she counted eight men total including Francisco. When he spoke, his voice was easy to hear.

As he read the safety sheets from a clipboard Emma saw an empty corner and moved over by the door. The car rocked and shifted across the switch tracks as the train eased onto the mainline, constantly causing her weight to move left and right. Inside, the car was comfortable, with a muted sound when the brakes released. Before Francisco concluded the meeting, he said, "Let's be safe out there this hitch, so wear all your safety equipment. We will have a new company man when we get to Junction. Be forewarned, he's old school and a real hard ass. Let's bring our A game. Believe me, in no time, he will get off our asses, and things will get back to normal. Copy that?" He looked to Emma, "Also, we have a guest, so I'll expect everyone to show her respect and help her, especially if she is doing something unsafe. But since Rudi had to leave, Emma volunteered to cook and clean the next few days. So show her some respect. OK, anyone else got anything, Chico?"

Chico said "That's all I got. Ten-four, chief." He stood, stretched, and gave her a big smile as he walked out the sliding door. She stayed in the corner, leaning against a refrigerator and waiting until all the men, including Roy, left the car. Francisco was going out the front door towards the front of the train.

She said, "Francisco, wait, please."

He nodded to her and said, "I'll be back. Stay here, ten four?"

"Yes, I'll be fine… uh… ten more." She raised her hand with her thumb up and smiled. He pushed the door closed behind her closing out the outside noises. Silence descended upon the dining car. Emma took a deep breath and half said, 'Oh God, wait have I got myself into?' She crossed her arms and took several deep breaths. Then as if afraid to she made her eyes look around the kitchen. She went to the large double sink and looked out the window, then she went to one of the dining tables and looked at the Salt Lake noting the glistening sun off the lakes ripples. Still uneasy, she walked across and looked up at the mountains on the other side of the car just as a fast moving freight train passed next to their track, shaking the train. It looked as though it would ram right through the dining car making her heart skip several beats. She jumped back, gasped, gripped the sink, and held on for a couple of minutes until the train passed.

She observed the kitchen layout, two elliptical windows over the counter, two refrigerators, and four dining table booths with bench seating. She opened a door by the sliding door and noted dry goods, cereals, pasta, and dried beans. Next, she went to the cupboards by the sink, where canned food and dishes were. More cupboards were under the counter and sink for pots, pans, and dish soap. There were the same windows at each table, and in the corner, she bent and looked. There were more cleaning supplies: a yellow plastic mop bucket mop and a couple of brooms. She pulled a broom out and started sweeping dirt into piles. The linoleum on the floor looked to have been a beige color at one time, but now it just looked like the color of the rail yard. She hoped that no one expected her to clean it like new again. The sink had a tall pile of dirty dishes, 'I can see why the last guy quit,' she mumbled.

She turned the faucet on and, while waiting for the hot water to heat up, moved the pile to one side of the sink and began soaking and scrubbing. After she cleaned and rinsed a pan, she saw the same burnt on food spots. She put it back in the sink and scrubbed it hard, but after a few minutes, it still looked dirty. In the cupboard under the sink, she found scrub pads. She rubbed and rubbed that pan, then rinsed and the spots were gone. She set it on the drying rack and looked at the pile. She pulled the largest pot from the pile and filled it with soapy hot water. While it filled, she flopped down onto the bench rubbing her sore hands.

She turned to look when the rear cabin door slid open. Francisco walked over to the sink, shut off the water, looked at Emma, and said, "We can't just be running the water here, this isn't home. What are you doing?" He crossed his arms and shook his head.

"Uh… I was just trying to help, and that pot needs to soak longer. I'm trying, Kiko." She wiped her brow and exhaled. She stood and pointed to the sink, "They left a big mess. I can see why the other guy quit on you."

"Really, you think that's why he quit?" he huffed. "So that you know, he didn't quit. His wife went into labor this morning. He stayed with us as long as he could, but we didn't get in town till you met us."

"Oh, I didn't know. I was just told he quit. Sorry, my bad."

"What do you want, Emma? Why are you here? Obviously, you are not a worker, so I can assume you are here just for personal reasons. What are they?"

"I do want to help. I'm a fast learner, and I really can cook. I wasn't lying, unlike my mom."

"Get your shit together, quick. This company man won't put up with any screw-ups. My job and my ass are on the line, copy that?" He put his hands on his hips and glared at her.

She looked down at her feet and softly said, "Yes, ten more, Francisco."

He chuckled, "That's ten four, not ten more, and another thing, in the future, while we are on this train, you will call me sir or Mr. Garcia. I am not your friend copy that?"

"Yes, sir, Chief."

"OK, just do your best, and I'll try to send one of the guys in to give you a hand. Sorry if I seem a bit harsh. I'm used to the guys when they screw off. The floor looks like it could use a good mopping. Do you know how?"

Emma pulled out the mop bucket, held it, and said, "Sure Kiko, I got this."

Satisfied, Francisco left her alone. She took the bucket to the sink and tried to fit it in, but it would not fit. She filled a pot with warm water and poured it into the bucket, then another and another. She could not figure out if there was an easier way to fill it. She plunged the mop into her soapy bucket of suds and then splashed it across the floor. She slapped it into corners and across, covering the entire floor. She stood in the water wearing her broken down high heels. 'Dang. No phone and no shoes. I never wear these things, and now where are my Hokas?' The back door slid open, and she looked up. Roy smiled from the entryway,

He shrugged and said, "You look like you can use some help." He looked at the floor. With a half chuckle in his voice he said, "What are you doing?"

She shook her head, shrugged, and wiped hair from her face, "Gee, Roy, I'm trying to mop this floor." She put the mop in the bucket, splashing more water onto the drenched floor. "Look at this. My shoes are ruined." She sat down, put her hands over her face, and sobbed.

Roy sat beside her with his arm around her shoulder, "I can help you if you want."

"Yes, Roy, I didn't know I had all this. What am I going to do?"

"Do you just want to go back, Emma?"

She turned her head and looked into his eyes. She looked away, "No, but if I don't do this, I know I will—"

He interrupted her thought, "Francisco will kick you off. Did he tell you that?"

She shook her head, took a breath, wiped her tears, and said, "Not that exactly, but I got the message."

"He's an asshole. Listen, if you want to stay, I can help you, but you'll owe me." He rubbed her shoulders and the back of her neck. She leaned over the table, his hands, found kinks and knots, and rubbed them till her tenseness faded. "First, let's mop this floor, ring that mop out and swab an area and ring it out some more, then I'll help clean those pots and pans."

Emma and Roy worked together cleaning for the next two hours. She set the clean pots and pans on towels along the counter to dry. In the corner of the counter was the base radio. Francisco's voice called the crew, 'OK, guys, get to your places for our first sweep.'

Roy picked up the microphone and said, "Copy that." He said to Emma, "You're on your own. I have to go to work now, but I'll be back for dinner." He put on his safety vest and his orange hard hat then went to the sliding door.

Emma let out her breath, "Dinner? What time is that at?"

"Seis." Emma shrugged. "Six." She nodded, oh. He smiled and closed the door.

The train resumed the grinding operation of the main line tracks at the blistering high speed of only ten miles an hour, slower than Emma's jogging pace. She opened the cupboards and rummaged through the supplies taking stock of their contents. By late afternoon, she had a pot of spaghetti sauce cooking and was heating water for the spaghetti noodles. She used the microphone and called Francisco. He asked "What's for dinner?".

She stirred the red sauce, added pepper, a dash of oregano, salt and dried basil, and then tasted her spoon. Just before six, she added more basil and pepper, then stirred the boiling noodles and turned the burner off under the sauce.

The door from the back slid open, and the crew shuffled into the car their blue jeans looked almost black from the grinding. They took turns washing up in the sink, laughing and kidding each other speaking in Spanish. The train blared its horn several times at road crossings, then at Provo, they switched off the mainline to a sidetrack and slowed to a smooth stop. The workday was over for the men but not for Emma. After dinner, there would be dishes and kitchen clean-up duty. The men sat at their usual spots. Francisco joined them for dinner as they filled their plates with garlic bread and spaghetti. While the crew ate, Emma scrubbed the dishes and waited to hear comments from the crew. After eating, the crew fist-bumped her as they brought their plates.

She asked Francisco, "Are we stopping for very long?"

"For the night. Why?"

She said, "I need to get a new phone and let my friends know I'm alright. This is where I go to school and where my friends are."

"If you leave, then don't expect us to let you back. I have a job position to fill."

Emma paused, leaning against the dining table. She looked out the window, then turned back to Francisco. She crossed her arms and exclaimed, "Why are you so mean to me?"

He smiled and shrugged, "What do you want, Emma? This is a real job; these men and I have real careers. Sure, we are not as good as you, but—"

"—but I never put anyone here down. That's not fair of you to say. I just need a phone, OK?"

She crossed her arms and stood firm in silence. One of her professors at school lectured the class on closing a deal, 'he who speaks last loses in the negotiation.' Emma found this advice true in all situations: don't over speak; silence can be a potent weapon. Married men for ages have felt the effects of the silent treatment from their wives. It works and can give a small person more power and strength. She stared into his eyes yet revealed nothing. Francisco waited another minute, then looked out the window at Provo. It was a warm summer evening; the freeway was jammed with heavy traffic, and the commute was well underway. Emma did not realize it, but at that moment, not everyone in her world knew where she could be or why.

After another glance out the window, he looked directly at her face, "OK, this one time, be back by 6 am or we leave without you. Now get some proper clothes and shoes, not just a phone." A little smile rose around the corners of his mouth when she left. He watched her climb down the stairs in her clumsy remnants of tattered heels, shorts, and a t-shirt. Emma waved as she wobbled off towards the mall a few blocks away.

Chapter 8

Emma went over her shopping list in her head hundreds of times on the train. She threw away her shoes at the mall entrance and went to Macy's. Her taste in clothes leaned towards the practical side; function at a reasonable price mattered far more than sparkly this or that or the over-priced designer stuff. She liked a good backpack instead of a bunch of purses. On the other hand, her mom ensured she attended her events adequately dressed and knowing her daughter's thriftiness she had outfits prepared and delivered by David the limo driver. Emma liked that and felt special. But for every day wear, she was a basic outfit girl. Though Macy's did not carry her Hoka shoes she found a pair of white Nikes with a green swish. After making her selections, she pulled her debit card from her shorts and paid the cashier.

The next stop was the Verizon counter. She hoped to get a replacement on the Chase family account, but it was too late, and they were closed for the night. Her debit card had a daily limit, thanks to her mother, so when she tried to purchase a phone from ATT, it was declined for NSF. She still needed a phone, and she also needed to get back on the train. If she could talk to Francisco, he would know what to do. She plopped down on a bench by a fountain as little kids ran and played around the fountain. She smiled back when a little girl stopped and looked up at her. After the kids left with their mom, her brows scrunched together as she pondered her dilemma. Where do you get a phone late at night? Then, an idea came to her, Martin.

She adjusted her new shoelaces, brushed her pants off, grabbed her shopping bags, and walked to the BYU campus. She cut through alleys, ran/jogged to a house, and knocked on the door. "Is Martin here?" she asked.

"Oh, Hi Emma, sorry he's gone till the fall. Is it important?"

"Can I use your phone to call him, please…? Remember me, I'm Emma. Where does his live?"

"I'm not sure, maybe Boise, here." He handed his phone.

She dialed, but it went to voice mail. She handed the phone back. "Thanks, but it went to voice mail."

"He'll probably text you back. Can you tell him I need to speak with him, please? Oh… I forgot; I need to use it to call Rachel too."

Next, she made another call, and the voice mail said, 'This is Rachel at the beep, you know what to do' "Hi Rach, it's Em, hey, I'm fine… sorry about your car today, that guy ran the light, and my phone broke in the crash, so I'm getting a new phone. Call you soon." She handed the phone back, "Thanks. Uh…"

"What's going on Emma?"

"My debit card is maxed out, and I need a phone tonight."

"Go to Walmart and get a burner phone. They got cheap plans." His phone buzzed. "Oh, it's Marty." He handed the phone back to her.

Emma talked with Martin, explaining her situation, and he recommended one of his burner phones in his room. With the help from his roommate, she found a box of phones and selected one and found the battery charger. Downstairs, a party started; she weaved through the crowded house to the front door. "Emma," one of the lady guests called out, "Where have you been? Did you talk to Rachel? She's looking for you and said you wrecked her car today." She handed Emma a drink, "Here, you need this, hon." The music changed tempos to a hard, rocking beat. Kids danced and whooped as they guzzled their drinks. Emma's friend grabbed her hand and pulled her into the mass.

After several drinks and hours later, Emma was too drunk to walk back to the train or to even stand. She lay on the arm of the couch next to another and fell asleep. The party went on until early in the morning. She rolled over, and the sun shined through the living room windows. Her mind cleared to realize it was daytime which meant it's the next day! She shot up off the couch, running for the bathroom. She grabbed her shopping bag and ran out the front door for the train. Her head throbbed and her vision blurred. She kept her head down, breathing hard, pumping her arms and legs. She held her phone; it was almost seven, and the train might have left. 'Come on, Em,' she told herself. The alley shortcut let out to the main street. Just a half mile till she turned the corner. Her lungs huffed, and her legs hurt, but it was just two more blocks. At last, she saw the rail tracks. The first block went by; her eyes followed the street sign as it neared, and she ran faster.

Ahead, the yellow train sat on the siding track. She just might make it if she ran a little faster. 'yes...' She waved to the men leaning on the back rail of the end car having a smoke. They waved back and shouted, waving their arms. She grunted and breathed faster and faster as she neared. The train's whistle blew three times, the engine bell rang, and Emma was still a block away, but closing the distance as it started to roll out. The diesel engine throttle rumbled as it gained RPM. Was she too late when they were leaving? One of the men, maybe it was Chico, yelled, "Rapido, Rapido." He stuck his cigarette to the side of his mouth and put a hand out.

She reached her hand up, and he grabbed hold. He pulled on her hand, but his hand slipped off. She fell off balance and stumbled on the railroad ties. She put her hand out to stop her from falling as she struggled. Her body sprung back up with her feet moving faster. She caught back up, and he grabbed her hand again and wrapped his hand around her wrist. He pulled her up the ladder. "Buenos dias," he said with a grin that covered his whole face.

"Buenos dias, sorry I'm late. Is Francisco furious at me?"

"Si, very mad at you, but the company man is even madder." He shook his head and said, "Is no bueno. I no wish to be you today." The men chuckled shaking their heads, no bueno.

Emma caught her breath then went forward to the dining car; she slip the door open in a moment of relief. The sink was full of dishes, the garbage overflowed, and spilled cereal, milk, and coffee dripped down the side of the tables. She shook her head and wiped her brow flipping her hair from her eyes. At the sink, she turned the sink water on and leaned against the counter. 'It's going to be a long morning; better make coffee,' she told herself. While the train ground the mainline, she cleaned the kitchen and mopped the grimy floor. She was washing the dishes when Francisco's voice asked over the radio for her to bring coffee up for him and the company man. She looked for the coffee pot in the cupboards, looked at the counters, and looked in the closet but could not find the coffee pot. She called back "I can't find the coffee pot.". After a few minutes, he entered and approached the cupboard.

He pointed and said, "Here it is. It's good that it wasn't a rattlesnake, or you'd be dead."

While she added water and coffee, he had words with her. "You're late. The company man has a tight schedule. You screwed our day up. Why? What was so important?"

Emma grabbed a water bottle and sat down at one of the tables. She shook her head and rubbed the back of her neck. She said, "I don't know; everything just went wrong, I screwed up. I am sorry. Please give me another chance to prove myself." She looked up with heavy bags under her bloodshot eyes, took a big drink, and rubbed her eyes. She looked out the window and mumbled, "I need some Ibuprofen."

Francisco shook his head, "You need to get your act together."

She nodded, "I will. Sorry." She looked up at him he stood with his arms crossed his eyes blazing through her his face set like granite with no expression. He picked up his clipboard and slid a form onto the table.

He pointed to it and said, "If you're staying, you must fill out the application form."

Emma looked at him and nodded, "Yes, I'll get it filled out as soon as I find something for my headache."

"I'll call Terri at the office, and she can process this ASAP." His voice trailed off, "This is against my better judgment. Ay, dios mio. I'll be back with my laptop." He handed her a pen.

Emma completed the application, and e-faxed it to Terri in Hasarco's Del Rio office. The train worked the main line between Provo and Colorado for the next few days. Emma screwed up, and she knew it was a big mistake to hang out with her old friends, but what was so wrong with doing what she wanted? It was her own personal time. Maybe this wouldn't have happened if she hadn't had those tequila shots. I should have stuck to beer. But she likes to drink tequila when she parties; beer slows a girl down and then you get all bloated.

Emma rubbed her temples and drifted off. She dreamed she was talking with Martin on a mountain top. 'Work, work, work. That's all they do on this stupid train, and they take life so seriously. Are these people half-crazy? It's so stupid just to work. How can a company expect its people only to work and have no personal life? Her head bobbed and hit the table. She looked up and took a breath. In the sink, she saw a pile of dishes and dirty footprints on the floor. 'The work is never-ending around here. Why can't things stay clean?' she asked herself. She put her head in her hands and shook her head. The door slid open. Diego tiptoed into the car, grabbed a soda, and slid the door closed behind him. She struggled for the rest of her day as she cleaned between making lunch and preparing dinner. Oh what she would have given for a pillow and a mattress.

That afternoon, she called Francisco, "I need to stop at a store and get some things to make dinner…"

He said, "OK, get with the suppressive water technician and have him drive you there. We will be stopping to change out some of the grinding wheels. Today, the driver is Miguel. Just call him; he's on the radio."

The slow-moving train eased to a stop on a sidetrack near Thistle, Utah. Since Thistle had no supermarket, she and Miguel drove to the Walmart back at Spanish Forks. On the trip, they talked, small talk at first, then he asked, "Senorita, por que… uh, why are you here and not with your rich family?" Tu es muy suerte."

She looked at him over that last statement. Lucky? I'm a very lucky girl to have so much?" she reclined with her seat back and turned to the side, "It's a long story. Have you ever felt that you did not fit in and that no matter how good you do, it doesn't matter?" Like the other men, Miguel was a Latino man in his twenties, yet he looked a bit older. He drove the work pick-up with the window down, his arm rested on the door, and the other crossed over the steering wheel. His posture struck her with intrigue. He drove conservatively and looked like he had been doing this sort of work for many more years than his age. He turned and saw her watching with a little smile on the edges of her lips; he chuckled.

Miguel said, "No, mi familia es muy importante." When he turned his head, she saw tired lines around his eyes and the edges of his lips, yet his hair was jet black, no grey hair showing yet. The late afternoon casts long shadows over the windshield from trees as they drove through the mountain. It set off a soft, dappled look. Miguel smiled and turned up the radio, tapping his hands on the steering wheel to the song. After a few minutes, he asked, "Senorita, que es… what's your plan?"

She laughed and shook her head. Ha, ya right." She turned the volume down and said, "Like the Joker said to Batman, do I look like I have a plan?"

At Walmart, they filled a shopping cart. Emma had fun grabbing several boxes of each item, Gallons of milk, jars of spaghetti sauce, bags of tortillas dozens of cans of beans and several packages of hotdogs instead of just one of this one of that. It was a novel way of shopping for her.

As they drove back, a deer ran in front. Miguel swerved and pumped the brakes. The truck avoided the animal, but then two more little deer followed mama deer. He threw the steering wheel to the left and then hard to the right as he locked up the brakes. The first little deer hopped across the lane, missing the front bumper by a foot. The other little deer hit the passenger door with a thunk. "Stop!" she exclaimed. He kept driving, and she again yelled, "Stop, stop, Miguel, you have to stop."

She waved her arms back to the little deer. Miguel looked at her, shaking his head. "Por que? Probably dead, so we have to go." He looked in the mirror, then slowed and stopped. After a semi drove past, he put the truck in reverse and rolled backward. She threw the door open and ran to the edge of the road. The deer lay so still she initially did not think it was still alive, then she lifted its head, its nose sniffed the air, and its eyes looked directly at her. She pushed her sunglasses up. "Come on, help me get it into the truck. Come here please, uh… por favor." She slipped her arms under its body. It kicked and moved, trying to run. They placed the deer in the truck bed, and it kicked again, splattering drops of blood on her new top and shorts. Miguel strapped the deer down so it could not get up and injure itself more. They jumped in the truck, and he hit the gas to make up time.

They arrived at the rendezvous spot on the sidetrack ahead of the train. Emma looked at the deer's injuries; it shook and tried to get up. She held the little creature and cooed as she scratched behind its ears. "Miguel, can you bring some water, please."

"Si," Where will you keep it?" She looked up at him as he handed her the water bottle.

"I'm not sure. Any ideas where I can keep it till it gets better?"

"No se." Boss man won't be happy; best to leave it here."

The train blew its horn several times down the track. Miguel looked up, "Best to not cause trouble and let it go here."

"No, it will die if I do."

"It was dead when I hit it, and you just gave it a little more time. I help you get it out of the truck."

"No, just stop, por favor… Uh… let me think."

Emma held the deer as it licked water from her cupped hand; its tongue was rough and tickled. She smiled and sang to the little frightened creature while it flicked its tongue like a little kitty. Her brothers had a dog long ago, but she was too young to remember. The story told to the kids was that their dad found a good home for the dog on a farm where he was very happy. She always wanted a pet. She asked for a bike and a puppy yearly on her birthday and Christmas. She did manage to get a bike for her thirteenth birthday, but never an animal to love or care for. She grew up with no needs, only wants. They moved about for her dad's career, and her grandparents from her mom's side of the family showered the boys with gifts and trips; she knew they were well off. She would occasionally be allowed to go on a vacation trip, but her brothers were so much older that they received the lion's share of admiration. Truth be told, it was a rare occurrence that she was included. She came of age without her brothers. They had moved on with life; her dad had passed away, and her mom was a career power boss bade with no time for Emma as a teen. She didn't even need to sneak out at night to party. Home became just a place to sleep when she was too tired. Now, in her little hands lay a shaking, scarred little creature whose very life was literally in her hands. She looked back behind as the train stopped. The large, imposing yellow behemoth intimidated her. She thought, 'I'm sure they will let me keep it. Who could turn this poor creature away?'

The company man yelled from the engine window, "Y'all git on up here; it's supper time. Come on, toots." He closed the window; the horn blew three short bursts. She looked at Miguel as he pointed to the woods on the side of the track.

Chapter 9

Francisco came around the corner in the dining car to eat dinner, but a box sat on the floor near the sink. When he looked down, the little deer poked its head up and looked at him. He looked over to Emma, shaking his head. She shrugged, finished serving, and put the pots and pans in the sink to soak. He motioned for her to follow him down the hall. From the kitchen, they went around to the left of the dry goods closet to a hallway. She wondered, 'What is he going to say? I assume he wants to yell at me away from the other men.' He opened a door to his stateroom and waved for her to follow. Emma, curious and unable to read his mood, followed.

He said, "Please shut the door and have a seat." He sat at his desk, his stateroom functioned as a bedroom and office, and as the supervisor on the train, he was entitled to one of the two staterooms. Emma smiled and remained quiet; she shifted her chair angle as he rummaged through forms. He asked, "I see that you have a friend tonight. Do you realize it won't last the night?"

"Perhaps it won't, but I or someone has to try to save it, sir." She sat facing him, showing no signs of happiness or sorrow. Her voice spoke from her throat, forced.

He nodded, "Well, you do the best you can, but if you want to keep it for your little pet till you can find a proper home, that's fine with me. You have our support, ten four?" He looked up at her with his big, deep eyes. He neither smiled nor frowned, then nodded for the second time. I have good news for you, Emma."

"What's that, sir? I could use some good news."

He slid a paper across the desk and said, "Read this."

She picked up the paper and read it silently. "Oh my, does this mean I have my first official job?" She looked up at Francisco, "Is this official?"

"No, it's almost official, but you'll have to pass some tests on the computer. One of the guys can help you answer the questions, but Terri has everything ready to submit, including a debit card to purchase hotel rooms and groceries for the crew along with a gas card. Pass this test and ensure your new friend doesn't die tonight." He stood up.

Emma's smile faded, and she hesitated to shake his hand, "But why are you doing this for me?"

"You earned it, Emma. Tomorrow, I'll show you around the train. Follow me, there's something else."

They walked down the narrow, short corridor to the stateroom next to his, "Here, this is your room. Normally, it's reserved for the alternate supervisor, but since he won't be here till Denver, it's yours. Bring your friend, but find it an appropriate home before we get to Denver."

She wanted to hug him but shrugged her arms, "I don't know what to say. Thank you so much for giving me a chance." He slid the cabin door closed behind him. Emma stood looking down at her bunk. A million thoughts flew through her mind, ending on her favorite Christmas. This felt similar to that. For just a moment, time stopped, and the world seemed to stand still in peace. She sprung into the air, flopped onto her bunk bed, and rolled over, kicking her feet and squealing into her pillow.

Later that night, she awoke hungry and craving a desert. She went around the corner to inspect one of the refrigerators wearing pajamas. After leaning against the open door, she grabbed the ice cream and dug into it with a spoon. After a few scoops, she shuffled back to her room and closed her door. Her privacy remained intact with no interruption, just like back home. She climbed back into her bunk and realized she felt normal for the first time in a while.

The following day, the train approached the eastern side of Utah, just a half day's journey from Arches, Canyon Lands, and Moab with vistas to the Colorado mountain range. After breakfast, Francisco and Emma had a meeting at the dining table.

He crossed the room and bent over, "I see your little friend made it through the night." He studied the bandages, then the eyes lifted back the lips and examined the mouth and tongue.

She cradled the baby deer on her lap while it drank a baby bottle of whole cow's milk. She hummed a soft tune as she pulled back the bandages and inspected its wounds. Under the bandage on the front side was a long gash she had glued together to cover the exposed bone. The edges were lifting and would need more superglue, she noted. On its little head, the ear had caught on the truck bumper and almost severed. She superglued to re-attach the ear. She unrolled the gauze and peeked under; she could not tell if she got it positioned correctly. The thick, long hairs made it hard for her to see where the edges were. She rolled the gauze back around the side of the head to hold the ear in place.

He said, "Impressive, you have a true gift."

"Thanks. I know it's still too early to say if it will live."

When she put the deer down, its legs shook as it tried to stand. He scratched its head.

He stood and said, "Tomorrow, we should be in Moab. The guys are excited, and the train's making good progress.

"Cisco, when am I finally going to see the train?"

Francisco rubbed his goatee, "Today, when we drop off this company, man. That might be a good time to show you the train. I'll have one of the men get you. Ten-four?"

"No, I want you to show me around. It's nothing against Roy or the others, just that well… it's important that you show me."

"I have a ton of work to do, sorry." He crossed his arms, looking at the deer. "My wife once gave me good advice when I first started on this train; I struggled."

Emma shook her head, "I never thought about it. I guess I just assumed you were the boss and always knew the right thing to do."

"Hardly. I learned what not to do more than what to do. One night, I called her from Pittsburgh, when I was frustrated and ready to quit, she told me, 'Cisco, just make yourself useful."

"That's why I want you to show me the train. Please…"

"Depends on when this company man leaves today. Oh, we pick up the next inspector in Moab, so that gives us tonight and a free day tomorrow."

"We don't work if there's no company, man?"

"We don't grind without one since they are here to inspect our work and ensure we don't set the forest on fire. So, once this company man departs, we'll have free time till tomorrow night if we are caught up on maintenance. The guys want to put on a sort of talent show tonight."

"That sounds fun." She chuckled.

After two long days with the train, Emma took stock of the many changes since the incident in the parking garage at the Hyatt. The event seemed like it happened to someone else, or maybe just a bad dream. That first day, she had been confined to the dining car with nothing to do except mopping, washing dishes, and making meals. Now, she had her own room and a pet. While she contemplated her new changes, the train ground half the morning before stopping. It startled Emma when they stopped moving. Then she remembered Francisco saying they'd stop to let the company man off at Green River. One time, her family went to a large ranch on the Green River for horseback riding and fishing. The boys loved going there. She didn't fish, but she liked riding horses.

She looked out the window, leaning against the counter on her elbows. She could see the Green River, and the town lay next to it. A major tributary to the Colorado River, the Green is famous for its white-water rapids, and it cuts through a deep canyon gorge as far as one can see. Emma noted that the sides of the gorge looked like a layered cake. The different types of rock layers, each with their own color, reds, greys, blacks, and tans, stacked on top of each other, creating canyon walls that soared hundreds of feet above the swift water below. Each layer told a story of the history of the continent, reaching far back into the Earth's past.

She looked forward, pressing her face against the glass to see ahead. The company man walked away with his backpack and computer bag, stepping over the rail tracks. She glanced at the clock; it was noon. The door slid open, the crew shuffled in, made sandwiches, then left. Miguel told her they were low on sandwich supplies and closed the door as he went.

Emma opened the sliding door and looked out to the town. Interstate 70 from SLC was near. The town was a magnet for tourists and passers-by. She decided to make a list and go to town. She went through all the cupboards and refrigerators and created a shopping list. The base radio squelched, "Emma, meet me up in the engine," came Cisco's voice.

Grinning, she picked up the handheld microphone, "Ten-four." Her hands shook when she tried to put the mic back in its cradle. She went down the stateroom passageway, passed to the front door, slid it open, and stepped out onto a porch outside. The summer air felt cool from the breeze blowing over the Green River. Her hands stopped shaking, and she relaxed. In front of her was the patio on the next car. She leaned over the side and saw the engine was several cars ahead. There were tanker cars, engines still to climb around to get to the front engine. In between cars were couplers that connected each car to the next. She wondered if you're supposed to jump across to the patio of the next car or step on top of the coupler.

Roy waved at her from the top of the rear tanker car. He yelled, but he was too far away. She waved back and sighed when she saw him climbing down. After a minute, he appeared at the door.

"Welcome, my lady. May I escort you?" He smiled and stuck his arm out for her. "Careful, you'll get the hang of it soon; it's easy." She followed as he stepped onto the coupler to each patio.

They went over patios and climbed a ladder on the end of the first water tanker. They walked across the top on a narrow walkway with a metal railing on the outside edge. Her hand gripped the metal railing, and her feet moved reluctantly forward, falling behind Roy. On the other end of the car was another ladder. They climbed down, crossed the coupler to the next water car, and repeated. At first, the heights and exposure frightened Emma, but she relaxed on the second water tanker. It took effort to climb all those ladders, and she had no idea how physical the job could be. After the third water tanker, they stepped across to the engine.

Finally, she made it to the front of the train. He said, "This is the front engine. We must go through the engine room, then come out on that catwalk and around the nose to a door. Don't worry; it's safe to do this. This is the rear door. She stood looking at the door. He said, "Here, use this latch."

Emma turned the latch and opened the door. A large round thing hummed, and a large grey colored diesel engine sat in front of it. Next to them, she saw a yellow control panel, and overhead was a series of giant fans on the roof. They walked on a narrow path leading around the diesel engine towards a sliding door. It idled with a loud drone, making it hard to hear another person talk. The air was hot and mixed with the odor from noxious gasses from diesel fumes and overheated electrical transformers. She followed him, walking across the area on her tiptoes, her shoulders hunched and her back arched. Her back and shoulders relaxed when she opened the sliding door to the engine's front catwalk that wrapped around the front end of the engine. Miguel opened the door, and she followed him inside.

To her left, she passed a workstation with a laptop on a desk behind a wall. She climbed steps to a raised area and turned around, now facing to the front able to see out the big windshield. She stood just behind the two driver seats. Miguel said, "This is where the driver and company man sit." Her gaze nearly missed Francisco; her eyes drew to the view out the view out the large front windows. She saw it all: the tracks, the people. Over to the side was the town, and tourists with various boats and rubber tube rafts were at a gas station. The streets and parking lots were covered with people on vacation. Who would have thought, let's drive halfway across America and play at Green River? Emma thought, 'This looks fun.'

"Wow, it's amazing, what a great view," she exclaimed.

Miguel said, "Here she is Cisco, she's all yours."

Francisco turned around and pointed to the empty seat. He said, "Grab a seat. I have to send this report, and then we can start on your tour. Thanks, Miguel. Tell the men to do the front half maintenance, and we'll call it a day."

He cut and pasted the spreadsheet files from their last segment along with notes, attached the company man's inspection report, and hit the send button.

"We have our own Wi-Fi system we hook up to satellites. So, no matter where we go, we can always communicate with headquarters, except in tunnels. It comes in handy usually when there's been an emergency."

Emma asked, "What do you mean an emergency?"

"Like a train derailment or maybe a tornado."

"I thought about your wife's advice, 'Make yourself useful.' I want to be useful, but I wouldn't know what to do. Look at all these thingy's here, screens and dials and… stuff. I could never learn what any of this stuff is for."

He chuckled, "It's intimidating. OK, see this lever with a handle on it? That's to make the train move forward. The farther you move it forward, the faster, and here is the brake. The rest monitors the train. The station below us by the door, that's for the guy whose job it is to monitor the grinding operation. We have cameras that point down to the rails and record it. Come on, I'll walk you through it as we go."

They walked through the engine cars, where he pointed to switches and where to shut equipment and engines off. Though she tried to comprehend, she soon tired of detail overload. She asked him just to give a basic overview of each car and its purpose. He showed her where to walk and how to climb over a water tanker car. She walked the train's entire length to the back end, where another engine was facing backwards, but just like the front engine. He said, "When we are moving forward, no one stays back here; its controls are done from our front engine, but if we switch it on, then we can take control from back here regardless of going front or backward."

"So, if the front engine was disabled, could you still run the train from back here then?"

"Yes." He nodded. He took her out to the front end, where a platform wrapped around the length of the nose like on the other engine.

Emma pointed behind them and said, "We had to climb over three water tankers to get to the engine. What do you use all that water for?"

"It's for fire suppression. Grinding causes a massive number of sparks; it looks like the whole thing is on fire, and at night, it's pretty cool to see. We man these fire hoses, follow the train with the pickup, to extinguish any other fires.

"OK, I get it. Now it makes sense. Don't you get homesick?"

"My wife lives in Mexico. I am gone for weeks or months. When I go home, it looks similar to this. Sometimes I get homesick, but I love my job."

Emma looked down the tracks and said, "I'm supposed to be a lawyer."

Francisco studied her face. She did not hide her feelings; instead, she wanted to show them. "Somehow, you are in the wrong body. Anyone can see it about you. I was against having you on board, but now I am beginning to understand how fate just brings people together."

She turned around and looked at him, noting his youthful looks were being eroded away by responsibility and long hours. The stress made him look older than his age, but he also looked more mature than his age. She told him, "I've had this crazy dream, more so lately, that I've never told anyone. My mom is a lawyer, and so is my brother Cody. I don't want to be an attorney like them."

"Oh, what kind do you want to be?"

"I don't want to be one at all. Every day, she gets on that stage or in front of news cameras, tells the audience what they want to hear, and never speaks the truth. She's probably never told the truth about anything since I've been alive." Emma inhaled and looked at his face. He looked off to the side, but when he looked back, she continued. "To make a long story short, I am the daughter of that woman who was on the news the other day when we met in the cafe. Senator Chase is my mother; if she knew I was here, she would ruin it for all of us. Trust me, you don't want to cross her. She is ruthless and very powerful."

"Why are you telling me all of this now?"

"Because, unlike my mom, I want you to know the truth. I trust you won't use it to your advantage. It's not easy being the daughter of a US Senator. When my brothers were growing up, she was still an attorney. They have no idea all the crap I have to deal with. Friends that use me, I never know if someone genuinely likes me for me or not or who I can trust. That's why I don't want the crew to know who I am, ten four Cisco?"

She leaned against the rail and caught her breath. When she looked up, he stared into her eyes and shook his head. "You know, I'm glad you told me all of this. I assumed there was a connection to that woman, but I never thought you would be her daughter. Wow. So, what are you going to do? What's your plan?"

She pulled her phone out, scrolled and swiped it, and then showed him, "See this? It's Bel-Rea Veterinary School in Denver."

"Ah, so that's why you want to go to Denver. Why don't you enroll?"

"Cause mom won't let me, and she's right, I must follow the family name."

Francisco laughed out loud. He caught his breath and said, "You realize now that you've told another person that means you must follow through and at least check the place out."

"If I do, I am sure it will piss my mom off, but by coming in this way, she will never know, and then I can decide if it's right."

"So, what are you saying here, Emma?"—

"That I want to work the summer and maybe start school in Denver in the fall. If I save, I can do it on my own money."

"I don't know if they will let you do that. You see, the other guy comes back next week. Sorry, Em, but Denver is the end of the line, unless Rudie stays home."

He tried to look at her, but he had to turn away. She held her face in her hands, trying not to sob. She gasped and struggled to hold it all back. Her breathing came in short gasps as her eyes welled up, and she buried her face in his chest. She heaved her chest in a jerking motion, fighting the tears her dark brown hair under his nose. He held her in his arms in silence. Minutes passed, and Emma emerged, wiping her eyes and nose.

"When I was little, I thought I would be just like my big brothers, but it didn't turn out that way. There must be something wrong with me because I keep thinking I know how things will turn out, and I'm always wrong. Here I go again. Why is it that nothing seems to fit? Why doesn't anyone care about me? My family doesn't, my dad never did, my mom... Ha, you are the first real person that does care, and you can't even—"

"—Wait, what did you say… about your family? Maybe because you are adopted or something like that. That would be a good enough reason for your family not to be there for you. Have you ever done a DNA test?"

She shook her head, "No, that's crazy talk. Besides, that's the same old cliché:' I know who my relatives and parents are. I need to do more shopping, and the guys said we are out of lunchmeats and juice."

"Here, take my card to cover the costs." He pulled his company card from his coveralls.

She waved her hands, her eyebrows crunched up, "No, I don't want anything. I can pay for this myself." She looked at her phone. It was almost noon, so she googled grocery nearby and selected Melon Vine Food Store. "Can I borrow the truck?"

"Yes, Diego is the on-duty driver today, so you can have him drive you to the store. He knows the area."

Emma climbed off the back ladder onto the tracks and returned to the pick-up truck. At Melon Vine Foods, she filled the cart with lunchmeats, 2-liter Coke bottles, and snack items. Fresh produce was in season, so she grabbed items to make an excellent fresh salad. And true to the store name, they had fresh melons in season, so she put a few in the cart. She rolled her cart to the checkout counter; the pile had grown high. She noticed that the cashier rang up three hundred dollars; it seemed that most of her crew purchases were three hundred dollars. She inserted her debit card and waited.

The cashier said, "I am so sorry, but your card was declined. Do you have another one you can use?"

Emma looked at the lady, "What, you must be mistaken. Please, try it again."

The cashier tried again, and it was declined. The lady took the card and cut it in half with her scissors. "Sorry, that's what it said for me to do."

Emma texted Diego to bring his card in with him. Behind Emma, the line grew by the second, with tourists' arms full of snacks, beer, and hotdogs. "Come on, lady," raised a growing chorus of resentment.

Emma's face glowed red as a hot poker while she awaited Diego. He handed the cashier the company card and stuffed the receipt into one of the shopping bags. He pushed the cart to the truck. Emma climbed in and slunk into her seat below the window, pulling her ballcap down over her brow. Diego looked over at her and put the truck in drive.

Chapter 10

Green River is a small tourist stop along Interstate 70 near Colorado and Wyoming. The location was part of Ute Indian land, the same tribe the state was named for. It was first made famous by the old-time fur trappers as a Rendezvous where, at the end of the trapping season, they would sell their hard-earned beaver furs to the fur company in exchange for credits, which they would quickly convert into whiskey and tobacco. Later, the old Spanish Trail passed through from 1829 till the 1850's. The settlement town first started as a river crossing for the US Mail. In 1883, the Denver and Rio Grande Western Railroad was built a train station. Quickly after that, a rush of people set up the proper town of Green River. Over the years, it served the military and railroad mining interests. These days, it caters to tourists and truckers. It sits at the entrance to Utah's magnificent national parks and Moab's recreation area. It still has that typical western town look, and if one looks hard enough, one might find relics from the bygone era of fur trappers and Indians.

When Emma and Diego returned to the train, they could not find anyone. After they put the groceries away, she checked on the deer, threw the door open, and ran to the patio. She asked, 'Where did everyone go?"

"Probably down to the river to cool off." He turned to leave.

She called to him, "Where are you going?"

He laughed, "To the river. Vamos."

She ran into her cabin, unzipping her coveralls while checking on the deer. Underneath she had on her shorts and a tank top. She jumped into her flip-flops and ran down the stairs waving, "Wait, wait."

They parked at the boat dock and looked for the other guys. Diego pointed in front, "Mira, Ahi ellos estan… Look, there they are." Their friends stood at the counter of one of the local river guides. He said, "We use the same one every year."

She looked at the sizeable photogenic sign, Sheri Griffith Expeditions. The sign had a picture with people were rafting through white water, sitting on the edge of large orange inner tubes turned into rafts. Diego ran to his friends, but Emma stood by the car. The men waved and called for her, but she stood motionless.

Roy came back and asked, "What is it, Emma? Let's go."

"You guys go on without me. I need to check on the deer. Have fun."

When she turned to leave, Roy stepped in front of her path, "What's the prob, Em?"

"Nothing, Roy, I'm fine. Have fun." Hundreds of tourists filled the parking lot, getting outfitted for rafting. Rafts and kayaks weaved and bobbed through the mass of people and cars on the way to the pier. She watched a raft slip into the water loaded with people and a dog. They were all high school and college kids like her, laughing and splashing each other. "I had a friend that drowned on one of these trips when her raft hit a rock and flipped."

Roy waved to the group and said, "Are you kidding me? We've never had an accident. Listen, I called my brother, maybe he can talk with you. We want you to come."

Emma looked over her shoulder, her face sweating under the midday sun, "Uh, I don't want to hold you guys up. I'll be fine."

Roy spoke to Francisco in Spanish; it was too fast for Emma to make the gist or hear any keywords. He patted Roy on the shoulder, who left and asked Emma her concerns. She explained her friend's accident, and then she heard her voice say, "If I go, something bad will happen to someone, but if I stay here, it won't. It's just a crazy feeling I have."

Francisco stared at her, rubbing his chin whiskers. She scratched her head and shuffled her feet. From behind, the men called to go. They had the raft in the river and waved one more time. "I know you want to go, but I understand. We don't want you doing anything you don't feel safe about, ten four?"

"I'd feel horrible if someone got hurt and I was there, but it's a perfect day." Looking back at that decision made her stop when approaching the raft. The vibrant red-orange raft bobbed in the water, and men clambered onto its sides each grabbed an oar. The guide handed her a floatation vest, pointed where to straddle, and gave her a helmet. Before she could internalize the events, they floated down the Green River into a canyon. Overhead, Pelicans soared with eagles. She looked behind and noticed the raft held more people than their group, and all were about the same age: girls wore swim suites and tank tops, and the men wore shorts. Their raft followed a convoy of others bobbing steadily on the river's surface.

In front, the canyon walls grew steeper and taller. The water turned frothy, with large waves cascading over the boulders.

The guide gave instructions in Spanish and English, pointing to other rafts and potential water hazards. With everyone on board the guide shoved off then settled in at the rear to steer. Emma paddled hard with the others as they drifted through the first rapids. The front of the raft shot upwards straight over the first rapid spraying the crew. Whenever they neared the rapids, their guide yelled to paddle hard to match the water speed. They clinched their thighs around the raft wall while gripping their paddles tight. Emma screamed as the rapids drenched them.

The guide yelled, "Faster; this was a big one. You guys dig deep, come one stroke, dig deep."

Emma paddled her hardest, digging deep into the river's green water. Their raft lifted, and her view looked directly at the canyon walls above. Swallows flew about building nests on the rock walls, dabbing mud, then swooping down over the rapids millimeters from the water, changing direction in the blink of an eye. It was beautiful, and she hollered like an animal. The front end came down, slamming with a big shudder while the rear end lifted high, tossing the raft sideways. Their guide pulled hard on his oars to get the front end pointing back downstream. He yelled for the right side to paddle hard and the left to hand on.

"Hold on!" he yelled Emma turned around and watched this sturdy young man with long big arms dig his oars deep and pull back to his lifejacket. It took strength and courage. He called out orders while remaining focused on the river, his voice never wavered nor rose high in pitch. Like an airline pilot dealing with stormy weather he remained calm giving the crew of tourists confidence not to panic though they were going for a ride up and sideways and once in a while even over. "Grab hold of the rope, and don't let go. Here we go."

Their raft flew over the next rapid sideways, tossing the right side upwards into the air and almost flipping them over. The crew on the left side, including Roy, Francisco, and a young couple, were thrown overboard. They hung onto the rope as the raft landed back upright. The guide yelled as he continued to work the oars to straighten the raft's attitude. The front end swung back in front in time for the smaller rapids, they rolled over them then relaxed. The guide and crew laughed and the floaters hung onto the rope splashing each other. Emma jumped into the water on her side, followed by Diego and the others. The guide eased the raft into a deep pocket of calm water and tied the raft onto a half-submerged log.

Under the water Emma opened her eyes, and reached out at a trout swimming in place, curiously watching her. The sunlight beams shimmered off the fish's scales, and she noticed several more trout glistening in the pool. Above, a cutthroat trout gobbled a fly at the surface and darted to the edge of a boulder. She went up, took another deep breath, and pointed to the others. They all dove and swam around each other like dolphins playing a game of tag. Roy chased after a large crawdad as it scurried along the bottom, trying to elude him by climbing under a tin can. When Roy lifted the can the crawdad swam away. He pointed to several good size whitefish feeding along the bottom, their skin shimmered.

After a picnic lunch of fried chicken, BBQ ribs, corn on the cob and potato salad, their journey continued for another hour through a series of smaller rapids. The high canyon walls faded away to a high desert plateau with short little stubby juniper trees dotting the landscape along with sagebrush on a brick-red colored rocky terrain, just like in the Roadrunner cartoons. Some of the crew swam with the raft as they floated to the pick-up zone. They rafted up to Swazey's beach and beached the raft. The crew raised their oars in a set of big cheers for their guide, the river, the day, and a last round for each other. Emma screamed her lungs out cheering and laughing. She helped raise the raft onto its trailer out of the water, wearing a towel. Warm again, she wanted to party.

The men laughed with the guide, reliving the near toss-over of the raft. Though they spoke mainly in Spanish, Emma laughed along. The young couple, Robert and Gabrielle from Minnesota, re-introduced themselves. They came west on vacation and went to Yellowstone Park when they heard about Green River. It was their first time being this far west, and since they had never seen canyons or mountains before. For them this trip gave them the most thrills and excitement. Everyone exchanged numbers and gave out lots of hugs and handshakes. It was more thrilling than they could have imagined which they kept saying all day. Roy joined the conversation and asked if they wanted to join their bonfire party. They accepted along with two others from the raft. Emma thanked the guide as the happy caravan climbed aboard the bus to return upstream to Green River. They sang, they laughed, and they teased everyone. Emma laughed harder than she could remember even peed her pants.

Back in town, Diego and Chico went to the state park to secure a picnic spot, and others returned to the train while Emma and Francisco went to a different grocery store. Francisco grabbed a shopping cart and pushed it to the butcher counter. Emma stood back as he and the butcher's assistant carried on in Spanish. He turned to her, grinning, and said, "This is my cousin, Jesus; we call him Chuy. He will pack us some ribs and chicken for our barbeque. In the winter, he works down in Del Rio. He will someday open his own shop when he becomes a US citizen.

Chuy weighed the ribs and chicken, added more, and wrapped it up; he and Francisco fist bumped. Emma put the wrapped meats in the cart, and Francisco introduced her to Jesus in mixed English and Spanish. Emma asked him if he always shops for so much food. He reminded her they were buying food for many people and that the leftovers would last a few days. He pushed the heavy cart up to the check stand. Emma said, "I got this, my treat. It's the least I can do for all you have done for me."

The cashier scanned the meats, jalapenos, beer, and corn on the cobb, "That'll be four hundred sixty-seven and eighteen cents."

Emma looked at Francisco. He nodded, and she pulled her own debit card from her shorts and inserted it into the machine. She put in her PIN and hit OK to accept. She shifted her feet and leaned on the little counter. After a moment, the machine clanked with a buzzer sound DECLINED. Emma looked down at the screen flashing in red, "There must be some mistake…"

Francisco shook his head, "Too much in the cart for your card to handle. "Here." He inserted his company card.

The cashier looked to Emma, "Sorry, we always get this. Who knows where the screw-up is? To be safe, you should call your bank." He handed the receipt to Francisco.

They stuffed the extra-large cooler with meat, beer, and ice at the pickup, then returned to the train to change out of their damp clothes. Francisco told her to bring warm clothes if the weather turned, but they were in SLC. Together, they rummaged through the work coats and hats, but even the smallest coat was still too big. He pulled up his laptop, and they checked the forecast. After such a hot day, thunderstorms often build out from the blue in minutes.

"Tonight, the blue skies should transition into a warm, starry night," she said, pointing to the screen. She asked him, "Have you thought about your talent?"

"Mine is music. Have you thought about a talent for the show?"

"Well, I thought it was singing when I was a girl. I tried ballet, but I wasn't any good. They pretty much just asked me not to come anymore. I liked kickball, though."

Francisco shook his head and patted her on the shoulder, "Little girls have their princess dream crushed too often by reality. My daughter is going through it, but that's how we learn what we are not." "We probably should bring a few things to make this night work. It might take a few trips to get everything we'll need. Come."

They went forward to the engine behind the front engine, "This is where we keep most of the stuff. Here, take this." He handed her a large and smaller case and took this light stand, too." He grabbed two cases and another light stand. They filled the pickup, locked the train doors, and drove to the park.

The Green River Park is large, sprawling over two hundred acres with overnight camp sites and picnic spots. It starts at the river and works its way westward. It's popular for campers and river floaters. Francisco and Emma drove into the park through the crowds of tourists that mingled on the road. It would be like driving your car through a herd of cattle in Texas. Emma searched the crowd for their friends. When they turned a corner, Francisco pointed in front. Emma turned to see, but too many people were standing in her view. She noted that they helped the men unload the truck; it was a lovely spot. It was covered, had a full-size barbeque pit, two picnic tables, and access to the river if they or when they get too hot, like right now. Over to the edge was a set of restrooms close by, she noted.

"Hey," she pointed to a group of girls by the restrooms. "I think that is Daisy over there… I used to know her when we were stationed in Kentucky. I'm going to say hi. I'll be right back."

The men watched as she bounded across the field. Roy twisted off a cap of Corona, tipped it back, took a big gulp, and wiped the sweat from under his hat.

Chico looked at his watch, "We should be eating about eight. Hey Roy, is she your girlfriend, or are you staying playboy?" the others laughed.

Roy said, "Me, playboys? Si… Emma, my girlfriend, no, I think she likes you more, Chico." They laughed again. "Come, Chico, and I will get some girls for our party tonight."

"No, no, no, last time Chico tried, he ran everyone out of the park. I think it should be Miguel and me this time. We are smooth."- the men laughed again.

Roy elbowed Diego when three young ladies approached. "Follow my lead, amigo." As the three walked past their picnic table, Roy dropped his cell phone in front of them. When he picked it up, he touched the screen. One of the girls, the shorter one on the side, said, "Oh, did you break your phone?"

Roy shrugged his shoulders, "Yes, I am sure it is broken," he showed her the screen and said, "Because it doesn't have your number." The girl blushed, holding her hands to her mouth.

Francisco chuckled with Chico at her blushing. He said, "Roy is at it again. It looks like we will have guests for the show. I don't know how he does it, and he is unashamed about it."

Chico said, "I think there might be more guests. It looks like Emma has a friend." He pointed over Francisco's shoulder at Emma, talking with a group of girls. "They look pretty hot, boss. Maybe we each have dates for the night."

They heard Diego ask, "Do you believe in love at first sight?" the girls giggled. One said no. Chico mouthed the words to Francisco as Diego said, "Shall I walk by again?" Chico said, "Maybe we get another table, so much company."

Francisco reached into the cooler, "We're getting low, amigo. Let's go for a beer run."

Later, at the barbeque grill, Miguel watched Emma pull back the foil and pocked at the ribs. Steam rose in a little plume as the fork went through the tender meat. She checked her watch; it was seven thirty, and the food was almost ready. She pulled the ribs off to the side and laid several ears of corn in their husk on the grill. Miguel shoved more hot coals together underneath. He looked at the sun getting low on the horizon. It was a large orange ball casting long purple-ish-blue shadows through the park. It was the golden hour when daylight became bathed in a veil of gold, and the shadows glowed a blue-violet hue. A catalog of Birds of the West flew about, singing and chirping, while some were in their nest, others searching for one last snack before bedtime. The park lights began to glow white as the previous swimmers returned to land, swatting at flies and mosquitoes.

Emma's old friend Daisy returned with another girl, and Francisco invited both to the party. She introduced her friend Brittaney, a married girl, and her belly showed a baby bump. Daisy sat down across from Emma next to Roy's other side. She smiled at him and asked for a drink. He offered water or beer, but she wanted something stronger: tequila. The two tables joined together; now, there was room enough for the eight men and eight girls with lots of food. Brittaney ignored that Roy was sitting with Emma; Roy was all she saw. Roy leaned across Emma as he talked with Daisy. Emma shifted in her seat and kicked at Francisco. She looked at her friend Daisy, conversing with the other girls at the table. She took her beer, tipped it back, and finished it. Roy's eyes shifted from Brittaney to Emma several times. Emma noticed and did her best not to make a scene. He tried to smile, but his brows scrunched when she spoke as though she were interrupting. Daisy had a higher voice that sounded like a girl's more than a woman's, but no man would have complained when her large, voluptuous chest sat on the table under a pink, low-cut tank top. No one could ignore the cleavage scene when she spilled her icy margarita drink down her front. The men offered napkins and watched her like vultures as she dabbed at her wet shirt.

While they ate, Daisy, a free spirit from horse country near Lexington, Kentucky, described back home with the green hills and the summer nights. She said, "At night, you could walk and walk and never need a flashlight. As you walk through the tall grass, there are so many lightning bugs to lighten up your path. Emma, remember the sleepovers and how we played outside the night until it was very late when they lived there."

Francisco rose and announced, "Tonight, we have a special treat. Forgive us while we depart to make certain preparations, but I assure you that your patience will be rewarded." He waved to the men to join. Some set up the lights while others tuned instruments.

Brittaney leaned over the table and asked Emma, "Who are you seeing?"

Emma shook her head, "No one. They are my friends."

"What, are you kidding? I'm sure you've had one or two by now. Come on, who are you trying to kid? Look at me." She leaned back to show her baby bump. "Well, tell you what, I'll make sure you get some tonight. I know that I am." She finished her drink, "Hey, can someone pour me another one I need to sneeze." She waved her red solo cup and turned her head away.

Emma said, "But you're—"

"—Pregnant," Brittaney blurted. "That's right, and from the right father, too. My husband is a fighter pilot in the Air Force. Now that I'm carrying his baby, I can do whatever I want or whoever I want. And from the looks of this group of horney young dudes, I might have to try them all. Hey Daisy, what is it that you always say?"

"You are only young once, and then your old the rest of your life."

"That's right, take it from your friend Daisy. It's better to enjoy being young while you're young. Think about that, or maybe you'll miss out and spend a lifetime of regret."

Emma sipped her beer and laughed along with the others. She said, "If my mom could hear this now…"

Daisy said, "Brittaney makes a good point, Em. Her father was Senator Warren from Virginia. Her father is on various boards of directors; people from that kind of power writ their own ticket and can pretty much do what they want."

Brittany emptied her cup and said, "That's right, Emma, and when I'm done being young, I'll follow my family's path in business. I'll be Senator Brittany, a leader for our country with the perfect family, but for now, I just have to have fun. Isn't your mom some big shot?"

Daisy said, "Tell her, Emma, no sense keeping it a secret. Notice how many people bend over to kiss your ass compared to some other girl that might be prettier?" The girls laughed. "Here's to our future. May the line be long for those to kiss our assess."

The sun sank over the desert horizon, saturating the land with its red light. Emma felt herself blushing the same color. Her throat felt dry and hot, reaching for her beer, but her cup was empty. Instead, she grabbed the one beside her and took a big drink. The ice-cold

Coors Light cooled her head. The girls laughed and toasted each other, 'here's to being spoiled and having fun! Whoo.'

Francisco returned to the table. "Thank you for your patience. Back in Mexico, we've had a tradition since our youth, and tonight, we would like to carry on our tradition and share with new friends in a wonderful setting that only God himself could have made. Tonight, we would like to perform various talents for your entertainment. Remember, we are not professionals nor amateurs, but we hope you enjoy it. First up is your boy, Roy. I believe he has a card trick," he looked over to a dark curtain, "He says he is ready,"

Roy came out from behind the curtain wearing a mariachi costume, enhancing his taller stature and good looks. Emma's mouth opened. 'Roy…'

"Good evening. As my brother said, when we were kids, we used to practice magic to pass the time. We knew a magician, the great Manta, or something like that." Francisco returned carrying a round folding table that he set it in front. Roy placed a new deck of cards on the table, shuffled it, and then asked his brother to cut it. Francisco stooped, looking sideways to see under the cards, then split the deck close to half. Roy scooted the table next to the audience, "Let's make this more interesting. OK, who would like to select a card from the deck?"

Emma reached into the deck and pulled out a card. He asked her "Show it to the others Emma, but not to me." She held up the eight hearts and placed them back on top of the deck. Roy shuffled the deck three times, each time showing a different face card. "As I go through the deck, I will attempt to determine Emma's card. He flipped over two spades, then a king of diamonds. The next card was the jack of clubs," He said, "The next card, I believe, will be Emma's." He grabbed the edge of the jack and lifted it above the deck, "Does anyone want to make a wager? Raise your money high, please."

The girls reached into their purses and pulled out twenty-dollar bills, five ones, whatever they had. Roy smiled, his eyes twinkling as he looked over to his brother. He looked at Daisy's hair, "Something seems to be going on with your hair." He reached into her hair, "Yes, see this… Here it is." His fingers pulled out the missing eight diamonds, and he snapped up the girl's cash they held out. "Let's call it a tip. Thank you."

He placed the cash under his sombrero, "Thank you. OK, next up," he pulled a silver dollar from his pocket and flipped it around the knuckles on his hand. It moved between each of his fingers, and then he flipped it over each of his knuckles down into his palm. "We won't do any of these cheap, easy tricks, like the disappearing coin trick." He opened his bare palm, but there was no coin. He checked his other hand, then up his sleeves, "I just had it a second ago. Did anyone see where it went? Where is it?" he held his hands out for them to inspect. The three girls and Brittaney examined his hands and sleeves, and then he tugged at his sleeve and pulled a long, blue-colored veil from his jacket pocket. "I believe we can make the coin reappear. What do you girls say?" He waved the veil in the air and let it land on the table. He asked for a volunteer to lift it, and Brittaney leaned forward and lifted it. There underneath was the missing silver dollar.

While the girls applauded, he pulled a white rope from his left coat pocket, stretched it out, swirled it around, and waved it in front of them. He let it drape over his left hand while cutting it into short segments using scissors. He bunched them together, waved his hand, and asked one of the girls to blow on them. Emma blew at his hand, and he reached in and pulled the same white rope from it to loud cheers from Brittaney.

She said, "Save it you might need that later, sweetie."

"Thank you, girls, you have been terrific." He took off his sombrero and bowed.

Francisco said, "Keep your eye on him, or he might steal your heart. Next up is the handyman of handymen, the nibble-fingered, the magnificent Miguel de la Rio."

Miguel stood under their work lights wearing a black silk coat and tails, a white starched button shirt, and a white vest and bow tie. His white cuffs flashed in the lights as he juggled a pair of white bowling pins with his right hand. He wore a formal black silk top hat, making him look tall and elegant. Francisco held a third pin and tossed it up into the air higher than the other two. Miguel juggled all three pins with one hand, threw it above the lights, spun around, and caught it by the handle behind his back. The table cheered. Next, he picked up a group of white balls and bounced them off the cement floor in an oval shape up to his two open hands. First, it was three, then four, now five balls zipping through the air and added two more. Seven balls hardly contacted his palms as he guided them to the floor. Emma tried to follow a single ball's path, but her eyes could not follow. Francisco added the side of an equipment case, and the balls bounced from the floor up to it. Then, to his right hand, he did this without losing any as he filled his hands with the balls. Ta-da! Miguel bowed, and the audience cheered and clapped.

Francisco clapped for his cousin standing at the end of the table, "Miguel, you still got it. When we were kids, a carnival came to town and taught us lots of fun things. Not one of those things was one that one of my cousins learned. Here is Diego.

Diego waved to the girls, holding a soccer ball under his arm and wearing a soccer uniform. The crowd lightly clapped. Chico played a salsa song on the guitar. Francisco clapped to the beat; Diego tapped the ball into motion with his right foot. He bounced it from foot to foot, then when the song grew louder, he bounced it up onto one knee, then up and down on the other knee, hitting it above his head, then the song paused, and the ball paused on the crown of his head. He held his arms out while it balanced, ready to roll off. The song started again, and he kicked it back up into the air, juggling it off his feet and knees, then over his head and back kicked it back up in front of him as the song melody played another time. The crowd grew and clapped; he was not done yet. He watched where the ball would land and focused on striking it with the right amount of force at the right angle and moment. Francisco threw him a second ball, and his body and feet juggled them in front to the tapping of the guitar strings with each strike. The beat increased; he kicked each over his head and back kicked them, bouncing like a string. He kicked one high overhead, spun around, and dropped-kicked the other ball. It curved and went into the goal across the field as he caught the first ball with his chest.

Francisco high-fived him and said, "That was pretty good, but he's a little rusty, just kidding, that was amazing." He clapped and then announced, "Next is a traditional song led by our Chico. He isn't much for looks, but don't let that fool you…" He picked up his guitar and joined the Mariachi band. Diego picked up a trumpet, Miguel was on bass guitar, and Roy and the others were on horns. Chico stood straight, dignified in his mariachi costume. He set his large sombrero on his brow and said, "Here is an old ranch song, 'Hermoso Carino,' It means beautiful honey that God has sent me to be destined, just for me." The horns did a quick tuning together while he sang the same note. Emma watched Chico, ignoring his crooked nose scars and poked skin; his energy and posture held her gaze.

He sang with a clear, strong voice, rolling his r's. The girls giggled at the table, and his strong voice accented his words, lending much passion to his voice. Miguel did a short melody solo on guitar, and then Roy played the same on his trumpet. Chico sang for two and a half minutes; he finished with a strong flourish of the last four lines. No puedo evitarlo y quiero gritarlo, Hermoso carino, que dios ha mandado, nommas para mi in one breath extending the mi upwards and faded it into the night. His audience felt the song's passion.

Emma cheered Chico, "I had no idea and all this time you never told me. You're so talented."

Roy's date and her two friends waved to Francisco, "Wait, wait, we want you guys to back us on a song we want to sing, 'Made you look.' By Megan Trainor."

Francisco tapped a rhythmic beat on his guitar body as the horn section worked out an arrangement, and the girls practiced their song and dance moves.

I could have my Gucci on. I could wear my Louis Vuitton, But even with nothi'n on

Bet I made you look….

The girls danced and sang the song with the men to a growing crowd of on-lookers. They extended their version of the song with a brief horn section solo with a run of loose dance moves.

Chapter 11

The following day, it was dark as the men began shuffling into the dining car. Miguel stood over the coffee pot, pleading with it to hurry. Francisco pulled a cup from the shelf, "We need to get over to Moab this morning. Have you seen any of the others yet?" He looked out the window over the sink. The brightest star in the morning, Venus, glowed on the horizon like a grand celestial torch.

The coffee maker wheezed as the last drops sputtered into the pot. Miguel mixed cream and sugar in his coffee, "Nada, I haven't seen anyone 'cept for you, boss. Shall I see if they made it back after last night?" He sat at the first table, rubbed his eyes, and asked, "Where's Emma? Is she going to make breakfast?"

The train was silent except for the faint drone of the locomotive's engines. Th interior constantly vibrated from the large diesel engines; Emma got used to that after a couple of days. Francisco rubbed his chin whiskers, "Hmm, guess I should wake Emma." He knocked on her stateroom door and waited. He looked down the hall toward the kitchen when he heard the door slide open. Low voices talked in the dining room. He knocked again, "Emma… you in there?" He put his ear to the door and called her again.

"Emma said, "I'm awake… Come in.""

He turned the latch and then slid her door ajar. "Em? Are you OK?" His hand searched for the light switch, "I'm going to turn your light on, OK?" She agreed. With the light on, he looked over to her bunk, where she sat with her arms wrapped around her legs, which she pulled up. Her back leaned against the wall. "Em? What's wrong?"

She pointed down to the box, "The little deer died. I assumed it was asleep last night, but it must have died while I was out having fun. I'm a terrible person." She leaned her head on her knees to wipe the tears on her pajamas. He kneeled at the box; the little deer lay curled up with its head lying toward the side. His hand stroked its soft fur. The eyes were closed. His voice was just above a whisper, "It must have passed away when it was asleep." He turned his head towards Emma, "I am so sorry about this… we must move out this morning. The men are looking for breakfast, but they can have cereal. Take your time, OK?" She nodded back under her tears. He slid her door closed.

Later, all but Roy sat eating cereal. Francisco asked, "Has anyone seen what happened to Roy?" He got up and looked out the window. "Here he comes. It looks like he had a wild night."

Heavy footsteps clomped up the stairs, and the door handle fidgeted, then slid open. Roy stood on the threshold, grinning. "Hola amigos," he laughed. He still wore his mariachi costume and waved his sombrero to the others.

"Get in here and get yourself cleaned up. There's work to do. The party is over, come." Francisco said.

"Where's Emma? I want eggs, bacon, and pancakes."

Francisco handed his brother a cup of coffee and pointed to the table, "Here, take this, go sit down, have some fruit loops. While you guys were out being a bunch of playboys, Emma helped me bring our gear back last night. I am just as tired as the rest of you, but we have work to do later, so get your selves together."

Francisco walked down the hall to check on Emma. She sat cradling the cardboard box with the diseased deer on her bunk. "We should bury it,"

He pointed and whispered, "Yes, but let's go out the front way and avoid the guys."

Emma whispered, "Did I hear Roy's voice just now?"

"Yes. Come on, get ready."

After they packed down the dirt mound, they added rocks to a pile. Emma laid some white-colored stones in the shape of a cross. They dusted their knees and hands. Emma kneeled on the grave and asked Francisco, "Why did it die? Was it because of me? She looked up at his face. Her eyes were dark as the night she pushed her messy hair from her face. The sunrise showed a natural reddish tint to her hair.

He said, "Come on, let me help you." She grabbed hold of his hand, and he pulled her up. "Look's to be another perfect summer day. How would you like to drive the train?" He put his hand on her shoulder. She leaned into his side, "Living is hard, Emma. Have you ever had a pet die before?"

"No... I've never had a real pet before."

They walked back to the train in silence. At the patio step, she stopped looking at her feet. He turned around, and she looked right, then left. "I'm just going to be a failure in my life. I don't know what I am doing, and you guys know how to do everything."

The horizon began to glow with a vibrant orange to the east as the sun poked over the horizon. She stood with her back to the eastern horizon; all he could see of her was just a silhouette. The desert air was cool, a breeze whipped up, and Emma shivered, "I want to be like you, Cisco. You always know what to do, but…? Geez, I don't know how to do anything. School is such a waste of time. I spend all day being lectured about things that have nothing to do with the real world or how to solve real problems."

He pulled his phone out, "Well, it's almost six, so if you want to be like me, you must get an early start. Come on; we are going to one of the most amazing places. It's so incredible that even if you didn't believe in God, you would after spending the day there. You can drive the train, come." He climbed down and pointed to the front of the train as they walked. It was a couple of blocks to the front; they climbed the ladder onto the platform to the door on the front nose.

Inside the train engine, he called the crew on the radio. His driver's seat was the right-hand seat. The company man sat next to the left side when they were there. He showed Emma where the throttle and brake were. She released the main brakes when he gave the 'all clear' and then began to push the throttle lever forward. He called the mainline. The train rolled on the track and then switched onto the mainline. Emma pushed the throttles forward, and the cars bumped and swayed while the train switched onto the mainline. Francisco pointed out the window to the oncoming train next to them, and she hung on. Not long after that, Emma again winced, gripping her seat as they rode over the river bridge. He stood at her side and pointed to speed and air gauges to watch. The engine shifted as it rode on the rails. Emma leaned back into the back of the seat and exhaled. As they entered the eastern side of Utah, the landscape began to reveal fantastic rock formations. Little scrub tress replaced the tall firs of the mountains. Cactus and sagebrush speckled the sandy ground. The forty-four-mile trip to Moab lasted under an hour without incidents or close calls.

The grinding train eased to a stop near Moab, Emma set the brakes and idled the engines. Their train cut through scenic canyons back to the Green River. Above and just behind was Arches National Park. In front was the tourist town of Moab, and a bit further back to the south was Canyonlands National Park. Francisco called on the radio to the crew, "Meeting in the chow hall." He turned to Emma and said, "We'll have a meeting and see who wants to do what. The company man is not scheduled to arrive until later." He led Emma through the engine, back out the side door, and down the ladder. Thy walked to the dining car on the side of the tracks instead of climbing over the water cars. Meadowlarks sang their songs, and crows and magpies flittered about as buntings and sparrows chirped, all in search of breakfast for their young. He pointed out that the railroad ties were old and twisted, and the gravel needed refilling. They climbed up to the dining car's patio and saw a family of mule deer walking to the river. The deer turned and froze, sniffing the air, then bounded at top speed into the sage. He slid the door open and joined the others.

With a fresh cup of coffee, he told the men, "Today is sort of a free day, and tonight we pick up our new company, man. He wants to start immediately, so be ready to work through the night. He's scheduled to be with us till Golden, so be on your best behavior, and we will try to get another free day or two in Denver. Some want to go to Arches this morning, while the rest of us will hang out here and wait for Chuy, who should be here in about an hour. Let's see a show of hands for Arches?" Francisco counted Emma's hand. He shrugged his shoulders at her. "As we all know, we have a buddy system."

Emma shook her head, "That's not fair. Come on, guys… Roy… Diego…Miguel!"

The men shrugged their shoulders. Roy said, "We have to work all night, and we're tired from last night."

Emma walked over to Roy, pointed her finger in his face, her head tilted, craning her neck, "Fine, I'll just go by myself. It's your fault for staying out all night, Roy. You knew I wanted to see the arches, but all you can do is think of Roy. I don't need you…" She turned towards Francisco and shouted as she slid the door open. "This is so unfair."

Why is Emma so upset?" Francisco asked Roy. He leaned over the sink and watched Emma climb in the pickup. "Whose day is it for truck duty?"

Diego said, 'Yesterday was your day, Cisco, which means today is Roy's turn."

Then, men stood in silence, all looking at Roy; he shuffled his feet and looked outside. Emma leaned against the hood of the large one-ton pickup. She lit a cigarette and checked her phone. She wanted to see the Grand Arch at sunrise, but it was now near 9 am. Her last family outing with her brothers was at Arches. That was a good memory, but like most things, other people come first no matter what she wants. 'Thanks, Roy, asshole. I better at least get to see the park today on the tenth year since that fun family trip.'

Roy said, "Can't one of the other guys go instead? You all saw her; she hates me now. Miguel, you like her, come on, bro, please?"

Miguel shook his head, "Sorry, Mr. Playboy, I have a date for the day with that Chica, Miss Daisy."

Roy crossed his arms and leaned against the wall, "Cisco, please, I'm too tired to drive. Come on and trade with your bro?" He turned and walked out of the car with his head down and shoes dragging over the dirt. Francisco heard the door lock chirp. He and the other men sighed and shook their heads. Chico asked, "What happened? All was so well last night. Diego and I visited with that crazy Brittaney bitch, we come back, and everyone is at each other this morning."

Miguel asked Francisco, "Did you sleep with her last night?"

"No. That's not what this is about. The deer died, and what's worse, Roy was out sleeping around with not one but three chicas and had the nerve not to come back till everyone was here, including Emma."

Diego shook his head, "Bro, we didn't know about the deer, and she didn't say anything."

Chico said, "That's 'cuz she's too upset. I will go with her if I know."

Francisco watched the truck turn onto the highway and head up the hill. "It's too late now, so everyone goes back to bed and gets some rest."

Later, Emma slid the patio door open and tiptoed to her stateroom. Her door creaked, then she tapped on his door and called out, 'Cisco… are you awake?'

He said, "Come in." He rubbed his eyes when she opened his door. He whispered, "You're back early. How did it go?"

She looked down, "Terrible. I tried to use my debit card but they declined it, and your brother, being the selfish asshole that he is, refused to pay my way. All we did was fight. Your brother is so selfish. I hate him."

"Sorry, Emma, but I warned you about him. Relax, lay down, take it easy, and get some rest." She nodded, and he laid his head back and sighed.

Chapter 12

Emma went back to bed after a discouraging morning, crying into her pillow. About an hour later, Francisco and his cousin Chuy, sat in the dining car drinking coffee. It was mid-morning, and the temperature was over ninety. After coffee, they packed an ice chest with sandwiches and drinks. The others slowly shuffled into the dining car to pack their coolers. The crew had free time to kill before the company man arrived, add Chuy and everyone was in for a great time riding Razors in Moab. Like Chuy said, it just doesn't get better anywhere than that. He reserved side-by-side Razor's for the half day and brought his. With their open cockpit, lots of power, and high suspension, the UTVs would go where few vehicles could follow. Th Razor used a Baja racer design. Whenever they passed through the area they did this with Chuy. They loved racing each other and following the leader over rock obstacles and up rock cliffs. Occasionally, someone would try too big of a challenge and roll their Razor to the jeers of their friends. That's when cold beer relives the aches.

Chuy and Francisco went outside to inspect Chuy's modified Razor. Francisco stood in front of the trailer studying Chuy's Razor. He said, "Even sitting here it looks like it's moving fast."

A lime green and black Razor was on a long trailer towed by a three-quarter ton Chevy Duramax. They toured around the Razor as Chuy showed the latest modifications to his tricked-out racing Razor. He climbed up the trailer and started it. Francisco unloosened the chains to the rear frame, and Chuy loosened the front-end chains.

They tipped down the wheel ramps, and Chuy backed his Razor off the trailer. The others came out to inspect his ride while Francisco returned to check on Emma.

"Emma… Emma, we are getting ready to leave," he tapped on her door.

He said, "Come on, let's go." She was in her pajamas. "Come on, Em…"

"Are you sure I should go? I don't want to ruin your fun."

"You won't. Have you ridden in one of these before?"

"No…" the edges of her mouth curved up. "Alright, sounds fun. Who am I riding with?"

"Well, definitely not Roy. Chico and Diego like to do things together, so that leaves Miguel or Luis. Rueben and Simon have to watch the train."

Her face turned to a frown, "Can't we go together? I need a friend, Cisco." Francisco could not break his plans, not even for a girl who pleaded for it. He smiled and held out his hands for her. She put hers in his hands. He said, "Aah, women make it so difficult, but why? It's just meant to be fun. I never understood my wife, even before she… she… and now I have two daughters, and I can't wait to have a boy, someone I can teach the ways of manhood to."

"Oh geez, Cisco… so what is happening with your wife? What are you not telling? You just might as well 'fess up now 'cause I'll learn, and then we'll have us a talk."

Francisco shook his head, 'Come on, tell you later, for now, let's go and have fun."

Francisco and Chuy roared out from the rental for the Hell's Revenge Trailhead, leaving a long rooster tail of dust in their wake. They first stopped at the Sand Flats Rec Area to meet with the others. Francisco took over the driver's seat for quick practice while waiting. He adjusted his face mask and sunglasses before driving over a boulder patch. The UTV leaned on its passenger side while the tires gripped the rock. They climbed over the boulders, and his body weight would have fallen into Chuy without the harness straps to secure him. He feathered the throttle as his left wheel followed the top of the boulder, and then the front rolled down off that boulder, and then the right front wheel rode up a large boulder, but the engine stalled out. Chuy laughed.

"Hey bro, this has a new deluxe suspension with more travel. You can take these faster. Try it, bro." he smacked Cisco on the knee, "Over there, can do that segment in second gear."

Francisco restarted and rolled out of the boulders, shifted gears, and went over a steep, barren sandstone formation, keeping his speed until he could not see below them on the cliffside. The tires gripped as he hit the brakes at the edge. Chuy waved for him to keep going, pointed below to the right, and waved no good that way. Francisco downshifted and eased down the slope. About halfway down, the angle lessened, he shifted, and flew over the bottom half, swerving around ruts and trees. Chuy lived in the area, memorized most of the trails and knew his equipment's limits.

They stopped at the bottom of a cliff and took off their helmets. Chuy laughed, pointing to him. Francisco looked at himself in the mirror, lifted his glasses, and pulled his face gaiter down. He shook his head, strapped his helmet, turned the Razor around, and sped up the cliff. The car roared up the face hoping and bouncing kicking up dirt. He timed his downshifts keeping his rpm's high. At the top, he dropped to first gear, spinning the wheels while creeping onto the red sandstone top. He set the brake and unstrapped the seat harness.

From their viewpoint, they saw the others coming up the trail. Below, the Colorado River wound its way through on the desert floor like a giant snake. Across the river up in the hills, he saw a few arches from Arches National Park, and in the rear mirror was the Rocky Mountains, their tall snow-capped fourteen-thousand-foot peaks.

"Chuy, you are so blessed to live here. Imagine being out here every day, but do you ever tire of it?"

"Never, bro. Hey, remember when we were kids back in Monterey? We used to ride horses and imagine we were cowboys. We chased after cows and rabbits. Imagine if we had one of these back in the day."

He watched Diego and Chico swing up next to them. Chuy yelled, "Hey bros, you ready to roll?"

Diego yelled, "Hell ya, we got this." He and Chico raised their fists, high-fiving.

Another UTV came along the other side. Emma sat in the passenger seat. Francisco leaned forward and yelled, "Is that you, Miguel?" Emma nodded with Miguel. "Hey, we are going to Hell's Revenge. Come on." He pointed to the left. Chuy tightened his helmet strap and rode down the trail followed by the other three Razors making a long dust trail.

The entrance to the trail is a paved single-lane road that quickly dissolves into sandstone. The caravan meandered through tight canyons, up steep hills, over large boulders, and down almost sheer cliffs. They flew down hills and caught air over mounds rising several feet before they landed on the other side, the long travel suspension compressing then expanding, each wheel moving independently making for smooth controlled landings at high speed. Strapped in tight, keeping their hands on the wheel and foot on the throttle being jarred required its own concentration. They stopped at a scenic overlook, a cliff just above the twisty river where pelicans and cranes flapped their large wings flying feet above the surface.

Chuy and Francisco, unclipped, walked back and pulled a beer from the cooler. The cold beer felt wet and so cold. Francisco massaged the back of his neck with the cold can. Chuy laughed, "Live for today, gone tomorrow." They clicked their beer cans and took a big sip. They leaned against the cooler; the others came over, each grasping a beer.

Francisco asked Emma, "Well, are you glad you came out?"

She wrapped her arms around his neck, "Oh my God, you guys are completely crazy. I think Miguel is trying to scare me to death."

Chuy asked, "Do you want to drive?"

Emma looked at Francisco, he smiled and took another drink. She shook her head, no.

Chuy laughed and said, "Come, just go down there and turn around in mine."

"Not with the others watching. I don't know how to drive one of these."

Francisco nodded, "It takes some getting used to, but go for it, Emma, come on. Trust me, you'll love it."

Bending or breaking under the pier pressure from Chuy, Emma climbed into his Razor's cockpit and Francisco helped her buckle in. Chuy gave her a rundown on the controls. She put in the clutch, but he put it in first and told her to give it some throttle while slowly letting her foot off the clutch pedal. She let her foot off but did not give it any throttle. The clutch popped and the car lurched forward then it stalled, she shook her head. Francisco and Chuy leaned against a rock sipping their beers talking. The Razor stood motionless then began rolling forward as she let it out slower but gave it too much throttle when her foot slipped off the pedal, jerking her backward and then diving forward.

Chuy handed Francisco his beer ran over motioning with his hands. He said, "Relax, it's made for this terrain, so just drive it like you would a car on the road."

Emma nodded and raised her thumb then grasped the wheel. She looked forward, took her foot off the brake pedal, and gave less throttle as she let the clutch out, and the car moved forward smoother. He followed next to her- and said, "You're doing it. Now let's go over there and turn around."

She eased the car around and shot back up the hill, shifting from first to second, then third. At first, the vehicle bobbed over the ruts, but as she gained more speed, the car seemed to float over the terrain. She hit the brakes at the top of the hill, and it stopped, almost running into the rear of the red Razor where Roy and Chico stood. Roy leaped out of the way. She said, "I meant to do that," She unbuckled the straps and climbed out and back into the red one with Miguel.

Francisco and Chuy fist bumped. He said to Chuy, "Thanks bro, I think she needed that experience, you should become a guide."

After three hours, the Razor caravan turned around and headed back down the Nine-Mile Trail. They rode under overhanging rocks, drove between cactus and sage, hopped over boulders in gullies, and stopped frequently for selfies. A day rewarded by Utah's rugged land of incredible beauty around every bend, ending at Moab. The hot afternoon gave the riders no relief from the mid-day heat, but no one wanted the day to end.

Instead of waiting for the others to return their rentals, Francisco and Chuy returned to the train and stored the UTV on the trailer. They shook hands with another chuckle and went into the dining car. Inside, they rinsed their hands and faces under the sink, then slunk onto the bench. Draining un cerveza, Francisco turned and looked out the window when the pickup drove up. After dropping four off, it swung around to get the others.

Francisco read a text from the office. "Looks like we are to meet the new company man back in Thompson Springs in the morning. Glad it's not today. Sure, you don't want to come back to work?"

"Nope, I'm good. Who would ever leave this just for a job? Since you're not working today, let's have a beer." He dug into the ice chest. "Got any in here?"

"No, not allowed to keep any on the train and you know how the guys are."

asked, "Who's your company man for this section?"

"His name is Turner. Do you know him?"

"Yeah, a real hard ass, be careful not to piss him off, and don't let him know we're cousins, I really pissed him off. He doesn't like Mexicans. You know the type."

"In that case, I think it's best to move the train tonight just in case he's early tomorrow."

Chuy, who used to be the train supervisor, agreed, "Si, bueno. But next time you return, we need to make it a few days of riding. I think you could get better with more time."

"Si, Chuy, bueno. So, what do you think of Emma?"

"Emma is a good person but doesn't reveal much about herself. Be careful, bro. There's much she's not saying, which could mean trouble. I don't want anything to happen to you."

"I copy that, Chuy. Looks like the gang is all here." They watched the others clomp up the stairs of the dining car. "Let's go in and cool off."

Chapter 13

The following day, Emma sat at the dining table, stirring her coffee, adding more almond milk, thinking of how the world went on without her. After a few sips, she opened the laptop, rubbed her temples checked her emails and Facebook page. She rubbed her eyes, yawned then took a sip, and choked; her mother left a message on her page. She shook her head, reading her mom's rantings about her being irresponsible by abandoning the family, and how her mom and her brothers had to go it alone while her daughter neglected her family while joyriding God knows where or with who. In fact, so irresponsible not even to let her family know where she was. She might as well have called her a spoiled brat, but she was by her nature careful with her word choices. Senator Chase succeeded, if her goal was to make her daughter feel terrible. Emma slumped and put her head on the table, ashamed of her selfish actions.

The radio called, 'Where's the damned coffee?' asked an unfamiliar loud, gruff voice. Emma lifted her head and looked at the counter; the pot was empty. Francisco texted her, 'Where are you? the pot is empty, and we are out of coffee.' She sat up and texted him, 'On my way with more.' She grabbed a coffee can and went to the front of the train, over the water cars, then through the engine to the front engine, walked along the outside to the front through the door under the cab, and climbed up the stairs to the coffee pot.

The new company man said, "Did you need a special invitation? We've only been asking for you for the last hour." He looked across from her, and then she looked back to Francisco. He shrugged and rolled his eyes. The old man shook his finger and said, "If you can't do your job, I'll find someone who will. Plenty of people would love to have a good job." He turned to Francisco, "You better get your crew in line real fast, boy."

Emma said, "I didn't hear the radio call for me until a few minutes ago."

The old man snorted, "That is the wrong answer. Next time, don't take so long, got it, Missy?"

Emma nodded, then went back down and out the door. She stood leaning against the front rail. The horizon towards the mountains looked almost as dark as the night. Thick, heavy clouds loomed over the peaks, sparking off lighting flashes. Behind the train, the cold front ended, and it was warm with a blue sky. She took a few deep breaths, returned to the dining car, started the coffee pot, and then shuffled to her room. She laid on her bunk and texted Francisco, 'Hey, I did nothing wrong. Why didn't you stand up for me back there?' She tossed her phone by her feet and curled up with her arms wrapped around her legs. Her phone chirped, a text from Francisco. 'Sorry, but I warned everyone to be on their toes, or he will cause trouble.' She shook her head, 'damn it.' She threw her blanket over her head; the stress made her tired and dozed.

When she awoke, she looked at her phone. At almost eleven, she threw off the blanket, stepped into her slippers, and ran to the kitchen. Dishes rose from the sink, and the counters were cluttered with more breakfast dishes. The floor had boot prints from all the grinding dust trampled inside, giving a dark blackish hue to the tan-colored floor. Her stomach gurgled, and she had to use the facilities; the cleaning would have to wait.

She took her phone and laptop into the bathroom and re-read her mom's ranting post on her site. She knew that if her mom knew she was on a train full of Mexican men, she would go ballistic. Apparently, her girlfriend Rachel did not tip her mom off. She texted Rachel, 'Hey, my mom is saying stuff. Has she talked with you lately?' she hit the send button and looked at the laptop, finger tapping the keyboard. Should she lie to her, tell the truth, or try to change the subject? She knew she had to send a response that would keep her mom from asking questions. 'This must be what it's like when a kid runs away from home.' she typed, then deleted it and typed, 'I am fine, Mom. Don't worry about me. Worry about your re-election campaign.' She deleted it. Next, she typed, 'I'll be home in a couple of days, just visiting a friend from school.' Her finger hovered over the post button. Back in the kitchen, she heard footsteps and voices. It must be lunchtime, damn it.

She finished and saw two of the crew members rummaging through the refrigerator.

Roy asked, "Where are the sandwiches?" from over his shoulder as he pulled out a 2 liter of Coke. Luis grabbed a bag of potato chips and poured himself some Coke. Their clothes were covered with dark soot.

Emma opened the other fridge, pulled out the sliced ham, sliced turkey, and pastrami, and set it on one of the tables. Then she brought mayo and mustard with a loaf of bread and slammed them on the table. "Here, I need to clean the counters and sink from your mess this morning. Why can't you guys clean up after yourselves? What are you, a bunch of little kids?"

Roy and Luis looked at each other and shrugged. She slammed the frying pan in the sink, threw dish soap, and turned the water on high. She grabbed a broom and swept the floor into a dirt pile blown around when the other men slid the door open. "Damn it…" she yelled. The men made sandwiches while she scrubbed dishes. After they left, she again swept the floor and set the clean dishes on the counter to dry on a towel.

She flopped onto the bench and wiped her hair from her eyes. She read a new text from Rachel as the company man entered the dining room. He looked over at her sitting and went to the coffee pot. "You're out of coffee," he said. She looked over to the empty pot.

"Damn, I just made a fresh pot too."

He grunted, hmf, "Well, you best get used to it, Missy, and while you're at it, you might want to clean this place up. It's a pig stye in here."

She set her phone down, filled the coffee machine, and hit the start button. She grabbed the mop and filled the bucket in the sink with cold water and soap. She splashed it across the tile floor as he sat at the end table. She swung the mop across the floor and then rinsed it out.

He said, "That's not how to mop a floor, don't you know anything? You're doing it all wrong." He took the mop from her and dunked it in the bucket, wring it out, swirled it in a circle above the floor so the strands would splay outward separate from each other, then swooshed it over the floor till it stopped cleaning. He turned it over, spun it in a circle, and mopped till the other side was dirty. He rinsed it and repeated. "Now put clean water in the bucket and give your floor a good rinse to remove the soap. That's how we did it back in the Navy." He chuckled. "Hey, I want to see your train card."

Emma shrugged, "I'm getting a new one soon. Francisco can tell you more about that since he talks with the office."

The old man limped as he approached her. He raised his finger and said, "You better tell the truth, Missy. I want to see your card and certifications by tomorrow, comprende?" He stared at her eyes, his eyebrows scrunched, his brows wrinkled, and his curved nose made sharper-. Emma leaned backward. She nodded and winced.

After he left, Emma's body went limp, and she sunk into the bench. Her shoulders heaved, her hands covered her head, and Francisco entered. She recognized his work boots at the end of the table, wiped her eyes, and blew her nose. "I suppose you came in here to yell at me too. Go ahead, tell me what a terrible person I am."

He sat across, his hand patting her shoulder and massaging behind her neck. They sat in silence for a long moment. She looked up and watched his eyes look upon the freshly mopped floor and then up to the counters. She sat motionless, awaiting for him to speak first. He went to his room and returned with a bottle of Advil. He put three capsules in her hand with a glass of water.

"My wife has it bad when it's that time of month. Sometimes, her cramps are so bad that she has to lie on the bathroom floor for hours, so the colder the floor, the better. Take these and go lie down. I'll get you when it's time for dinner; go sleep." He held his hand out, and she looked up. He winked when she put her small hand in his. He helped her to her feet and down the hall to her room. She slid under the covers and sunk into the mattress, half asleep before her head touched the pillow. He closed her door, grabbed his raincoat, and returned to the front of the train.

The afternoons in the Rockies are known for their ferocious sudden cloud bursts and wind squalls. It happens when the the desert floor heats and this hot air rises, forming white puffy clouds by mid-morning. By the afternoon, the updraft heats those cumulus clouds into enormous, cumulonimbus thunder clouds. The strong updraft currents, mixes with colder air aloft creating super-cell storm clouds which suddenly release powerful storm squalls.

Francisco wore his rain jacket and climbed over the water tankers when a burst pounded him with heavy rain and hail. The high winds pushed him inside the engine door. He leaned hard and pushed the door, and it closed with a loud bang. He grabbed a soda from the mini fridge and went to the cockpit. "Wow, it started raining just before I got here." He opened his can and took a sip then he looked out the front window. The wipers beat overtime in the heavy rain. "It's really coming down now."

The company man said, "Yeah, and that's going to bring our work to a halt for the day,"

"What do you mean? Can't we still work on this?"

The company man stood up. He was half a head taller, "Not if I say so. I've been watching that man's cameras. The work is shit and will have to be re-done. You can tell your office it was the bad weather and Miguel not paying attention to his job."

Francisco said, "Re-done? What part are you referring to?"

"The whole damn thing since we started, it's all crap. Do I need to make a call?"

Francisco looked out the window, then said, "No, we will start over."

The company man added, "But not until this storm passes. And let me give you some advice. You have a green crew here, so stop coddling them. They are grown-ass men, so you better quickly whip them into shape. You read me, Señor Garcia?" Francisco leaned back because the man pointed his finger at his chest as he emphasized his words.

Long ago, Francisco's stepfather, Steve, taught him that many white men would be like that and not to take it personally but to stay up on the ridge away from their arguments. They only pick arguments they can win. With that advice, he said, "Yes, Sir." He and Miguel reviewed the day's work footage at Miguel's station. Often, there will be a section of rail that they go back over, but not the whole day's work. He leaned over Miguel's shoulder and had him pause the footage. They checked the other camera angles and studied the measurement graphs.

While grinding the rails helped to reduce train derailments, improves safety, and reduce vibration and a train's lifespan, but if over done, it can have serious adverse effects that lead to premature replacement of rails and an increase in derailments. Grinding is measured in tenths of a millimeter using a Laser Profile Measurement System and performed in real-time. Once the equipment is in place, the system performs the grinding work with minimum operator intervention.

Francisco's stepfather was a white American trucker who often worked on his semi-trucks. Francisco learned never to cut corners when working on equipment that others' lives depend on. Another lesson he learned; you don't want to end up on the news. While Chuy and Francisco learned about diesel mechanic skills, his half-brother Roy lived a different life. He was the only offspring of his stepfather. Later in life, he apologized to Francisco for being too hard on him and too easy on Roy.

Miguel said, "We have a few places that can be gone over, but the rest is good, boss. Call the office and show them that we did it right."

Francisco rubbed his chin, "It's Union Pacific's call, so let's hang on to this just in case this old fart goes too far, for now. Let's meet up in the dining car. Ten-four."

He grabbed the radio mic and said, "Crew safety meeting in the dining car in ten minutes; everyone must be there." He shrugged and lowered his voice, "Thanks, Miguel, good work. Just go along with him for now, text me if he gets too crazy. He called the company man and said they'd restart as he requested when the weather let up. He had a crew meeting after he eased the train onto the sidetrack and stopped.

Emma watched the door as the men rushed inside from the storm. Over by the sink, she saw Roy talking with Francisco in Spanish when the company man entered. All eyes turned and watched as he shook the rain from his jacket and hat. The background noise from the rain pelting the metal car made everyone yell while standing a foot apart. Francisco spoke first, but Emma could only hear his voice and could not discern his words from where she sat. She didn't care, so she sat against the wall while he spoke from the center of the floor. The men nodded and shuffled and flexed their knees. The old man stood motionless, his arms crossed, she wondered how he could stand so still for that long. She heard Francisco say copy this and copy that a few times, along with a ten-four or two. Next, the company man spoke. He puts his hands on his hips and spoke with a strong voice.

Usually, when people criticize others in a group, they start with a compliment or two, but this old man must not have heard of that etiquette; instead, he came out with his complaints. He pointed to Francisco, "I have serious doubts that your leader here is qualified to run this train. There is a serious lack of discipline and neglect of the job. I reviewed the work with Miguel here, and the rails were not being properly ground. I've given a casual inspection of your grinding cars on the way back here, and the grinding wheels are worn out, several motors I doubt even work, and your spark aprons have too many holes and could result in a fire. Now, I understand that you are just here to do a job, but I am responsible for doing it right so there are no future derailments and we don't set the whole place on fire. Before we restart the work, I expect the grinding equipment to be fully operational. It's what Union Pacific is paying all that money for. When you think this train is ready to resume, I shall make the final determination."

The men looked across the circle to Francisco, and the old man's eyes looked at each man, and then they stopped on Francisco, too. The old man said, "That is all I have to say about that, dismissed."

Francisco asked the old man, "Sir, if we are done here, may I have a word with you?"

The old man puffed his chest out with his hands still on his hips. With a smirk, he said, "Sure."

Francisco said, in my stateroom.

The old man followed him to his room, "Please, close the door, sir. Allow me to clarify a few little things. With all due respect, this crew works for Harsco, not Union Pacific. Second, it is my responsibility to do any inspecting of this train. You are the customer and will not perform any such inspections of this train's condition or personnel."

The old man, not to be one-upped by a young mouthy Mexican, shook his finger at Francisco's chest, "Listen, you little maggot, I was running trains long before you were a little shit in diapers, you best shut your lippy mouth right now, or I'll be making a couple calls then you'll be out of a job along with the rest of your gang."

Francisco pulled a drawer open on his writing table, plucked a copy of a document, and thumbed the pages, stopping at page five. His eyes studied the page. He smiled, put it back in, and closed the drawer. With a smile, he said, "Sir, I welcome any disputes that you may want to share with my company, and with respect for your position, I did not correct you in front of the crew, but you will never dismiss my crew again. Now you go do whatever makes you feel more superior, but I advise you to read the contract."

The old man leaned his face within an inch of Francisco. His eyes turned red, and his grey scruffy whiskers hid a reddish-pale complexion. "You think you're so smart but have not heard the last of this." He balled his fist and waved it under Francisco's chin.

"Sir, please remove yourself and calm down before you make an even bigger mistake than threats, for I shall be forced to make a few calls of my own. Now leave, and let me not hear of you harassing my crew ever again. Ten-four?"

The old man threw the door open, it slammed against the wall as he stormed out. He stopped at Emma, "I want to see your rail card by the morning, Missy." He flung the back door open. Emma ran to her room and locked her door; Francisco heard her weeping. He pulled out his cell phone and dialed. 'Hey Terri, not good, so we have that crazy old man that Chuy had problems with. He has gone too far, and now he is harassing Emma, amongst other things… I suggested he reread the contract… I am sure he is making some calls trying to have me removed… he— he— we have to re-do our work from today, and he thinks he is going to inspect our equipment… it's ruining morale, and the men are terrified of him… yes, I told him he has no authority, but that just made him angrier. Miguel and I reinspected the footage, and a few spots can be gone back over, but… Call me when you find out, thanks. Oh, about Emma's card… OK, thanks for the update. I'm sure you are. Bye.'

After the call, he went to the fridge to rummage for something to eat. Roy came in and asked, "Where's dinner, Cisco?"

Francisco shook his head, "Emma is not feeling well. For now, we should just make ourselves something unless you want to go to town and pick up some pizza or something."

"Speaking of her, you need to get rid of her, bro, 'cuz it's her fault."

"Her fault? What are you talking about, Roy?"

Roy raised his voice and waved his finger at his brother's face. "If she had done her job right, the company man wouldn't be taking all this out on us."

"Calm down, little brother. It's none of our fault. You know, it's just an old, angry white dude that hates brown people, trust me. Just relax."

"Calm down? Really? If you don't do something about her, I guess I'll have to, bro."

Emma entered the dining room, "I'm not surprised at you, Roy, but if it improves your life, then I shall leave. Francisco, will you take me to where I can get a ride back home, please?" She wiped her nose and slung her backpack over her shoulder. "Goodbye Roy, thanks for everything. You're such a great man."

Francisco crossed his arms, "Roy, you are out of line. Apologize to Emma, and remember who the boss is in the future."

"Hell no, I won't be lectured by you, bro. Fine, we'll see how it goes when your crew calls in sick. Sick of your shit with little Missy Emma here. I'm taking the truck to get something to eat."

They watched out the window as five of the crew climbed into the pickup and left. Emma rummaged through the fridge, "Let me make some dinner." She pulled out cold fried chicken, macaroni and cheese, leftovers frozen green beans, and a two-liter of Coke. She heated the food in the microwave and set two plates out. They sat and ate their leftovers in silence, and he texted back and forth while she took a few bites, then pushed her plate forward and looked at her Facebook page.

She broke their silence, "I just don't get it. How can someone be so attractive and then be so cruel?" she wiped tears from her phone screen. He shook his head and shrugged. "But he was so nice and so funny. I get that mean old man, and why is he so angry… Yes, I beg to differ, but at least I get it. But Roy… why is he so cruel?" She shrugged and scrunched her brows, looking down.

A phone chirped with a text. They looked down, it was Francisco's phone. He read it and leaned back, 'Thank God…" Emma looked across at him, "It's your license. Terri just sent a message that she emailed it a minute ago along with your certs, too." He shook his head, wiped his brow, and then leaned back. He knew the one thing that the company man could raise a dispute over was Emma's license. Francisco has the discretion to bring her on board as long as she is confined to her role as the cook, but with some embellishment of his story, the company man could cause harm to Francisco.

Emma leaned over the table and patted his shoulder, "Thank you for trying to help. You didn't ask for any of this, and it's all my fault, and I have to say, Roy is right."

"What are you saying, Emma?"

She leaned back and wiped her eyes, "My mother is a US Senator, my older brothers are successful, my father was a war hero, and I'm just a nobody without them." She pushed her cell phone towards him and pointed to the screen. "Look at this: my mom's re-election is almost guaranteed. See, here she is with my brothers."

He leaned over, picked her phone up, and zoomed into the picture of the three of them on stage. He asked, "How come you're shorter? Your mom looks about five feet five, but your brothers look over six feet. What are you?"

"Almost Five one," she said. "Yes, they are taller, but they are boys. Mom is five four. She told me that the girls in the family are shorter than the men."

"Do you have a pic of your dad?"

She flipped through pics and then handed it. He looked at her dad, wearing his uniform in his thirties, it was taken while on tour in Afghanistan. His face was clean shaven and tanned, his hair cut short, and ribbons and medals adorned his jacket. He said, "He is quite handsome, but it's hard to see the resemblance I can't tell what his hair color and skin color are."

She grabbed her phone back.

"Look, Emma, I never told any of the guys who your mom is, but of all the people I have ever met, you wield the greatest power. You could pick up your phone and do many things that the rest of us could never do in our lifetimes. But with that power comes responsibility, and you know it. Never have you used your name or influence with us. I admire that about you, but someday, you could run for office because you have the right name. You're not some nobody college student, so you need to give your future serious thought on what you want to do."

"Did I tell you that I want to go to the vet—"

Vet school, I remember, but what else will you do? Will you follow your family at some point? Your real problem here is not vet school or any other, and you need your family to tell you what they think you should do. You're stuck in a time warp."

"Maybe you're right." She looked away and rubbed her head. "I've never stood up for myself, but I remember as a little girl, when my brothers did well, my mom always bragged about them. I'm sure she doesn't care about me as much. She probably just hopes that I don't embarrass the family. What do I do?"

Francisco looked at the door. Roy slid it open, followed by the others carrying pizza boxes. Francisco whispered, "Meet me in my room. I have something for you to read." He went over, picked up a slice of pepperoni pizza, and walked to his room.

"Hey Emma, want some pizza?" asked Diego. She reached around behind her to the other table as he handed her a slice.

She took it with her and tapped on Francisco's door. 'Come in.' she turned the handle, checked down the hall, then slipped in. "It's in here somewhere, just give me a second." He pulled his drawers out then looked under his mattress, "Oh." He opened his closet door and stood back, "Here it is." He handed her a hard-cover book minus the dust jacket. "It's one of my mom's favorites to read. I use it when I'm trying to figure things out."

She read the title, "The Art of Failure. What?"

"Emma, if you want to join the world of doers, you must learn a few things about the power of failure. No one gets it right the first time, no matter who they are or what they are trying to do." The book was thick with ink drawings and maps. Emma looked at a two-page timeline. "Trust me," he pointed to the book with a nod. "Steve told me some things before he passed away. I was just a teenager, but I still use those things today with that company. I had to support the family when he left us, and Roy was too young. I went to work at thirteen as a diesel mechanic helper, changing oil and tires and fixing things on the big rigs. He had my little sister when he was sixty-five. I quit school to make enough for the family. It was just enough to keep us from being evicted. I didn't know what I wanted to be, but I knew what I didn't want, and as Steve taught me, sometimes it's more important to know who we aren't than who we are."

Emma looked at the pages, "What did you know you didn't want to be?"

He paused, "Well, I didn't want to be in a gang like many others and knew I could work harder than most kids. So here I am, sort of."

"That's amazing, Cisco, what a hard life you've lived, and me… I'm crying over nothing. Thanks for the book and the talk. I appreciate it very much." She returned to her room, changed into her pajamas, climbed into bed, and opened her new book. She opened it to the title page and read a quote, '*Knowledge can never replace experience which only comes from doing.*' She nodded her head and turned the page. After an hour, she yawned and pulled her shade back. Above were stars twinkling. She rolled over and turned her light out.

Chapter 14

It was a brilliant sunny morning the next day; crew morale was higher than expected, and after an early breakfast, the men worked on the grinding equipment. Emma ran hot water over the dishes and pans, refilled the coffee pot, and then moved back to the window screens, bathing the dining car in sunlight. After a quick sweeping, she grabbed the mop, spun it, and dropped it center down, as the old man showed, then gave her mop a good rinse and repeated. She finished, stepped outside, looked back at the floor, and smiled. She turned when footsteps shuffled across the rail gravel to the dining car. It was the old man; she gave a tight-lipped little smile as he walked up the stairs.

On the platform, he said, "Ah, just the person I seek a word with."

She shrugged, 'Today, I promise. Terri back in the office said the fax machine was down yesterday and will email or fax them to Francisco."

"Humph…" he snorted. "Fine, play your little charade, but payback is a real bitch." He walked past her, across her freshly mopped floor. He poured black coffee with no creamer or sugar. Emma's face puckered when he took a sip, then looked across and laughed. After another sip, he looked around the dining car, "Humph… well, this is a big improvement. This morning, Missy, bring me your documents." He tromped down the ladder, spilling no coffee.

She texted Francisco, 'He just left, again demanding to see my documents, help.' She walked outside to the train's rear and then around to a pair of men. One held a large stone disc wheel, and the other rotated a huge wrench. He looked up and said, "Buenos días, Emma." It was the quiet one, Luis. Soot covered his coveralls and gloves, and grease and soot smudges marred his face. He wiped his eyes and cranked the wrench till it stopped, then leaned against it and pushed another inch.

She asked, "Are you guys replacing all the grinding wheels? How many of these grinding wheels are there?"

Luis said, "One hundred twenty grinders this train. Today, we're replacing just the worn ones and some spark skirts. See, this one has holes burned through it."

His partner pushed a lever and lowered the grinding carriage till it almost touched the rail track. He leaned over, looked at the wheel and the rail surface, and motioned for Luis to turn another nut. "Bien," he waved. Then pushed the lever and raised the carriage back off the rail again.

Emma looked down the length of the train and saw Francisco and Miguel underneath one of the cars up ahead. "Gracias." She walked to Francisco, and he and Miguel looked like they were looking at a camera. She squatted and asked, "Hey, did you get my text?"

He cleaned the camera lens and held the camera's body while Miguel tightened it in place. They compared the angle to the opposing side camera. They tilted the camera mount, then moved it slightly and retightened it. He wiped the lens again and blew the lens off with a can of compressed air.

He crawled out from underneath and sat, "What happened?" he asked.

"I saw that old man again this morning. He said, "Time is up to show him my documents, or he will give me the boot. Did you get them yet?"

Francisco and Miguel chuckled and shook their head, "Emma, yesterday you wanted to quit today, you want to go on; what is it tomorrow?" He shrugged his shoulders at Miguel, stood up, and said, "Relax, you're fine. We are just messing with you. Terri sent everything." He took off his gloves, reached into his coveralls, and pulled out an envelope, "Here," was all he said.

She held the envelope in both hands, her mouth agape, "Congratulations, you are now official."

Emma held the envelope to her chest, "Oh my God, my first job!" she wiped her eyes.

Miguel said, "Welcome to the team," and held his hand out. He asked, "How long will you be staying with us?"

Emma shook her head, "Uh, I don't know, at least till Denver, Cisco. Can I stay on till the end of summer, please?" Her hands grabbed at his collar and tugged.

He looked to Miguel, "It's all right with me, but when I leave, Miguel will be the one to decide those things. Chuy passed it to me, and I will pass it to Miguel next."

"Leave! You can't leave; we all need you. No." she pleaded.

He chuckled and patted her shoulder, "Emma, in the four years I've worked here, we traveled across America three times. I am tired of all the constant travel, which is a younger man's job.

I'm ready to try something new." Emma shook her head no. He said, "Calm down. I am incredibly lucky to have had this opportunity. All of us came from nowhere, even Roy, and this was our first decent job for all of us. For me to be able to move on is a good thing." Miguel agreed, and they both patted Emma's shoulders.

She said, "That old man said the floor looked good. How did you guys learn how to do all of this stuff? I mean, like, was there a school or classes? How?"

Miguel chuckled, "Just by doing Emma."

"Even driving the train? Come on, there had to be a bunch of teaching involved."

Francisco said, "We learned from each other."

"Well, I want to learn too; teach me. Before I graduate, I want to know at least how to do something that's real."

Francisco climbed back under the train's body, "Come down here, and we'll show you how to set-up the cameras. Emma climbed underneath in her shorts; the rocks dug into her knees. Francisco said, "Go get a pair of coveralls and some work gloves; Miguel will help you."

She came back dressed like one of the crew in grey coveralls, an orange reflective vest, a ball cap, and small leather gloves size small that were still big on her. They showed her the camera system from the bottom up to the train engine. Up there, the high-definition monitor screens showed the view in minute detail. Miguel showed her how to run the system's complex array of buttons at his station and the drivers, she learned the correct sequence for turning the system on and off. Once she could repeat it several times, he showed how to gauge the grinding and followed him around the engine. As he pointed to the different systems, she stood close to him to hear over the drone of the running engine. He showed where to fill the engine oil coolant, then the most important gauges to look at, and their max readings. Her brain absorbed most of it quicker than most of the crew did, but she could not comprehend what was happening inside.

Next, she walked over to a significant grey thing with giant wires coming from it. Miguel told her the generator made electric power at 600 VAC. They followed the power lines to a large electronics cabinet that converted it to DC. He took her under the engine and pointed to a locomotive drive wheel. Just like in an electric car, these drive wheels had electric DC motors to drive them. In the box was the drive motor; every wheel had a drive motor on the engine. The diesel engine only was there to produce the electrical power to run the drive wheels. She looked at the drive systems. She went back into the engine room and followed the energy path. All that big support equipment for the engine, such as the radiator, was not to run the train but to keep the engine running. She had no mechanical knowledge, so he showed her an animated YouTube video of how a diesel-electric engine works. Since the late thirties, when diesels came into service, they began adding more energy-reclaiming systems. Yes, for all their high technology, a nineteenth-century steam locomotive can still pull pound-for-pound produce the same amount of power. Still, they are big polluters with low energy efficiency, making them inefficient and forcing them to become obsolete.

After a second YouTube video, Emma changed out of her coveralls, washed her hands and face, went to the dining car, and made sandwiches for the crew. When she closed the refrigerator door, the old man slid the car door open, "Well, little Missy, are you ready?" He held his hand out and scowled at her.

His hand was calloused with crooked fingers that matched his large, crooked nose. She smiled and said, "It wouldn't hurt for you to be a little nicer, if you even can remember how." She reached into her shorts and handed her Rail Card with yesterday's date. The old man held it to the light and studied the card for some time. He showed his approval with a snort. Next, she showed him her certification booklet. Satisfied, he nodded, let out a Humph, and scratched his head.

He said, "Missy, I reckon I had miss-read you, my apologies." He gave her documents back with a little smile.

She said, "Thank you," and put them back in her pocket. She asked, "When we start back up, they will train me on the rear firehose station, so maybe you can give me a few pointers."

She watched him stand half an inch taller and scratch his head. Under his burly mustache, it looked like he was smiling. She said, "May I ask you a question?"

He nodded, "Sure."

"Why do you dislike Francisco so much? Chuy even said he used to be terrified of you."

He laughed and leaned against the sink counter, "Oh, Missy. First off, I don't hate Mexicans. Hell, my departed wife was half Mexican, but Francisco does not respect old school. I know he is very smart and good with the men, but he needs to follow orders. He runs this train like a bunch of pirates. Chuy was worse. At least with Miguel, I know he will listen, so when Mr. Garcia leaves and Miguel takes over, I know he will keep things in line. If I hadn't leaned on Garcia, he would have been perfectly happy to cut corners and do a half-ass job because he spoils his crew too much. Take my advice, Missy, when you are in charge someday, don't try to be friends with your workers. If they can't cut it, you need to cut them from the herd. Also, never hire anyone you cannot turn around and fire, so avoid hiring family."

Emma doubted his advice and opinions, but she remained quiet as he spoke, mostly out of courtesy and partly out of fear. In the last twenty-four hours, she had learned more about life and engine systems than she ever thought she could understand. She thought of her mom as the old man lectured her. Maybe she should send her mom a message. Her new role as part of a team that 'did things,' appealed to her. When the coast was clear in the dining car, Emma went to her room, flopped on her bunk, and exhaled. When her pulse lowered, she looked at the nightstand, and the book almost leaped into her hands when she saw it. Her fingers flipped through pages, and she read caption after caption and looked at photos. It was two, and she had maybe an hour or two before she needed to start making dinner. She leaned against the wall and began reading. She might read a whole book in school in a few days, but reading like this was fun. She read slowly, even re-reading specific passages and phrases. After another chapter, she wanted to find Francisco to discuss it. The train jerked backward, then forward, the brakes released, and the car swerved gradually like riding a boat floating on the water. She lifted her blind and saw the foreground gliding across her view. They were on the move.

The following two cars in front were grinding cars, and then two tankers were in front of them, then the two engines to power the grinders. Should she climb up to the front engine and watch what they do, or should she go to the back car and learn to use the firehose? She left the dining car at three-thirty and combed over the rear water tankers through the grinding cars and engines till she reached the crew car at the back of the train. Chico stood on the rear patio. He said, "Hola, Emma."

She asked Chico, "Will you guys teach me?"

"Si senora," Chico and Diego nodded with big smiles. They showed her the water valves and how to turn the water pump on and off. Chico opened the valve on his hose station and sprayed the tracks behind, pointing to the sage brush near the rail on his side. Diego helped her open her water valve, and her hose fired water from the nozzle under pressure. Pivoting the nozzle on the mount, she tried aiming at her side of the rail. When the brush ignited, she tried to hit it as they passed. Her nozzle made a slow turn as she reacted, but Chico knocked the fire out with his station. Wearing just shorts and a little top, she got wet from the misting. Next time, she would remember to wear a rain jacket and a hat. It was a sweltering summer day, and the cool water mist felt refreshing.

With Emma operating his fire station, Diego used the opportunity to call his mom back home. The inside of the rear car had a crew rest area and facilities, along with a microwave and mini fridge. Emma peaked inside and saw him sitting on a couch, dialing while sipping a Mexican Coke. Chico called her back to her station. She extinguished a sage brush then Chico asked for a break. Emma stayed out a few extra minutes to appreciate both men.

That day, Emma learned the value of making oneself useful; it was a mantra of Francisco's that the old man did not appreciate. Was that because the old man didn't want to seem weak to his crew or because he just saw others as inferior? She would ask Francisco. When Chico returned, she looked at the time and said, "I have to go and start dinner. Thanks for helping me, guys."

"What's for dinner?" he asked.

"Chicken tacos." The man grinned.

Chapter 15

Later that night, when dinner was over and the dining car scrubbed, Emma went to the patio and texted Francisco while enjoying some night air. The train continued its grinding operation after dark. She leaned on the railing, looking up at the night sky. She used an astronomy app to see where the constellations and planets were while holding her phone at the sky. An incoming text from Francisco, since he and Miguel switched out he could meet her at the dining car. She went back inside and turned to the next chapter in her book. Her eyes moved around the page, unable to concentrate but not ready to put the book down. She flipped a few pages, looked at some pictures, and, with her other hand, began tapping on the table. Then she put the book down and went to the fridge. Her fingers tapped on the table as she studied the contents three times. Unsure of what to grab, she pulled a Coke and sat down. Francisco came down the hall and went straight to the fridge for a water bottle. Emma leaned forward on her elbows over the table and set her phone to the side.

He smiled and looked at the book. "How's the reading coming?"

She shrugged and said, "Nah, I'm not feeling it tonight, but I do want to talk. Why are you leaving the train? What's your plan?" Her brown eyes locked on his even when she took a sip. He winced and scratched his head, then rubbed his chin. "Well, nothing lasts forever, and I've been raising a family on the road and trying to have a wife, but it's not working out. I had to decide, family or the job. So, I decided family comes first."

Emma nodded, "I get all that, but what are your plans? What will you do?"

"I won't worry about it; I have many options. We live in the US, but I will move back to the other side of the border and work on this side. My main worry is my wife and I are getting divorced. She cheated on me too many times. We were sweethearts since junior high. I never thought she could be this way, so it is time for me to go home and fix things for the kids."

Emma leaned back and looked out the window with her arms crossed. Although it was a warm night, she shivered. "I am so sorry; I had no idea. If there is anything that I can do, please don't hesitate to ask. I want to be a friend, no, not that, not just a friend. You are like the kind of brother that I don't have, and I need you." She laid her hand on the table next to his. He smiled, took her hand, leaned forward, and kissed her head.

"Thank you, Em. I am not leaving yet, maybe not until the train returns to Del Rio, Texas. We still have this summer and lots for you to do and learn. Ever been to Junction?"   "Where?"

"Grand Junction, it's in Colorado. That's our next stop, maybe tomorrow afternoon. You will love it there. I'll ensure the crew has the night off; there is much to do. Emma, can I ask you a personal question?"

"OK…"

"What is it that you want? You are not married, have no kids, and until now, no job, so what is really going on here?"

She looked out the window and shook her head, "I don't know, something about my life doesn't… Sometimes, on this train, it feels like I'm living someone else's life. So, I guess I am on a quest while trying to stay away from my mom's crazy schedule, especially with it being a re-election year."

"Did you tell her where you are or what you are doing?"

"No, not yet. I told my friend Rachel not to worry, that I was fine, and that I was visiting a friend, a boy I know from school, Martin. If I say anything to my mom, I already know what she'll say, then I'll feel bad and leave."

The base station speaker called, 'Garcia, come to the front of the train.' He looked at Emma, "Urgh… It's the company man… I wonder what it is this time." When he left, Emma checked her Facebook, then looked at posts from her friends, selfies of girls being cool. She rolled her eyes and saw Rachel's post from a party. Her phone chirped, a text from her mom. She looked at the screen; her lips tightened, her nostrils flared, and brows scrunched. Her hand shook as she typed a response, then she deleted it, looked around, took a breath, typed a response, and hit send. Then she texted Francisco and stared at her screen for his response. It chirped, and she put her phone down, slid the door open, and took a couple of deep breaths. Her brow glistened from a sheen of perspiration, and now, inside, it was too hot. After a minute in the cool air wearing only a tank top and shorts, her arms got goose bumps. She slid the door closed, grabbed her phone and book, went to her room, and flopped on her bunk. 'Urgh…' she screamed into her pillow. Why did her mom change, it was as if she became a different person.

Early the following day, as she lay half-wake, she rolled over to read her new messages. After a few minutes, she turned her phone off, lay on her back, and dozed back asleep. When she awoke, she got up and went to the dining room. It was four-thirty, time to prepare breakfast for the crew. She hauled eggs, bacon, and hashbrowns from the fridge, kicked the door closed with her knee, and set everything on the counter. She cooked the crew eggs or omelets to order, a sure favorite with the men and the old man. Since making her mom happy was impossible might as well do something to make the men happy. Most wanted the chorizo sausage, cheese, and peppers in theirs. Emma knew how to make tall, fluffy omelets. On top, she garnished them with cilantro, pepper-jack cheese, and salsa fresco, and sometime with sliced jalapenos.

At last, she made one for herself and stood over the sink, eating it while soaking the dishes and pans. Then, she gave the floor a good sweep and took the last bite, the cheesiest bite that she had saved for last. Hmm, she savored the flavors. After the quick mopping, she brushed her teeth and crawled back into her bunk. Her body melted into the mattress as she pulled her favorite pillow over her head and pulled her covers up. Tired yet satisfied, she fell asleep. For Emma, a cheesy omelette made it is easier to sleep.

When she awoke, there were text messages from Francisco, her mom, and Martin. Francisco needed her to watch a video and take a test for a certification. Her mom sent another scathing text, not as long as the night before, but it got directly to several points. Either Emma returned home that day, or she would make her. Next, she looked at the Facebook message from Martin. He said Rachel messaged him asking about Emma being with him, and he didn't know how to respond. She looked through her Google pics and found a selfie of him and her out shopping. Maybe she could post the pic on her page if the background was vague. At least the picture was recent, and the weather looked similar, but it was from a store in Utah. Anyone who could zoom in would see the store name and know it was not from Martin's location. 'Oh well, maybe he can photoshop it,' she thought.

She messaged him, 'Hey Martin, I need a huge favor. Can you do something with this photo so it looks like we are together where you are?' Knowing that her mom would check her page, maybe this charade could buy her another week. If her mom knew the truth, she would flip out, and who knows what she could do. She hit the SEND button and then curled her arms around her legs.

***

Later, at Walmart, Luis pushed the shopping cart while Emma walked along the side as she grabbed items from the shelf. She stood on her toes, reaching for a bottle of dish soap on the top shelf, a woman pushing a cart stopped and asked her where the Sauve hair shampoo was; Emma just shrugged. She turned and tried to reach the dish soap, but the woman tugged on her work vest and said, "Excuse me, how rude of you to just turn away like that. Where is the manager?"

Emma said, "How should I know?"

The woman said, "Well, we will see about this…" She pushed her cart to the end of the aisle, found a clerk, and then pointed back. From the corner of her eye, Emma noticed the woman pointing right at her. She asked Luis, "What's wrong with her?" He shrugged his shoulders 'No se." then he pointed back down the aisle to the woman, followed by a manager.

The woman said, "There she is, that rude worker of yours, so you better have a talk to her."

Emma turned around, "Me? What are you talking about, lady?"

The manager said, "You don't have to get hostile, young lady. This is a family store, and we don't treat others that way."

"Me? I was minding my own business; what are you talking about? I'm just trying to get that bottle of dish soap up there, but I can't reach it."

The manager handed her the bottle and said, "There seems to be some confusion. Who's your manager?"

Emma pointed to Luis, "He and I work together. My boss is Francisco Garcia, oh the vest... I work for the railroad, not for Walmart. We are in here shopping for the crew, and our train is just parked down the road."

"So, you want us to believe that you work for the railroad and are in here shopping for a train just down the road. Maybe we should have a talk with security; wait here." He held his hand out while he called on his radio, "Code blue aisle 34. Don't try to run off. We are going to have a talk with security, and they will determine if we should get the police involved."

Emma bit her lip, and Luis shook his head, "Miss Emma, this sort of thing happen to us when we are in the white part of town. Maybe we should leave before they call the cops."

"No, I refuse to run, we've done nothing wrong. We are in the right, and this is a form of harassment. There is no need to escalate things, Mr.… Hodges, let me show you my proof that I work at the railroad."

"That won't be necessary, miss. Security is on its way and they will handle this matter."

The security team arrived and escorted them off to the interrogation room. She and Luis showed their driver's licenses and rail cards from the back room. The guards made copies but refused to let them go.

"We had a complaint that you tried to assault the woman when she caught you shoplifting."

Emma shook her head, "Look at the footage, then tell me what we did wrong, nothing."

"We will show it to the police and let them decide. Sorry, but it's procedure."

Over the years in school, Emma learned when to use her famous name. One time in junior high, a Circle K manager accused her of shoplifting cigarettes and within a minute, the matter was dropped with an apology from the store owner.

"Do you guys want to hear a funny story?"

The security man turned while standing motionless.

"Can we have a private conversation? Luis, here, is not part of what I want to discuss. I assure you will want to hear what I have to say." The manager nodded to the security men.

When alone with the security agents and the store manager, Emma said, "Do you know who one of the United States Senator of Utah is? I'll give you a hint: it's a woman whose last name is Chase."

She scrolled through her Google pics and selected pics from the Hyatt Convention Center. "Here she is just a few days ago on the stage running for re-election, which she will. I took this picture from the stage wing." She showed the security guards her mom. "Now, here is another picture just moments later with her kids." They leaned over her phone and looked at each other. Emma said, "Now, this is the best part because this is where you guys and the store manager apologize to Luis and me.

The manager again nodded; Emma smiled. Power can be as addictive as any drug ever concocted, which was why she avoided this sort of confrontation. The second security guard shook his head. This does not prove anything. Who knows who took those pictures. You're not getting out of these charges just by showing a picture."

Emma put her phone in her pocket and turned to the store manager, "You don't strike me as stupid as that Neanderthal, and you better hope that I don't file charges against you, but that depends on what you do in the next two seconds." She smiled when sweat dripped off his forehead. "One… two."

It didn't take Emma long to sort out the false accusations made against her and Luis. As she pushed their full shopping cart past the security guards out the front door, Luis laughed, "Miss Emma, I have never seen anybody do that before, so tell me, what did you show them on your phone? Do you have a magic phone?"

"Well, Luis, nobody is treating us like that and getting away with it, not as long as my last name is Chase.

Chapter 16

The train ground the rails into Grand Junction, Colorado, arriving late that afternoon. As promised, the crew had the night off and chose to eat at a brewpub, giving Emma the night off in the kitchen. The journey to Denver was just two more days away, yet it seemed to her that she had spent weeks or months with the train, and now it was ending too soon unless she could stay for the summer. Standing over the sink, rinsing her mop before giving the floor one good swabbing, she pondered, 'what will life be like when I go home? Will mom tell me she's proud of her daughter for managing herself under very trying conditions?' She spun the mop and set it centered on the floor, swishing back and forth. 'No, instead, she heard her mom's voice berating her for poor decisions and immaturity, and then, to make it all so clear, why can't you be like your brothers?' Her brothers were successful; what mother could not be proud of their success? 'But what,' she wondered, 'what was that difference? Was it because I am just a girl? Does mom hate girls and only likes boys? No, come to think of it, her brothers never included her and her Dad was not doting either. And then that time in the third grade, he showed up at school to pick me up, drunk. I wanted to hide. He never acted that way when the boys were little. Why did he fight with mom so much? Was I a bad kid?'

The door slid, breaking Emma's inner thoughts, "Oh, hi," she said.

Francisco and Miguel stood at the door as she rinsed her mop. She said, "I just have to grab my backpack." She returned from her room, "Have you guys decided where we are eating yet?"

Miguel said, "We will meet the guys at Fourth and Main Street."

Francisco said, "There are several on the strip, so whatever one they are at."

She looked at him, "You seem different…"

"I'm fine; come on, let's go. I'm starving, and I could use a cold beer."

The truck honked; Chico drove back to get them.

There are fifteen brewpubs in Grand Junction, and six are located a couple of blocks from one another on the main road; called, the strip. Grand Junction is an excellent place for tourists to set as their base camp. It's close to Moab to the west and Vail to the east. Summer and winter fun, Junction has it covered. There are fossils in the hills, digging for dinosaurs, fishing on one of its three rivers, hiking, biking, and brewpubs to recharge. The whole region is an outdoors person's paradise.

The pickup cruised Fourth Street, slowing to look for their friends. Emma sat in the backseat across from Miguel. Like Emma, he was young, but unlike her, he was married and soon had a baby. She looked at him; he looked young but was a man. She was no further along in life than when she was a little girl. The idea of marriage, husbands, and kids was an obscure idea far from her orbit. She couldn't imagine being married with kids. Maybe her mom's comments were true, perhaps she was a lesbian?

Chico pointed to the Goat and Clover Tavern on the right, "They were over there, following some girls." He turned left, "I think they were going over here." He pointed to Trail Life Brewing.

Francisco said, "No… I don't see them, so maybe they went to the Feisty Pint."

Miguel said, "Si, Diego's back there, so that must be the place."

Chico parked and met up at the patio, where three round tables were grouped. The trees along Colorado Avenue dappled the afternoon sun, lessening the day's heat. Luis pointed to Emma and raised his glass, "Here comes the girl with the magic phone. Amiga, let me buy you a beer."

Francisco leaned to her ear and whispered, "Ah, you have fans here, so should we tell them who you really are?"

She chuckled, "Not if I'm sober, I won't. Here comes Roy, watch this."

Roy asked, "So what ability do you seem to have? Luis said that Walmart had you guys in the back and were calling the cops." His head tilted while he studied her face. They laughed, but Roy crossed his arms and tapped his foot. Her stomach turned, causing her to bite her lip. With eyelids, half closed, her mind's eye went into overtime. Oh, the things she thought of doing to Roy for being a vindictive asshole, but she knew she'd just play nice and not create a scene. 'I just want him to turn his dark, life-sucking gaze somewhere else. Why can't he just leave me alone?'

Her shoulders heaved with a shrug. She said, "I took a pre-law class and knew our rights. They had no reason to detain us, and I just showed the manager the law. I also told him that I would slip and fall, charge them for assault, and then sue him and have his job." She looked at Francisco. He nodded and laughed with the men. Everyone had a good laugh except for Roy. He still sat with his arms crossed. Emma winced for a microsecond, turning her head away, and then Luis handed her a beer. Emma took a sip and noticed several college-age girls roaming the area. She thought, at least Roy's attention would be detained for the rest of the night. But to be sure, he was no friend and not to be trusted alone. His anger simmered just below a thin veneer. Just a poke below the surface and up boils the monster. She made a note to herself to ask Cisco why Roy seemed so angry and ready to attack yet was so fun and smooth with the ladies.

True to form, as soon as the young ladies walked by, Diego and Roy began flirting, and soon after, they bought them drinks. After the drinks arrived, Chico joined their party.

Francisco's phone chirped, and he said, "Hey, you might like to hear this, Emma. The company man had personal things and will have a replacement tomorrow."

"Who is it?" asked Miguel.

"It's Justin, bro." He told Emma, "He is the coolest, a great guy, and you're going to like him, maybe like him too much..." He waved for the server and ordered, "Two fiesta burgers, chicharrones, chips and queso, two fiesta tacos, and three plates with another round." He turned to the others and said, "Buenos tardes, I just received a text from Terri. Good news: tomorrow, we get a new company, man." The men asked who. "It's Justin." He saluted the group with a big smile. The men cheered and slapped each other on the back. "Also, tomorrow's safety meeting will not be until seven-thirty. Enjoy yourselves, but not too much."

After a few more drinks and a plate of nachos, Francisco said, "Come, let's see how many gutter balls we can throw."

Miguel stood, "I'll go."

Emma nodded, "Sure, count me in." She looked across the tables, but the others' attentions were preoccupied.

They walked along Colorado Avenue, looking for a taxi. Emma said, "Hey, Cisco, call an Uber for us 'cause this phone of mine is too basic."

He leaned against a wall, clicked on the app pointed in front, and said, "There's one."

***

When they got out at Orchard Lanes Bowling Alley, Emma exclaimed, "I haven't done this since I was a kid."

People of all ages stood in the long shoe line. Emma said, "I didn't know bowling was so popular; look at this place."

Her first ball did not roll good, instead, it just did a slow roll off into oblivion.

Miguel told her, "Maybe your ball was sleepy and fell asleep."

After a good laugh, Francisco aligned himself with his well-chosen ball. He held it before his eyes, then stepped forward, shuffling his feet as his right arm drew the ball straight behind him. He took one last big gliding step that stopped before the line, snapping his wrist from underneath the ball to the right side of it like a professional. The ball skidded down the alley, curving away towards the gutter, and then, about halfway, it began to swing back. It hit just behind the front pin, knocking all but one back corner pin with a loud whack sound. When his ball returned, he lined himself to cut the angle to the pin. He stepped and threw another curve ball that started in the middle of the alley, then curved off to the left, nicking the pin. He waved his hands as the pin wobbled. He jumped on the floor, but it only wobbled to a stop.

Miguel and Emma laughed. Then, his first roll looked like Francisco's first roll. He had two pins left standing, one in each back corner. Francisco shrugged, "Tough break, bro."

Miguel took a sip and grabbed his ball. His toss hit solidly on the right corner pin. It flew across but was behind the other corner pin, leaving the left corner pin wobbling. Both ended the first frame with nine and Emma zero. Emma placed the ball between her crouched legs in the next frame and shoved it forward. It rolled straight into the pins. It was slow but managed to knock seven over. She rolled her next ball off to the side, and it only hit one of the three. She got eight pins for that frame, then raised her fist and screamed. Both Miguel and Francisco rolled strikes. She jumped and cheered each time as if it were her strike.

Later, at the last frame of the game, Miguel was ahead by five, Emma finished with eighty-three, and lastly, it was Francisco's turn. He rose, focused down the alley, lined his feet, and rolled a solid strike. Emma started cheering when the ball crashed into the pins with that whack sound like a baseball bat hitting a home run. His next roll curved too shallow, leaving four pins wobbling. His final roll went at the headpin curved to the right, missing the pin on the left, knocking the other three down, but it was enough for him to move into the lead.

Miguel said, "You must give me a rematch, bro."

Emma got up, "I'll grab another round." While she waited at the bar for their pitcher of beer, she checked her Facebook page. Rachel sent a message with a link to a news report. The article was from a local SLC news reporter about a car accident. The driver, an unidentified young woman, ran from her car after when it ran into another car at the intersection. The police hoped someone could identify the woman, but there were concerns. After watching the news video, Emma read her friend's message, 'OMG Em, they have your phone. People will look—. Her stomach knotted, and the room dimmed; the bartender served the pitcher of beer and nachos. Emma looked across the counter; as her head throbbed, her ears heard a wobbling drone sound and swirling ambient sounds as lights flashed bright white, and then everything faded to a dull red. She felt the numbing embrace as paralysis removed all feeling from below her hips. Her legs became like infants unable to stand, while her head felt overwhelmed and lightheaded. Her body swerved and veered, then landed on the cheap indoor-outdoor carpet. Her body lay motionless with one arm underneath.

The bartender said, "Call 911." He ran around and bent over her.

Emma sat up and said, "No, don't call 911. I am fine. No, don't do that. Please, just help me up." She held her hand out. "Please. That's all I need."

The bartender shook his head. "No, you shouldn't move just stay there. Don't move."

Miguel came to the bar to check on Emma and the beers, "Emma, what are you doing?" He turned to the bartender, "It's OK, she has these fainting spells." He pulled her up. She leaned on the bar while he held onto her. "See, she's fine. Come on, Em."

After a moment, she said, "Here's the beer. Sorry, I apologize, it was a long day." She handed the bartender her debit card. "It's been a long week. All of a sudden, my mind felt exhausted. I didn't know having so much fun can be so exhausting. But I'm fine, really."

She started the next game, but lasted for two frames before her body became chilled and nauseous. "Cisco, take me home, please." He and Miguel nodded, then held her hands. "Can you get my phone for me?" Miguel Uber'd a ride back to the train. They rode in silence while Emma leaned her head onto Francisco's shoulder. He said, "She must be going through some heavy family shit."

***

Emma sat in the dining car back on the train as Miguel served her tea. Francisco sat across, studying her face as she sipped. "Can you talk about it?" he asked.

She asked, "Do you have my phone?" Miguel pulled it from his pocket. She scrolled to her Facebook page, "Here it is. Rachel, my school friend, sent me this link. It was Rachel's car that I was driving when I ran into the café and met you."

Francisco leaned over the table, and Miguel watched the news video over Emma's shoulder. The reporter explained that the driver involved in the hit-and-run accident was not the car's registered owner but authorities believe it is a possible car thief running a red-light. The Reporter finished with the news update that a cell phone had been recovered from the suspect. Though it was broken, the police detective in the interview believed they would uncover the identity of that mysterious young woman. Emma's hands shook as she held her cell phone.

"They're going to be looking for me now. Am I a fugitive? Did I break any laws? Maybe I should call my mom, or turn myself in."

Miguel looked at Francisco, who nodded back and shrugged. Francisco said, "Her mom is a US Senator—"

Emma blurted, "—Elizabeth Reid Chase is my mom, and she is the last person I want to talk with right now." She wiped tears and buried her head in her hands, her shoulders heaving as she sobbed. "I didn't do anything wrong. I am an adult, and I just want to be free to live… This is where I want to be here because I feel safe here, not judged but appreciated. Besides, who else would take me bowling?"

Miguel asked, "Cisco, she is a senator's daughter? Our Emma?" Francisco nodded. "We must help; we can't let them take her like that. Look at her; she's a total wreck."

Francisco said, "You're right, I agree, but it might bring unwanted attention if we do. Families are at stake, and we need to think about it."

Miguel said, "We are on this train, and no one knows Emma is here or where we are. We can keep it a secret a few more days till Denver, right?"

"You're right, and as long as none of us or Rachel rat her out, her secret will be safe. But we should keep her out of the public.

Emma, stay with the train until we get to Denver. It's just a few more days."

"Yes, I will. What'll I tell Rachel? What if they ask her questions about me? What should she say since it was her car and I borrowed it?

Francisco rubbed his chin, "As Miguel pointed to, as long as she doesn't know where you are, let 'em ask questions. We can clear it up in two days without involving the train or the crew."

Emma nodded and said, "Yes, I'll send her a text so she doesn't say too much when they find her. Maybe she can run off with a boyfriend and not answer her phone a few days."

She rubbed her forehead. "Did you make chamomile tea? I feel tired." She finished her message and went to bed.

She called back down the hall to the men, "Do I have to get up early?"

Francisco chuckled, "Not unless you want to. Good night, Em." She collapsed on her bed before she could change into her pajamas. She dreamed of Dorothy and the Wicked Witch from The Wizard of Oz. In her dream, she wondered why some people are so mean; are they made that way, or born that way?

Chapter 17

The next day, with Justin, the new company man aboard, the train steadily progressed towards the Rocky Mountains. By dinner, they passed Glenwood Springs and were deeper into the mountains only an hour from Eagle. For dinner, Emma made two kinds of burritos, then wrapped each in foil, each with a seared jalapeno tucked inside. For herself, she made a less spicy chicken burrito. The train worked continuously the entire day without stopping, aiming to be in Eagle that night. She took an Insulated cooler with dinner forward. She climbed the ladder on the first water tanker after the dining car. The sky grew dark with pregnant, low clouds that soon would compress against the mountainsides like wringing out a soaked sponge.

In the late afternoon, she strode the catwalk along the top of the water car without wearing a jacket. The temperature dropped, so her arms got goosebumps, and she shivered. The car's metal surface felt cold and damp, she glanced up, bad weather was imminent. Her eyes looked from the sky back to the train cars in front. She still had another water car, two grinding cars, and two engines remaining. Already, she had hiked for ten minutes, if not more. Undeterred, Emma gripped the handrail, leaned forward, and stepped quicker. She told herself, damn, I should've wore my coat. At the front end of the other water car, she climbed down the ladder and into the back door of an auxiliary engine.

It was loud inside the engine compartment. but warm, and at least she stopped shivering. The large generator hummed, giving the sense of static electricity tingle, making her wince as she passed. She shifted the cooler to her other hand to get around the large diesel engine, opened the door, and immediately regretted not wearing a jacket. With her head down, she went around the first engine's outside catwalk to the front, grabbed the door handle, and turned. Her hand slipped off the smooth metal. Urgh, she tried switching hands and turned it again. It almost opened, and her wet hand slipped off again. She banged on the door, shivering rigorously. Desperate, she banged harder. The door opened and inside stood a man who looked like the personification of the Colorado Rocky Mountains, wearing a big smile under his two-week-old beard and Stetson hat. He seemed seven feet tall and handsome.

He tipped his brim up, looked at her face, and then into her eyes. His smile grew, and he said, "Here, let me get that for you. Hi, I'm Justin, and you must be Emma. Come in before you get yourself cold." He placed his jacket around her shoulders. "Wow, you mean to tell me you climbed over the train in this weather to bring us dinner?" Inside, they walked up the stairs to the front cabin.

Emma stopped at Miguel, "I brought burritos and some hot sauce that I made. I'm going to miss you."

Looking up from his computer screens, he said, "Thanks, muchos gracias." He hugged her. "Well, we knew this day would come, Emma." He unwrapped his burrito and nodded at the seared jalapeno. "Ah, Bueno."

Emma told Justin, "Some burritos, fresh salsa, and guacamole are in the cooler. I made enough for everybody, so help yourself, there's lots to go around." She went to the driver's seat and said,

"Hey boss, got you some food? Wow, look at that view ahead. Do you ever tire of all this?"

Francisco said, "Tire of this, nope, the views are incredible. I am tired of all these long hours and being away without seeing my family. Last year, I was out here for ten months. Now my wife hates me, and my kids are growing up without their dad."

Justin said, "Cisco says that you go to BYU, so what are you studying?"

Emma could not help but smile when she faced him. While he sat, they were head-to-head as she stood beside him, and he smelled like a forest. She smiled bigger. "Uh, just some pre-law crap, but lately, I've been thinking of going a different direction." Francisco nodded with her. She shrugged, my family are lawyers and soldiers, but…"

"He nodded, but… you would incur their wrath for going a different road. What is it you truly desire, Emma?" Her mouth was agape, and her brown eyes grew and sparkled. Her body wanted nothing more than to melt into his chest.

"I want to go to veterinary school in Denver. I think animals like me more than people. Knowing Cisco and the men helped me realize many things about myself."

Francisco said, "Sorry to interrupt, but we still need you to do the H2 S course. Maybe you can help some guys who don't read English, too. Tomorrow, we go through Moffat Tunnel just before Denver, and it's very important that you know how to use a respirator."

Justin nodded, "See, that's why Cisco is such a good friend. I'm going to miss him when he leaves. He's an excellent leader. Hey Cisco, what'll you do when Miguel takes over?"

"Oh… it's hard to say. My cousin has an autobody shop in Houston. I used to work there, and my other cousin has a yogurt shop in Del Rio. He wants me to franchise with him."

"Yeah, sounds good… why am I not buying it, Cisco? I don't hear your heart in what you are saying. Emma wants to be a vet. I feel her passion and can see she is more of an introverted loner type."

"Hey, I'm not a loner, I have friends, lots of—"

"Oh, I'm not saying that you're some recluse. I can see you like being here, and that fits you." Again, Justin paused with a smile along the edges of his mouth. Those lips Emma stared greedily at them. His smile grew, making his already blue eyes twinkle like sapphire gems.

"You know what I just realized? This is the first time Cisco has avoided giving a truthful answer. why are you avoiding the question, Cisco?"

Francisco shrugged, "Ah, you are getting to know me too good. Now, my wife will be jealous."

Emma crossed her arms, "You're avoiding the answer. Come on, I said what I really want to do, your turn, boss."

"Alright… I want to learn to write movie scripts. It doesn't matter what my day job is, but I want to learn to be a writer and travel to great places like right here. Look where we are. This, to me, is amazing."

Justin nodded, "Yeah, you're a real people person, so I can see you doing that. Well, good luck, Cisco. Let me know when you sell a script, and we will have a great party."

Emma said, "Wow, I wouldn't have guessed that. Well, I'm sorry, guys, but I better get back and relieve the guys at the back. It was nice talking." She looked out the front train windows again and returned to the dining car with her cooler. It rained, but it didn't matter because she wore Justin's jacket.

Back in the dining car, she changed into pants, grabbed her own jacket and hard hat, and went to the back of the train. If not for the overcast heavy clouds, the scene to the west would have the setting sun, but instead, the flat grey colors just reduced their colors as the day faded to dark. She relieved Diego first, and then when he finished with his break, Chico took his break. While she was alone with Chico, hosing the tracks with the water cannon, a fire started to her right. Chico called and pointed over to her right. Her hose missed, and the brush fire erupted bigger. Chico called forward, "Hey, stop the train. We need to go back a few feet."

The brakes squealed as the train slowed to a stop. The fire grew with every second fanned from the upward evening draft in the canyon. Due to quick thinking, they extinguished the fire before it could burn the forest down. Chico told Emma, "Sometimes the spark skirts get holes in them, and if the right spark gets out like that, it can make a fire, especially at this time of year."

Diego came back, "What happened?"

Chico pointed to the charred brush and said on the radio, "Hey, Cisco, I'm going to hop off for a second. I think we need to change a spark skirt." He climbed down, ran forward to the grinding cars on the driver's side, and returned. He grabbed his mic again, "Yep, we have one that needs fixing when we stop. We're clear back here."

The train blew its horn and rang the bell. The brakes released; Emma could hear the engines as it began climbing. Four engines, two at the front and two at the rear, roared as it tried to regain momentum, the drive wheels spun and screeched on the steel rails.

Emma told Chico, "Cisco says we have to do H2 S class.

"OK, can you help me? I don't read English too well."

Emma said, "Sure, Chico." Well, I guess I better get back. See you guys in a couple of hours for another break."

Back in her room after a shower, Emma flopped on her bunk and reached for her phone. There was a message from Martin and two from Rachel. She checked her Facebook page, and her mom left a coded passive-aggressive text that Emma interpreted: get home now or wherever you are, and I will make you regret it. Emma had practically worshipped her mom and her friends a few days earlier. You do one thing that serves your interest, and that's when you find out whether people care for your interests or just their own.

She read Martin's text, 'Hi Em, how's it going?' A man of words, she chuckled. She typed, 'Hi Marty, hey can you do me a couple of favors please? First, can you post a Photoshop pic of us together at your parents' house on your Facebook today? Also, my mom is up to something, but I don't know what. She's insisting that I come home like yesterday, or else.' Love you, thanks. Em. She read it out loud, made some spelling changes, and then hit SEND. Next, Emma read Rachel's text, 'Hey, your mom called, so where are you? Call me, please.'

She set her phone down, crossed her arms, and took a drink from her water bottle on the bedstand. She took a breath and picked up her phone. 'Hey, sorry, but I am with a boy, one you know, and we want our privacy. I am fine.' She hit SEND.

Her phone chirped, 'Hey, so you know the cops have your cell phone and are trying to break into it. When your mom finds out you're the girl on the video, she is going to have a shit fit.' After she read it, Emma took a shower. The clean water rinse away the day's dirt and relieved yesterday's sorrows. Back in her room, she looked at her pajamas and then at the clock and put her clothes back on. She typed, 'Thanks, Rach, I'll talk with her.'

She returned to the dining room with the company laptop, completed the H2 S course with a cup of tea, and did the online course for Chico. She texted Francisco, 'OK boss, I did the course and Chico's too. I did not know that the smell of rotten eggs was such a big deal. Wow.' Her phone chirped with a text. Francisco said, 'Meet me when we get to Eagle next hour. We have to use the respirator mask to complete the training.'

Emma's phone chirped, a text from Martin. 'Hey Em, here is what I came up with at the last minute, so let me know if you need any changes.' Then, a pic file began downloading, and after a minute, it paused. Dang, internet, she grumbled. She took her phone to the window and waited for the picture to download. No change. She grabbed her hat and coat and went on top of the nearest water car, but nothing downloaded. She climbed down and headed to the rear of the train. Eagle is located near Vail and several other great ski areas on the western side of the Rockies. During the winter months, its population triples.

"Hey, do you guys have any internet back here?"

Chico and Diego looked at their phones. Diego nodded, "Si, I do."

"Damn cheap service," She said.

Chico said, "I have nothing. It must be the mountains blocking our signal. We should be in Eagle in a few minutes, and there is a good signal."

Their radios squawked. Francisco said, 'That is a wrap for today, boys. We are staying in Eagle till morning. Does anyone have eyes on Emma?'

Diego returned the call, "Si, back here, Cisco."

"Tell her there is a Costco, which stays open another hour. We can get you a ride if you like, so see me. I have a Costco card."

Emma went to the front of the train as Francisco applied the dynamic braking. He said, "Hey, here's the card. Can you get more muffins, too? I like the double chocolate ones, Miguel likes the blueberry, and Justin likes everything, and ate the rest of them."

She nodded, took the card, and stuffed it into her pocket. "Hey, who's taking me?"

Justin smiled, "Well, this just might be my lucky day. I'll get to drive you there." He came around the corner holding a can of Pepsi."

Emma's phone chirped; her text picture was finally downloading. She looked at Martin's Photoshop skills, then enlarged the picture, looking at the edges of her with him in front of the background of his parents' house. It all matched. Maybe her mom won't be able to tell that it's a fraud as long as she gets to Denver—just one more day to hang on. 'Hey, great work, Martin. I owe you a big favor for this. Now, if she asks to corroborate my story.' She shared the pic with her Facebook page, adding a caption underneath; we are so happy. Then she hit the POST button and left with Justin.

The store was nearly empty of customers, so they pushed the cart freely up and down aisles stopping at the meat aisle, grabbing chickens, pork roasts, lunch meats. They loaded cases of soda and water, laundry detergent, and toilet paper. He pushed the cart while she shopped. They finished shopping and paid with her new company card, They hung out at the food court before leaving.

While he ordered them some pizza slices and a soda, she checked her Facebook page. It worked. Her mom wrote, 'I didn't know you liked boys. I assumed, with you being a Tomboy, that you were gay. Maybe you should bring him over for dinner. Emma chuckled as Justin handed his bank card to the cashier for the food, "What is it, Emma?"

"Oh, nothing… well, my mom thinks that I'm a lesbian."

She wrote, 'Well, Mom, it's not that I'm not gay, it's that I have found I like this boy. Sorry I've disappeared, but we had just this opportunity. I will be back home in a few days.' Justin leaned over the table, taking a big bite; nearly half of his pizza slices doubled up in one big bite. With the charade working she looked at Justin, the mountain man. What a hunk, and there she was, sitting right next to his big, rugged body. Lesbian… ha, what Emma was attracted to was not what she was used to being around. Real men had her undivided attention.

"What are you doing tonight?" she nibbled at a slice, then took a little sip while her eyes never left his face.

He wiped his face, "Oh, I reckon I might get a room and crash out, Denver tomorrow, Darlin. It is the end of the line for you. Will be sorry to have you leave us.

"Actually, I have been talking with Cisco about staying on for the summer. But I need to visit that Vet school for the day. His body shifted, and he put his arm around her shoulder and pulled her closer. Her head leaned on his arm, the back of her little hand touched the skin of his hand, and then her face blushed. He smiled and looked forward. She said, "What are you thinking?"

"I was thinking what it would be like to grow old with you. You have a perfect soul that makes me happy. Strange, it's like that old cliché, but I feel like you've been in my heart my whole life."

Emma's eyes held his gaze as she took another drink. Her eyes studied his features; maybe she had never wanted to forget the moment. The day of the week, time of day, where they were, what he was wearing, his hair, all of it became sealed in her memory forever. "We better get back," she said in a soft low voice. "Otherwise, I can't guarantee your safety if we stay here another minute." They shifted their eyes to break the magic spell. She turned back, and held her hand and he smiled.

Justin spoke softly, just above a whisper, to her ear. He said, "I can wait, Darlin." He reached over with his lips and kissed her head below her hat. He helped her to her feet and pushed the cart to the pickup truck. The night air felt cool and crisp for a July evening at the edge of the parking lot in the fir trees, a big owl hooted. In the sky, hawks swooped down at the parking lot lights, snatching flying moths and other big bugs that swarmed around the glowing lights while frogs and crickets serenaded each other. Justin opened her truck door and helped her up. She buckled her seatbelt, leaned over, and started the truck as he pushed the cart away. He hardly said a word as he drove with his left hand, and his right hand held her hand.

Before they drove up to the train, he stopped and kissed her. After they unloaded, she packed the food away, said goodnight to him, and went to bed. She tossed and turned most of the night, unsatisfied. Lesbian, ha, her mom knew nothing about her. Emma was happy and loved by the train crew. Maybe for the first time in a very long time. She knew that was the easy part; the trick would be holding on to that feeling. What will her mom think? Would she support her new happiness? When they arrive in Denver, she will be alone with Justin, and then she will know her truth for sure. With that last thought, her conscious mind closed off, opening the gates for her subconscious to begin the planning stage.

Chapter 18

Emma awoke early, hungry and feeling that she had just fallen asleep, time to make breakfast. She flipped the eggs, added salt and pepper, and checked her phone. Still, she had no bars of signal nor Wi-Fi. Amazing, in the twenty-first century, none of the crew had any signal either. The phone will have to wait. For now, she served eggs to order, pancakes, bacon, freshly fried hashbrown potatoes and sipped coffee between orders. Good morning, Diego, Francisco, and Chico. She wanted to sing and dance. She said good morning, and they said buenos dias. Everyone understood the other's phrases. She leaned over the sink and looked up. The clouds had thinned overnight. Venus hung in front of her view just over the ridge, its brilliant light making it the perfect morning star. How fitting that the ancient Greeks started their day with their goddess shining down so brilliantly, she bemused with a little chuckle.

She sat across from Francisco as he devoured his breakfast. It reminded her of last night when Justin gulped his pizza. The more ferocious they plunged into their food, the more her fork was compelled to pick at her plate with an occasional bite. Maybe it's part of her being a Libra, always balancing the world around her. "How was your night, Cisco?"

"It was good. Some of us played pool at the bar down the road."

"Where's Miguel this morning?" she asked.

"Oh, he wanted to say goodbye. We dropped him off at the bus terminal, and he went home. He'll return in two weeks unless we make it to Del Rio first. He wanted you to know that you always have a job even if neither of us are here." She held his hand; they smiled and sipped their coffee. Emma cupped her mug in both hands, warming her palms. She told him about her Facebook page and how she fooled her mom with the pic. He nodded that Martin did a good job. It looked like she and he was there with his parents. She tried not to smile so big or look so happy, but she wanted to tell him all those things; she was reluctant. What if he didn't approve? What if he, like her mom, criticized her instead? After his cup was empty, he got up to leave.

She held his arm, "No, stay. I have something to ask or say or … sit, please. Here, let me pour you some more.

"I'm in love, Cisco. This is truly the best I have ever felt in my entire life. Do you see how happy I am?" He studied her eyes, rubbed his chin, and nodded in silence. "You're not saying anything. Is that good, or are you just trying not to disappoint me?"

"I can see, and yes, I am very happy for you. You truly deserve to be happy and to fall in love. What can I do to help?"

"Thank you, Cisco, thank you so much. You don't know what that means to me. We plan to meet up in Denver for a romantic few days. With Miguel gone, it looks like you're stuck with us a little longer."

"I am not ready to leave Emma, maybe at the end of summer. I'm putting Chico in Miguel's spot since he is the senior crew member. Actually, I asked him to take my spot, but he turned it down."

"Why would he do that?"

"He said he doesn't want the headaches. He makes enough and lives in Mexico on his time off. Not everyone feels the same desire about getting promotions or money. Chico likes an easy, simple life."

The train began its work before sunrise, or as Justin said, when the rooster crows, grinding the rails as it climbed higher into the mountains towards Vail. The train made slow progress climbing the ridges into the mountains and had to redo several sections. By lunchtime, they neared a valley in the mountains. Emma cooked chicken burritos to take to the men at their workstations for lunch. A routine she worked out and the men liked. She'd vary the burrito ingredients daily and make a new salsa. Since there was no cellular in that area, she left her phone in the kitchen and made lunch deliveries, saving the front engine delivery for the last. It was noon on a Sunday. Tourists flock to the small little alpine villages, creating too much noise, some locals will tell you. A double-edged sword is that the money tourism brings into the coffers helps with many improvements that would otherwise be neglected, but it increases traffic and noise into the later hours of the night. Without tourism, many towns and their heritage would vanish.

Emma leaned her body over the sink, in front she saw Avon, another small rustic tourist town. She looked at her phone. Ah, finally, she had a cellular signal. She hopped over to her Facebook page, and while she waited for it to load, she noted a bald eagle perched at the top of an old dead tree nearby. Beyond her field of view must have been a river or lake. Avon is located near the ski area Beaver Creek, just down the road from Vail.

Her eyes wandered back into the kitchen and rested on her phone screen. She saw a message from her mom, but she saw a news video link posted from SLC before she read it. A special new bulletin with a police detective for missing persons was interviewed about a missing young woman, a college student at BYU. They showed footage of the car crash and Emma staggering into the café where she met Francisco and Roy. Then, the video showed them leaving the back door with one of the men holding her hand as they ran out of view down an alley. The police told the reporter we didn't know what happened to her or where she was. We do know the identity of the family being contacted—more news to be released shortly.

Emma grabbed her phone, forgot the burritos, and ran to the front of the train. She ran inside, breathing fast, her body shaking. "Emma," said Francisco and Justin.

"Here, it's real, and I'm going to jail. You have to help me." She held her phone and replayed the video. Justin held her arm to keep the phone from shaking so much. He looked at Francisco and back to Emma. "See, they have a search, but I'm not lost."

Francisco nodded and said, "You just don't want to be found, and there is no law against that, Emma."

Justin said, "The way you charged in here, I thought a swarm of hornets was after you. This is not a big deal, and we'll speak for you if you want. Tell them you started a new summer job that requires lots of travel."

Francisco said, "Right, and you have your rail card to prove you work for the rail company…"

Emma shrugged and looked away.

"What happened to your rail card?"

"I don't know. I lost it, I think. We went bowling, and I had it, but then I thought it was in my shorts pocket, but I didn't see it."

Justin said, "Well, Cisco will just order you a new one. It's no biggie; I'm sure it is on file."

Francisco nodded, "Yes, it's on file. Tomorrow, I'll call Terri when we get to Denver."

Justin asked, "Hey Darlin, where's our lunch? We have been up here drooling for one of your home-cooked burritos. Never mind, tell you what, how about I walk you back to the dining car?"

Over lunch, Emma told Justin how she met Francisco Roy and got herself a job with the railroad. While they ate, her phone began beeping, chirping, and vibrating for her attention. He said, "You might want to take one of those calls. It could be important."

"Oh... mostly it's my mom, she is demanding that I come home."

"Or else what, Emma?"

"I don't know the answer. I just know that she is a very..." She looked at her phone, "There was an update to the story. The female reporter stood in front of the State Capitol building. Emma leaned over her phone, turning the volume up. 'There has been a new development in the missing young woman case we reported on earlier. With us now is the mother of the missing woman, none other than our own US Senator, Elizabeth Chase. The police have identified your daughter as the missing woman in the earlier video. Have you been in contact with the authorities?"

"Yes, I have been in contact with the FBI, Utah State Troopers, and the Federal Marshals office. We will find my daughter and bring her home safely. We don't know at this time if this is a kidnapping, but the police have informed me that a group of men abducted her."

"Has there been any contact with the people who abducted her? Have they made any requests? Has there been a ransom?"

"I am not to discuss the case details at this time. My daughter is out there somewhere, and if you hear this now, I will bring you home and bring the evil villains to justice. I am offering a reward for any information that helps with my daughter's return."

"How much are you offering Mrs. Chase?"

"The family will pay up to 100,000 dollars."

"You heard it first here on KFXX channel seven news. I am Alicia Dragger, reporting live at the state capitol, back to you guys.'

"Your mom is Senator Chase? Really?"

"Sorry, I was going to tell you before we go to Denver. I didn't know that it matters who my parents are."

"Normally, with me, that's true, but in this case, everyone is in great danger, including yourself. We have to come up with a plan, so let's tell Francisco since he's in charge." He stood up, stretched his back, and walked her out the front door. After the door slid closed, the bathroom door opened. Diego looked down the hall, flushed the toilet, and slipped out the back door.

Francisco said, "It's your decision, so whatever you decide, we will support it. I can call Terri and get you time off to go home to sort things out."

Emma leaned on the control station, sighed, and shook her head, "But that's just it. For my whole life, my mom has decided everything in my life, and I never knew what it's like to make my own decisions or live my own way. This is the first time I've gone out and just done what I want to do. I am an adult, technically, being responsible, so why do I again have to do what she wants? It's just so she looks strong for family values right now. I'm just not ready to go back to that life."

"You're right, Emma. Look how far you've come since last week. Now you're stronger, happier, and you make yourself useful."

Justin asked, "Does anyone know you work for the railroad or are here?"

"No, I haven't told anyone yet."

"OK... Cisco, if no one knows where she is and she is an adult, what's wrong with dealing with this when we get to Denver? Emma can make some calls and talk with the local police to assure everyone and keep her job."

Emma added, "And, check out the Vet. School." She grabbed Justin's arm and smiled.

The base radio station called, it was Roy, 'Hey bro, we need to stop soon. We are almost out of water on the front tanker.' Francisco held the mic and shook his head. Well, this sucks. "Copy that, Roy, thanks."

Justin looked at the map. The nearest place is back behind us, but the next one in front would be in Vail. Maybe this water tanker's gauge needs to be fixed. He pointed to the monitor screen and tapped on it. "Ever visit Vail before Emma?"

She said, "Was here for skiing a few times during winter break, but not in the summer."

Justin patted Francisco, "Hey, how about dinner while they fill the tanks? What do you guys say? I'm buying."

Francisco shook his head, "Naw, I don't want to be a fifth wheel, you guys go. It shouldn't take us too long."

Justin said, "The guys know what to do. Come on, Cisco. Besides, there's something that I want to discuss with you."

"Very well, 'How about you, Roy?'"

Roy said, 'Go ahead,'

"Hey, can you guys handle that if I run to town to take care of something?"

'Yeah, go ahead. I'll call if we have any questions.'

"Thanks, Roy."

Francisco shrugged and shook his head, "I guess you'll just have to deal with me being the fifth wheel to ruin your romantic getaway." He leaned out from his seat and called to the third station, "Hey, Chico…"

"Como estas boss?"

"We need to stop for water. Can you give the guys a hand with it?"

"Si El Jefe."

Francisco called the mainline and changed their route plan to be diverted off to Vail. The track dispatcher said, 'Just let me know when you are ready to switch back, but you're clear to divert.'

The Harsco rail grinder slowed and switched off the mainline onto the Vail spur line. The pickup was parked near the front; Garcia went into the engine. "Here's the truck keys. Can you put some air in the front driver-side tire?" He handed Francisco the keys. "Where are the guys at?" he asked.

Emma said, "In the back. Do you want to go have dinner with us?"

"No, I'm good. Are you guys bringing food back?"

Justin nodded, "Sure thing on me, bud. Any request?"

The restaurant was popular in the winter and always packed. Now, in the summer, business wasn't hectic. As the three relaxed during the dinner, Emma checked her Facebook for any new developments. As she looked, Justin got up to buy a round, and then Emma kissed Francisco, holding his face in her hands. She said, "I always wanted to do that, just to feel closer to you. You're the brother that I always dreamed mine would be. Thank you, Cisco, for everything." They turned and watched Justin walk back with three mugs of beer. "God, even his walk is so sexy. I am so attracted its magnetic I can't stop it, and you know…" she leaned closer and whispered, "I don't want to stop wanting him. But don't tell him. Men can turn into a holes when they think they are that great."

Justin said, "OK, boys and girls, Darlin, did you learn anything new?"

"Not yet, we were talking," she said.

"Well, guess what, you're famous, Em. Yep, they have your mug shot plastered all over that giant TV above the bar. That news video… it made it to the main news wires. Yep, it won't be long, and some assault team will bust down this here door and save you from the bad men."

They enjoyed a sit-down dinner of wood-fired pizza and beer. Emma almost forgot her predicament when she sank into the booth, pulling her ballcap low. Her hair was pulled back in a ponytail tucked through the back of her ballcap, and she was wearing a Harsco Rail jacket, looking different from the young, abducted woman on the news video. Francisco received a text from Roy, 'Hey bro, tankers are topped off.' He nodded as he read it.

After their dinner, they returned to the train. Francisco and Justin went to the engine, and Emma went to the dining car. She slid the door open inside, and the crew sat at the tables laughing until she closed the door. Roy turned and stood before her, and the room became silent. Emma stopped and looked at each of the faces. Some looked away, some looked at Roy, but none looked at her.

She said, "What's going on, guys?"

Chico said, "Nothing, we are just talking, so everything is good."

Emma turned to Roy, "Chico says everything is good, is it, Roy?"

He scratched his head and smiled. "Sure, whatever."

"That's good. I thought maybe there was something else for a second, but since all is good, I'll just go to my room." She closed her door and texted Francisco. 'Hey, something is up with the guys. I don't know what it is, but it involves me.' She grabbed a new set of clothes and went to the bathroom. She turned the hot water up for the shower, slipped in, and soaked her head, neck, and shoulders under the hot water. The nervous tension receded. After a few minutes, she turned the faucet off calmly and relaxed. She heard voices from the dining room, and she tensed from the sound. After getting dressed, she came out with a towel wrapped around her wet hair. The men were still there, along with Francisco.

"What's going on?" she asked.

Francisco said, "The men heard about you in the news. It seems your old boyfriend Roy here has been trying to throw you under the bus, but he needs the other men to agree. Apparently, he holds a grudge against you."

"I don't hold any grudges, I don't feel any loyalty to sluts and whores, the police want information about you, and since we are law-abiding citizens, some of us, that is... should help our friendly police in their efforts."

Chico shook his head, "Tell her the real truth. You want the money is the only reason. Emma, I would never turn on you. You're like family now."

She looked at Francisco, "Who else is with Roy?"

"Diego and Luis." He pointed to them.

"Can we have a word, Cisco... guys just stay here; we will be right back." She waved for him to follow her. In her room, he closed the door. "Your brother just called me a whore back there and a slut. Nevertheless... I have an idea. What's wrong with you guys collecting a reward? Hell, my family is rich. 100K is nothing."

Francisco rubbed his chin, "I don't know, Em... is it legal?"

"I can check with a friend, but then everyone can share. Let's talk with the guys."

She followed Francisco back to the dining car, and he said, "Amigos, Some of you want the money more than you want Emma's friendship, while others want to stay loyal to their new sister. We understand how both of you feel, and neither is wrong now. Emma asked if she could speak to the group." He sat down next to his brother.

Emma looked at the men, "Hola, Buenos noches, and to think just a week ago I knew zero Spanish, a week ago I had never had such good friends as you are… mi familia. So… Roy said some words, some I agree with, and the others hurt. I am not a whore or a slut; in fact, we have never had sex or anything more than a couple of dances, but Roy was the reason why I am here, and I will never forget that. He also said he wanted to make some money by being disloyal to me. Maybe he has a good point. Why not share in the reward money for my being recovered? After all, my family is very rich. I don't trust my mom; she is a very powerful US Senator, and as I am learning about, a narcissist who will stop at nothing for revenge or to get her way. So we should think about this first or not, but you could be sorry."

The men looked at each other and then at Francisco. Roy asked him, "Hey, Bro, are you going to try to stop us?" All eyes looked to Francisco, and he took a breath, "Roy, you are a grown-ass man. I used to wipe your ass when you were little, and now I see that you don't need to ask my permission."

Francisco's face became solid like a granite statue, but his eyes never left Roy's face. Roy leaned away from his older brother but was boxed into the bench and pinned to the wall.

Francisco lowered his voice, "You go ahead and turn on your friends, but you will never have me for a brother. Money is a terrible reason to be an asshole, and only really selfish assholes would do such a thing. Steve would be ashamed."

Roy shoved his brother, and then they jumped out of the booth with Roy swinging a right. Francisco ducked, knowing where on his face Roy was aiming. He rushed Roy, grabbing his throat with his hands and tackling him onto the table. Roy short-punched his head and chest while Francisco used his upper body to wrestle Roy against the wall with his fist at his throat. Roy spun away, leaping off the bench as the other men grabbed his shoulders, yelling stop, bro. Francisco climbed off the table and wiped his lip, "Enough of this, we still have a job to do. Everyone, go to your stations. We are going to Denver."

Chapter 19

After the makeshift crew meeting about collecting the reward money on Emma, the train was back online, grinding the switch tracks and spur lines around Vail. Emma offered to relieve the men on Firewatch, but they did not want her to help; instead, she set her alarm for four-thirty and went to bed. The train ground the rails through the night, so the men were tired and hungry by daybreak. They shuffled into the dining car in one's and two's, their faces and coveralls dark with soot. Emma stepped away from the sink as they washed up for breakfast. She poured pancake batter on the skillet and flipped another row. She set bacon, a stack of pancakes, and three eggs on a plate. Diego washed first, and she handed him his plate and said buenos dias.

The men ate silently while she finished making extra for the front of the train and herself, then took her cooler. The morning star shone just above it lay a layer of clouds blocking most of the early morning dawn. They climbed over the water cars and then through the engine cars to the front door. While the men ate, she picked at her plate. Francisco said, "How are the guys this morning?"

"Not too bad, though most did not speak to me. Roy hates me."

Justin said, "I doubt he or anyone can hate you. More like he is building a reason, selling you out for the reward money?"

Emma looked to Francisco; he nodded and said, "It's likely the case, Emma."

She shrugged, "Well, I think if I just don't talk with anyone back home, then the whole crew can split the reward, and I can keep my rail job. But… then again, I know my mom, and she is not going just to write a big check for my safe return when I was here working the whole time and was never abducted. It's weird that they came to such a conclusion."

Justin put his arm around her, "Whatever you decide, we'll help, ain't that right, Cisco."

"Just let me know what I can do to help."

"Thanks, guys. I'll talk with a legal friend today and see what he says. What are we doing today?"

Francisco looked at the map. "Let's see… today, the men will sleep a few hours, and then we will do some maintenance on the grinders and work our way to Moffat tunnel. We have some spur lines to grind along the way, so Denver must wait another day."

It was the end of June, yet the alpine air remained chilly and damp. It seemed it could snow on the tops of the fourteen-thousand-foot summits. Before the train could enter Golden, it would have to pass through the Moffat tunnel in the mountain range's heart. The seven-mile tunnel was wrought with hazards of the seen and unseen. Many game animals use the tunnel to avoid prey or escape freezing blizzards, only to tire and pass away inside. Animal carcasses decomposing in a confined space give off hydrogen sulfide gas, H_2S. It's an obnoxious odor that smells like rotten eggs at low levels. But at higher concentrations, it overwhelms the olfactory senses. The odor becomes undetected to the nose, and that's when it becomes a deadly gas known to kill humans and mammals after less than a minute of exposure. At high concentration levels, people die after one breath. The crew relied upon their gas masks and good training to work safely inside the tunnel.

The mainline dispatcher gave their train permission to switch over the spur line. Francisco said, "Copy that." Eased the train through the track switcher while grinding to the spur line, then set the break. "OK, guys, that's it for now, get some sleep." He checked his phone messages, "Hey, Miguel made it home and took his wife to the hospital just in time. She is in labor now."

Justin asked Francisco, "Do they know whether it's a boy or girl?"

"He said that they knew it was going to be a boy. I like to know ahead of time, myself."

Justin said, "Well, I want to be surprised when I have a baby. How about you, Emma?"

"I can't even imagine babies or weddings; I'm still just trying to make it through school."

Justin chuckled, "Well, Darlin, when you're in love, neither school nor job matters because your body is just gonna want to make a baby."

"Sounds like you have a lot of experience in that department. Were you married before? Do you have kids?"

"I was married once. Five years ago, she miscarried the baby. After that, she lost interest and filed for divorce."

Francisco said, "So sad, sorry to hear that, but you're still young and can start over." He smiled at Emma.

Emma looked at her phone, "Not to change the subject, but I have a message from my legal friend, and he says he doubts it would be legal unless it were a tip from an independent source. The trouble here is I am not being abducted or held against my will." She texted him thanks. "Well, it doesn't look like the crew will cash in on this reward scheme. Roy will be so brokenhearted."

While the crew slept, Emma, Justin, and Francisco replaced the worn grinding wheels on the front grinding cars. Justin held the heavy grinding stones while she handed Francisco tools. After a couple of grinding wheel swaps, they increased their rate. Francisco said, "This is the last one, geez, I'm starved."

"What's for lunch, Darlin?" Justin said with a grunt as he lay on his back, holding a heavy grinding stone on his chest. "One, two, three." He pushed it up into the spindle. Francisco spun the nut, securing it onto the motor's spindle.

"I guess now that we're done, I should go make some lunch. What would you gentlemen like?"

Francisco stood up and brushed his coveralls off, and she wiped his backside, "Oh, nothing special. I'll just have a couple of sandwiches."

"Sounds good, me too." He walked Emma back down the train. Emma, our date in Denver keeps getting pushed back, but it's been a good thing, allowing us to become better friends. Have you called your mom? Maybe that's all she needs to drop all of this. If I talk with her, do you think it could help get her to call off the dogs?"

"To be honest, I don't know. This... Well, it's just not her normal self."

After lunch, Emma said, "I think I'll just go take a quick nap before the guys wake. It's been a long day." She laid her head on the pillow in her room and fell asleep. It was mid-afternoon when she awoke to her door knocking. She put her shorts on and slid the door open.

Francisco asked, "Hey, have you seen my brother?" He leaned into her room.

"Roy? No, I haven't. What's going on?" she hopped on her bunk and put her socks and shoes on. "Where are the guys?"

"Outside." He motioned over his shoulder. "Has he called or texted you? Did he say anything?" Emma followed him down the steps to the railyard. Across the tracks were some of the crew talking with a different worker. The railyard worker said he did not see anyone leave, but he just got to work an hour ago, so maybe they could have left before then.

Emma said, "Where's Diego?" She pointed to the train. "He and Roy hang out. Maybe he knows something."

Francisco said, "There he is." He called out to Diego and waved for him to come over. Diego jogged across the tracks over to them.

"When was the last time you said, Roy?"

"This morning, when we went to sleep after breakfast."

'Did he say anything?"

"No, we didn't talk. I am just as surprised as you are that he left."

Emma asked, "Has anyone checked his room yet? Did he take anything with him or leave some sort of message."

Diego said, "I knocked on his door."

Thanks, Diego, "Come on, Cisco, check his room."

Emma and Francisco jogged back to the crew car at the back of the train. They climbed the stairs, ran down the corridor between bunk rooms, and pushed the door latch, but the door went ajar. Inside, the light was on in the tiny bunk room. In most houses, a crew bunk room would fit easily in the average bedroom, but on a train, where space is a premium, a small closet of a room is all most workers get. She looked in the little drawers in the closet; his work clothes lay piled on the floor, and most of his civilian clothes were gone. Francisco sorted through the pile. "It looks like he took what could fit in his backpack and left the rest. Is there a message?"

Emma said, "Oh yeah, there's a big message here. Damn, it." She looked at Francisco, "I'm afraid for Roy. He went to get the reward money as greedy and selfish as he is."

Francisco sat on the bunk and rubbed his head. "That makes for a new problem for us, Em. Now they will know where we are."

Emma said, "Sorry, I never knew your brother was this selfish. It reminds me of my mom."

"Your mom?"

"Well, all of this is because she needs all of her kids up on the stage for her reelection speeches, and with me missing. She runs on a family values platform, showing she puts family values first. Now I see how phony that is."

"Sorry, you must leave before trouble comes. It's just a matter of time until Roy tells them where you are. Some of our guys are legal, and others are not; one or two may have expired work visas. If people come snooping around, it will cause trouble."

"Please, Cisco…" Emma grabbed his arm, shaking her head. "No, don't make me go. Please, I think I can straighten this out. I just need a little time. We will be in Denver tomorrow, and I promise I will get off the train as soon as we get near the city before trouble can come." She studied his face, "I'm pleading with you. Please don't send me away. I need you right now more than I ever needed anyone. Leave it to me, and everything will be all right." She kissed his head and held her arms around his neck as she sobbed. Francisco wiped her tears from his cheeks and shook his head.

"Damn Roy, why does he have to be that way? He only cared about himself all his life except to show me up with our mom. I would buy her flowers he would find out, and guess what he'd do?"

"Buy her a bigger bouquet?"

"Right, and put cash into her account or pay her cell phone bill. He's always showing me up every chance he gets. Now this. Go, get on the train and stay on it until we get to Denver."

That evening, they parked the train in a different town's spur rail, and Emma stayed away from the public's eye. Her phone revealed no news updates. She lay on her bunk and read Cisco's book, the Art of Failure. She crawled off her bunk and shuffled her feet to the kitchen to make a sandwich and grab a Coke. When she returned, there was a message from her friend Martin. She dropped her phone as she read his message. The room swirled and blurred her senses, confused her hands lost feeling and were numb. When she came around, she ran to the bathroom and vomited, wiped her mouth, and then vomited again. The floor felt cold on her knees, and the toilet's stainless-steel bowl was cold on her hands. Her head again spun around and around. She cupped her hand under the faucet and rinsed her mouth. Then her stomach lurched again and shoved its empty contents upward, and stomach acids spewed forth. She grunted and gagged and lay on the floor next to the toilet. She wanted to cry out from her suffering, but instead, she embraced her fears and the anguish her mind's fears were imposing on her body systems.

After several minutes, she rolled onto her knees, rinsed her mouth with more water, pushed her hands down, and climbed onto the toilet seat, her legs shaking. She hyperventilated and pushed up to her feet while holding the door jamb with her hands. Holding onto the doorway, she shuffled to her room across the corridor. She slid her door shut, fell onto her bunk, and re-read Martin's message.

'Hey Em, I don't know what ya did, but the FBI are searching for ya. Let me know if I can help.'

Emma shook her head and mumbled, 'the FBI... Mom, what did you do? How could she be this way?' After a deep breath, she pulled her curtain back and thought, 'Outside is the next town.' She saw several building lights, porches, car lights, and street lights. She leaned her face to see to the right. A man walked his dog, smoking a cigarette on a path not far from the tracks. It must be the residential part of town. She shut her curtain and fell back to her bunk.

Later in the night, while everyone was sleeping, a loud banging sound woke Francisco. The banging came from the dining car's back door. He saw a civilian man and opened the door. "May I help you, sir?"

Emma heard voices in the dining area, slipped into her slippers, and shuffled to the dining hall, where Francisco and another man argued. Francisco shook his head, saying, "No, this is railroad property."

The angry man shouted at Francisco, waving his hands and smashing his fist in his other palm, then pointed to the right side. He shook his head and waved his cell phone in the air. "Some of us have to get up early for work, move your goddamned train, or I'm calling the cops. Move this train now."

Francisco again shook his head and said no. The man called police dispatch, "Get a squad car out here at the railroad yard and make them move their train. They are disturbing the peace of our neighborhood. The tracks are over by the Willow Point Apartments. Thank you." He pointed at Francisco, "The cops are coming. Now you're going to move your train or risk going to jail, so move it before they get here."

Emma called Francisco, and she said, "Hey, can he really do this? We don't need the police getting involved. This could be risky."

Francisco agreed with her and returned to the angry man. He said, "The police can't make us move because this is railroad property. But if you insist on bringing the police into this, fine, we will wait, but you can wait outside and off of our property. You are trespassing, sir."

"So, you think you are going to get your way? We will see about this. I'll be back."

Francisco and Emma sat on the bench for half an hour, but the police never appeared. They both went back to their bunks and fell asleep. Not long after falling asleep, they awoke to loud banging noises on the side of the train. The wall next to Emma's bunk boomed. She woke up and ran to Francisco's door. He said, "What is going on? It sounds like we are under attack."

They ran to the dining door and threw it open. Outside, a mob threw sticks and rocks at the train. One man grabbed a railroad tie, and two more helped move it next to the train. They rammed the end into the side under Emma's window. "She said, "We need to call the cops."

"But you said not to get them involved."

"That was before these people started World War Three." She ran outside yelling, "Stop this at once, or you will be charged with destruction of private property and spend your sleeping hours in jail. Get off this land, go home."

Three bigger women surrounded little Emma, closing in on her, yelling and screaming, pulling at their clothes and hair. One shoved her off balance, and another grabbed at her hair. Emma yelled at them to go home. Two of the men joined and surrounded her. They shouted obscenities, and the rest of the mob continued to throw rocks at the train. Francisco ran to Emma; the women turned and threw rocks as he approached. One hit him on the leg, and another rock hit his head. He put his hands up and blitzed in, grabbing Emma's arm and rushing through the mob, knocking the men out of their path. Diego and Chico ran to the steps and helped them into the dining car."

He called the police and the office while they locked the doors. Diego asked, "What is going on?"

"I don't know, they are from another country, and maybe that's how they deal with problems, but they demand we move the train because they have to get up in the morning for work, and they say it's too noisy." He looked out the window, "They are still out there, all of them, and here comes the police."

Chico said, "It looks like half the police station has come."

Red and blue flashing lights streamed through the dining car windows. Francisco looked out the window, shaking his head. Emma saw his face, color changing from red to blue and back. He half said, "Here they come." He unlatched the handle and turned to Emma, "Maybe you should disappear till they leave."

She shuffled back to her room and watched through her curtain with her window ajar."

The mob came to the dining car and demanded to speak to the police. Two officers spoke with their mob while one talked to Francisco. He went outside and pointed to the side of the train and then to the mob. Two officers looked at the side with their flashlights. The two lady cops came over to Francisco along with the mob leader. He waved his arms and shook his head. The angry man did the same but in a bigger motion. Emma sank onto her bunk. The mob waved their hands and yelled at Francisco. The police pulled him away, and they entered the dining car together.

Fransisco told the officers, "We have the right to be here, see where they damaged my train. I want to file a complaint, and they threatened me and one of my crew. Arrest them. They are nothing but a bunch of vigilantes."

Emma peeked out her door. The female officer called the male officer over to the sink. After a moment, they told Francisco, "Your train was not too damaged. It would be best for you to move the train. We will stay here to ensure nothing else happens. How long do you need to fire it up?"

"It already is, but I just have to get track permission and find another place to stop. We need half an hour." He shook his head and looked out the window. "I can't believe I have to move because of them!" He shook his head, breathed, and said, "Fine, I'll call track dispatch and see if there is another place we can stop." He picked up the base radio and switched channels, "Track Dispatch, this is RMS 10 come in... 'go ahead RMS 10.' Track Dispatch requestion a different track to stay for a few hours, currently at mile post 0175. 'Stand by RMS 10... Proceed to milepost 0189.' 'Thank you, Dispatch.' "OK, they get their wish, and we will move down the line. They assaulted me and one of my crew. Are you going to do anything about it?"

The lady officer asked, "Are you going to press charges?"

Francisco put his head down, "I won't be this way again till next year, and I'll make sure not to stop here."

Chapter 20

After a long, stressful night, Emma yawned as she flipped pancakes just a few hours later. One missed and landed on the edge of the griddle. "Damn it," she scraped it off and pitched it in the trash. The men sat at the tables, drinking coffee and playing on their phones. Francisco filled his cup and stood beside the tables, "Well, that was a rough night. Today, we will work the rails through the Moffat Tunnel. We hope to make it into Golden today. Use the staggered buddy system in the tunnel. Remember, if anyone goes down and you rush to save your buddy, you're going down too. Ten-four. Also, is everyone comfortable using their respirator?" His eyes addressed each person, who in return nodded, and Emma shrugged, her eyes trailing away from his look. Francisco asked, "Has anyone here heard from Roy? Did he say anything about leaving or where he was going?" The men shook their heads and said no. "Before he left, did anyone hear him on his phone?"

Chico said, "He must have left to collect the reward money, but he said nothing to us." The other men nodded and grumbled. Emma refilled their coffee cups and made another pot.

She said, "Maybe I should have said who my mom was before. I am truly sorry if I have harmed anyone here. When I met you all, I fell in love with the notion of freedom, and over the last several days, you have treated me better and been more family to me than my own. I talked with a legal expert, but by then, Roy had run off to collect the reward money. My friend said the reward would be disqualified since I was not lost nor abducted and that Roy wouldn't collect anything other than possible fraud charges. We want to stop him, but he won't answer his phone."

Diego said, "So, there is no reward? What was all that on the news? I think you lie, and now you tell me what I saw with my own eyes is not real."

Francisco climbed to his feet with his hands in front to stop Diego's line of thought. Emma nodded and said, "Diego, what you saw was real. My mom has offered a reward for information that leads to my safe return. My legal professor says that since I am not being held against my will, my friends can't just claim they found me when I was with them the whole time. Do you see? I wanted you all to share in the reward, including Roy, but it will be grounds for fraud, a major felony with years of prison time."

Francisco said, "Diego, if Emma did not care nor if she wanted to go back, she would just go, but she cares and wants to be here with you and Chico and—"

"—That's right, Emma is here with all of you and does not want to be returned home, but instead, she wants to make her own home, maybe even here in Colorado." Justin said, "Diego, there are laws against fraud, and someone as rich and powerful as the Chase family is well protected, so you would not win that fight. The bottom line, none of this is Emma's doing. She is here like all of you to do a job few are willing to do. We don't get into why we are here; we all have stories about why we're here and what motivates us. But what does matter is how we do our job and if we are on time and reliable, right Chico."

"Si, that's all I got, boss."

Justin nodded with a fist bump, "Ten-four. Now, if you need anything, you can go to Francisco. I've known him for a few years, and he has grown into one of the best men I have had the pleasure of working with. For any other concerns, my door is always open. Good communication keeps the ship afloat. Sorry to interrupt you all's meeting. I just came in to talk with Emma for more of her special coffee. This stuff's great." He raised his cup to Emma.

Francisco chuckled, "OK, guys, today we are going to work the area through Moffatt into Golden. Check your equipment, make sure you have your PPE, and have a safe day. We roll out in ten minutes."

Francisco whispered to Emma as the safety meeting broke up, "Meet me up front." She gave a little nod with her eyes, then turned to look at Justin. He hugged her as soon as the door slid closed, "Good morning, Darlin."

"This is our last day working together for a while," she said.

"It's been a good one. The company approved my vacation request, so I am all yours for the next week." They shared a smile.

She said, "That is great. I can't wait for us to get to Denver. I'm making burritos for lunch; do you have any requests?"

"I like everything that you make, Em. Whatever the other guys are having is fine with me; just don't make mine as spicy as theirs. When we get to the tunnel, please don't leave the car until we get out on the other side. Promise me that, OK?"

"OK… I promise I won't get myself killed." She yawned. "That was crazy last night, so has that ever happened before?"

"With this job, you never know what will happen; that was crazy. Try to get some rest before lunch." He looked out the window, "Sun should be up soon." Then he went forward, and she stood at the coffee pot. After a minute, she shuffled back to her room in her slippers, slid the door closed, and lay on her bunk. She looked at her phone for messages, then lay curled into a fetal position and slept for hours.

The train backtracked to the town from the night before, then lowered the grinders and headed for the tunnel at ten miles an hour, blowing the horn at the wildlife on the tracks. Deer leaped high and bounded from the tracks, elk ran to the side, and rabbits zigzagged with a final big bounce before getting caught by the wheels. Big horn rams jumped to the side, then stood and watched, ready to ram the train should it decide to come in their direction under a canopy of Ponderosa pines and spruce forest. Hooves kicked up pine cones as they disappeared into the forest. Magpies and crows squawked as the train approached. Higher up the slopes at ten thousand feet was the land of Aspens, those magnificent trees with white bark trunks and blazing red leaves in the fall. The train rose from the desert bottom through the temperate zone and then to the sub-artic near the peaks where snow falls any day of the year. Francisco opened the valve that lets sand pour on the tracks in front of the drive wheels, providing a firmer grip on the rails, a common practice for starting and going up inclines.

When Emma awoke, she reached for her phone and saw several messages. Rachel told her she heard about the news about the reward money and wondered if she could collect it. Martin told her to call him, and Francisco wondered if Roy was okay. 'Amazing,' she muttered, that Francisco can care so much for someone who cares only for himself. Unlike Francisco, He made quite a good first impression, and then there's Justin… OMG, what a hunk with a heart of gold. To think, at one time, a couple of years earlier, she had contemplated a serious relationship with her friend Martin. He probably could never rescue her from a swarm of puppies, let alone change a flat tire. A capable man with a big heart was far more attractive and desirable; even her mom would approve. She texted Justin. 'Thinking of you when I woke up, Denver tonight, can't wait.' She read her text and made a couple of grammatical changes. Oh,' she gasped. She called Terri at the office. The call could not be completed as dialed. Dang, mountains were in the way AGAIN! She texted Francisco, 'I need a few days in Denver, and you said I could. Is it still OK?' she read it, then added, 'How do I make Wi-Fi phone calls?' then tapped send.

After a sandwich, she relieved each man on the fire watch at the back of the train. As she sprayed the rails, she looked around for fire flare-ups and hit them before they got out of range of the firehose. A large herd of elk ran away from the train, the little calves bounding their hooves, hardly touching the Earth, as if they had wings. It reminded her of a Red Bull commercial. Within half an hour, black dust covered her boots from the grinding. She watched Chico return from his break, and he walked with a limp on his right hip. She always meant to ask him about it but never felt comfortable discussing personal things with the men, except for Justin and Francisco. It would even be difficult for her snooty mother to criticize Justin. Even her brothers would like him, but what did she find so attractive about him? That her family would maybe finally approve of her own life choice. Her phone chirped a text.

She looked up and said, "Got to go. They are calling for me at the front. Do you guys need anything before coming back next time?"

Diego leaned to turn his hose left and right, "Just come back before we go into the tunnel."

Emma went to the front of the train, climbed around, and went to the front door. Again, Justin was there to greet her. Up in the cab, she brought them foil-wrapped pork-verde burritos and half a cob of corn. Justin took a big bite, smacked his lips, and wiped his mouth edges, "Hmm... delicious, I was starving." She watched as he devoured the first burrito without taking a breath. He smiled and nodded, and he chewed the final bite. He told Francisco, "I'll tell you what, she is going to make someone a good wife someday, man; that was good."

She reached into her cooler, "Well, here's another, but it's chicken and Pico de Gallo. See what you think of it." She crossed to Francisco, holding a plate of burritos with grilled jalapenos. He chomped into his and nodded approval, then bit into half a pepper.

Justin watched, "See that... I don't know how you can handle that much heat. Were you raised on them as a baby? How old were you when you ate your first jalapeno?"

Francisco wiped his mouth, "Hmm... my mom says I was maybe a year and a half old."

Emma shook her head, "Good golly. I can't even eat them at my age." She looked at her phone, "Did you hear from Roy?"

He looked out the window and shook his head in a low voice, "No…" He asked, "Hear any more about your situation or from your mom?"

Emma looked through her messages, but there were no new ones yet. I tried calling but might not have the Wi-Fi calling set up correctly. Can you show me?" She handed him her phone.

He said, "Just go to settings then here and select Wi-Fi calling, then make sure you are on the Wi-Fi network, and it should work. Try it."

"You did it, it's ringing. Calling my mom."

'Hey mom… I'm fine… no… no…. I'm fine, please don't do that. I saw the news report; no one had abducted me. I don't think I should tell you that. Has anyone tried to claim the reward? A man named Roy Garcia… how about an anonymous claim from a man with a Spanish accent?" Oh… and… so what did he say? What's the number? I don't have the number because my phone was broken, so I'm borrowing a phone. Text this number, Mom. I miss you and will see you soon."

She looked at the men and shrugged, "I guess she had to go and hung up without saying goodbye. She set her phone down, rubbed her eyes, wiped her cheeks, and blew her nose.

"My mom said that someone that might be Roy called the number and will text the attorney's number for me to call him for any information. That was a hard call to make. What did I do wrong? All my life, everyone told me how lucky I was to have such a great mom. Looking back, I don't think she ever loved me like my brothers." Her phone chirped. "Got the attorney's number, so I'll see what he says." She took a sip of her Pepsi can. "Hello, Mr. Goldich, this is Emma Chase… I am fine… no I am not being held… I have a question: has anyone called in to claim the reward money? Oh… did they give a name? What did their voice sound like? Uh-huh… OK…. Did they say they would contact you again? I am trying to clear up a missing person, a friend I met last week who, since the news report, has vanished. I want to be sure he is OK, that's all. OK, I am fine and will call tomorrow, but no. I am not kidnapped or abducted. Proof? Like what sort of proof? Did my mom get the FBI involved? Oh! That's scary to hear."

She hung up and turned around, 'Well, she did get the FBI involved as we thought. They refuse to believe that I am free. It's crazy. Roy might have been the caller, and he'll get details to meet with the attorney with proof that I'm still alive."

The train stopped to fill up with fuel at the Union Pacific filling depot. They stopped along the siding track in Avon. Francisco's phone beeped, "Hey Mike, yep, need to top off the back tankers. Yes, the front ones are good. Thanks, see you in a minute."

"What was that about?" asked Emma.

"Water tanker is here to top us off on the back tankers. Come on, you got to meet this guy. He's quite the character." Justin was filing his report from the last day's work. She followed Francisco back down the tracks to the rear water tankers. He pointed to a large semi-tractor with a tanker trailer. "That's Mike. He has a driver for his pickup camper, and he drives that big rig following the train. He gave the driver hand signals and maneuvered the truck just where he wanted it, crossing his arms above his head. Whoosh, went the airbrakes. He gave the thumbs up to proceed. "You know, Emma, by the time this summer is over, and you go back to school, and I find a job closer to home, you're going to be able to be one of the crew, and about the only difference is you know how to cook and you look good doing it."

"I don't think I'll ever know how to do what you do. I'm so impressed."

Diego and Chico met Mike as he climbed out of his truck. They grabbed hoses and connected them, and then Mike connected them to the first water car. He turned a valve handle and then walked to her and Francisco. She whispered to Francisco, "He looks like a biker." His sunglasses were the Ray-Band's famous in the '60s. He wore a blue bandana, ponytail, vest, and cowboy boots. He was taller than Francisco, thickly built but not heavy, with a grey goatee.

"Hey Cisco, como estas? He gave Francisco a warm handshake. So, you're the girl I've heard about. Hello, I'm Mike. I hear you are a good cook. How much would you charge me for lunch and dinner daily? Truck stop food gets old after a while."

"Uh… it depends, do you just want what I make for the crew, or do you want to make your request? I've been making the crew burritos, pork verde, chicken, and carne since they have been working long hours at their station with no time to eat."

"Yeah, that sounds great—"

Francisco interrupted Mike and Emma, "—Whatever you feel you can afford, our company pays for ours, and we cook some meals for the company man. Come to the dining car when you're done, and Emma will get you something for the road."

"Where's your next stop?"

"Well… we hope to get through Moffatt tonight and stop somewhere along Boulder Creek part of Denver for sure by tomorrow."

Emma asked, "How much water does your truck hold?" she pointed to the tanker.

"This one holds about nine thousand gallons, a little less than one of your water cars. Hey Cisco, I saw the funniest thing on the way over here this morning. Do you know that single-lane road over by the river? I just filled up and got on the road, and this cow was walking right down the middle of the road. I beeped at it, and she moved faster but, for some reason, was going to stay on the road. The other day, by Wintergarden, I was riding my bike down the pass, and a cowboy was herding his cows down the road. I must have spooked them, and they took off running and slipping. Cows were skidding off the road. I was surrounded in this stampede of about a hundred heads."

Emma's mouth opened, "What… really?"

"Sure, here are some quick pics I snapped as they skidded past. She leaned over to avoid the sun's glare. Check this out: they flipped on their backs when they started running." On the screen, several black cows were skidding off the road as the cowboy and his horse rode along, whistling to his dog as if there was no concern. He turned the camera and showed the rest of the herd running towards his bike, and then he veered through the herd down the hill.

Francisco stepped aside and called his mom. Emma tried to hear the call, but Mike had more fun with wildlife stories. She tried to smile and nod at the pauses. Diego waved to him to shut the pump off. When he turned, she wandered closer to Francisco as he walked and talked his way back to the engine. He waved back to Mike, "Catch you tomorrow on the other side." Still on the phone, he prepped the train for departure, fired up the engine and built air pressure, pushed buttons, and flipped switches. His voice remained calm, and he never had to repeat himself. Emma thought, now this is real multi-tasking. "OK, Mom, I love you. Tell the girls I love them and give them a big hug. Si, adios."

The radio squawked, 'RMS 10 is confirmed for one hour on mile marker 0257 to mile marker 0285; my name is Rachel.' Francisco grabbed the mic, "Copy that, Rachel. RMS 10 is clear for one hour from mile marker 0257 to mile marker 0285. Chico said from the back of the train, 'We are clear to the rear.' Francisco nodded; copy that, Chico, and we are clear to the rear." Dispatch train RMS 10. We are clear to the rear from the siding at mile marker 0257." The lady's voice confirmed they were on the main line for the next hour proceeding to Granby.' "I copy that we are clear for one hour from mile marker 0257 to mile marker 0285 at Granby Rachel; thank you."

He set the mic on the base. The brakes clanged and whooshed as the air was forced from the air tank into the brakes to release them, and then the train crept forward. Emma held the handle on the control panel as the cab swayed and bumped while they built up speed. Francisco moved the throttles up as the train crossed from the Wolcott sidetrack onto the main line. They would follow the Colorado River to Granby, then after the next freighter passes, hop back on the main line and grind their way through Moffatt Tunnel into Tolland, then follow Boulder Creek into Denver by the next morning.

"That was my mom. Roy called her and told her he'd buy her a new car." He shook his head. "No matter what, she always sticks up for him. I guess I better send her some money to help with my girl's expenses this week."

Emma said, "So, Roy thinks he's collecting the reward and keeping it all?"

"Looks like it, Em. Has your family said anything new?"

She looked at her phone, "Uh… no… don't see anything here. It just sickens me how good you are and then how selfish Roy is, and he will get rewarded for being that way. It reminds me of my mom."

"How's that, Em?"

"Well, my dad is from the Chase family. My mom went to law school, worked hard, married the right man, and used his family and influence to get elected. My dad never had that desire. He was happy being an officer in the Marines. He was so miserable when he retired, and they fought every time they were together. After he died, she used that to help her get elected. Now I can see that, like Roy, Mom has no morals or scruples, and just like Roy, she always seems to benefit. It seems to me Roy is her kid, and I'm your stepdad's kid."

Francisco chuckled, "Hey, you're my little sister then."

Justin leaned over and patted her shoulder, "Sorry to hear all of that, Emma. We all have skeletons. Some have them under their bed, others in the closet, and the rest leave them lying around for others to trip over. Maybe your family harbors a secret or two; if so, it will eventually come out. And when her skeletons come out, please, hon, don't stop being your beautiful self; promise me that much."

Emma looked out the window and nodded, fighting the tears of her family's coldness. All of her life, all those birthdays and holidays, report card days, and sports days, her brothers were superstars in the family while she was shoved off to the side, like the little kid at Thanksgiving eating at the little kid's table. Windblown snow capped the peaks high above. She said, "That's my family. The tallest is my mom, the two brothers, and that barren rock that fell off the side is my dad."

Justin and Francisco looked at their feet, and the floor swayed long before anyone could speak. Emma smiled and hugged each other, "I love you, Cisco, and I love you, Justin. Let me go make dinner for the crew, and I know they are getting hungry." She kissed Justin on his cheek.

They watched her go. Justin said, "Man, she is going to be some kind of woman."

Francisco said, "Si, she already is. She means that she loves you."

"The feeling is a mutual partner. Another day, and we are home free. Hell, what can possibly go wrong after all of this?"

Chapter 21

While roasting meats for more burritos, a peaceful calm washed over Emma as she sat alone on the bench in the dining car, accompanied by just her thoughts of simple things. The colors of trees, the smell of the forest, and the sound of forest birds chirping at trickling brooks. She let go of her phone, and it fell, making a thud on the table, waking her back to consciousness. She stretched and yawned, then checked her phone. There was one message; it was from her friend Martin. He also left a voice mail when his call did not go through. After Emma read his message, she felt like she was in a flooding river about to go over a waterfall, and no matter how frantic she swam for the bank, the river still swept her down the middle of it closer to the precipice.

'Em, call me when you read this. MP.' There was another news report link. Her finger shook the nearer it got to the link. She texted Justin, set her phone down, and heated tea water. The front door slid open and closed, "Hey, Darlin," he hugged her, and she put her arms around him.

"Justin, I thought it was maybe over, so I guess I was just lying to myself. There's a text from my friend and a link to a new news video. I'm not able to watch it. Will you sit with me for a few minutes? I'm sorry to ask you for help like this."

"I have to get back up there; can you bring your phone, and we can look at it up there?"

"I don't want to have others see me as a wreck. I am petrified of what this might be, please." She buried her face in his chest. Her brown hair fell over his arm, and he stroked his hand through her curls. Without a word, they sat on the bench and held her phone out; he clicked on the link. She kept her head down towards the floor, and he held her hand. Her hand squeezed to the words of the reporter.

"Well, Em… here goes," he hit play. The reporter interviewed Martin at his parents' house, and he showed the photo that he doctored to make it appear that Emma was there. Her mom pleaded on the TV with tears for her daughter's safe return. Emma squeezed her hand in his while her mom spoke to the reporter. He stopped the video.

'Lies, all lies, and you are right here with me and know it's all lies. Why are bad people rewarded for being liars and cheats?" she said, "Continue, please."

The reporter interviewed the state patrol captain, who said he was utilizing all resources for a positive outcome. The reporter asked, 'What about the fact that Emma Chase did call in and say that it's false?' that's what kidnappers get their victims to do.' But she sounded convincing. Do you have any leads on whom the abductors may be or where?' Emma sat upright, "Hold on a sec…" she blew her nose, "OK, go."

The reporter then interviewed the family attorney, 'We have breaking news; there has been a reliable tip that the kidnappers are of Mexican decent, and they are on a train somewhere in Colorado.' The reporter said, 'Do you think they are illegal aliens?' 'We are not eliminating that possibility.' She asked, 'Does that mean you will send a swat team to rescue Emma Chase?' Yes, it is possible, and we are working with all the authorities now.'

"Holy shit Emma, what the hell…"

She said, "We must warn the men before it's too late."

He looked out the window, "Maybe it's too late already."

"No, don't give up, Justin. Maybe you can help straighten this thing out. They will listen to you."

"Whatever happens, Emma, I'll be there for you. At least Roy didn't tell them which train we were on. That might buy us a little time."

"We need to talk with Roy and get him to admit the truth to the police." She texted Francisco and hit SEND. She said, "Maybe Cisco can think of someone in contact with Roy who can send a message."

"That would be their mom, but Cisco won't involve her. It would bring embarrassment to all of us but not to Roy somehow. He has gold fever on the brain. That reward is too irresistible to him."

Emma stood up with her arms around herself, looked out the sink window, and then returned, "What if you called your office? Maybe they can clear this up, or maybe we should call Harsco, and they can prove I work here and am not being abducted or held or anything against my will."

"Do you have your rail card handy?"

"Let me go check," she ran to her room, "Damn it!" she came back waving her wallet, "Look, it's empty. Someone came into my room and took my company debit card and rail card, and I had a few dollars. It's all gone." She threw her wallet on the floor and screamed. "Roy did this, so now it's personal because I didn't sleep with him, and I corrected him in front of his friends back at Moab. He has had a grudge against me ever since that day. Unbelievable how evil some are."

The door slid open, and Diego looked inside, "Como estas?"

"Come in; we are fine," said Justin. He lowered his voice, "I have to return to the cab. Come forward with me."

"No, I have to make lunch right now. I'll bring you guys something soon." She walked with him as far as her stateroom, "I need to change, so I'll see you soon." She hugged him. "Thank you."

The train followed the Colorado River north for half an hour before swinging east. Justin said, "Hey, we might have a problem here. Just half an hour is left before we run out of track time. Can we make it to Granby?"

"At this rate, no is the short answer. If we pick up our speed, we can, but then we will have to backtrack at some point, putting us in Moffat tonight and Denver tomorrow. This rail section has needed more grinding from that cold winter. I saw Emma texted, what's going on?"

"Oh… she showed me a news link. Roy told the family attorney Emma was on a train. Have you tried to call him off? Maybe tell him that there won't be any reward."

"Yes, I tried, but he won't listen, and now he won't answer his phone."

"This is no joke, Cisco; he is playing with fire and will get in trouble. I will do all I can to protect you as a witness that nothing happened, and she is an employee, though I never saw her rail card for myself."

"She lost it?"

"Well, she couldn't find it, and when she showed me her wallet, it looked like someone had been through it, just to make matters worse. I think it was Roy."

"You don't know that. Sure, he is gone, but Roy is no thief."

Relax, man. I didn't say your brother is a thief; I just said he took it out and probably threw it off the train so that Emma can't prove she works here. He wants that reward money bad enough to do irrational things to get it. You should tell your mom; she can call Roy and have him stop this before it's too late."

Francisco's face turned red, his eyes blazed. He pointed his finger at Justin's chest, "You leave my mom out of this and stop picking on Roy because we don't know if he has done anything. Aren't people innocent until proven guilty? My dad Steve said that's what makes America better than the other countries."

"Well, hang on, look at the evidence…"

"No, you stop right now and just stay out of my family's business."

"Fine, but if anything happens to Emma because of your shithead brother, it will be your ass that I'm coming for."

"Hey, I'm right here. Do you want some? If you don't go for it, then shut your mouth. You're on my train."

"Stop it, you two, stop right now. Cisco let go of him. Justin, back off." Emma pulled them apart. "What has happened to all of us? This is crazy." She told Justin, "Thank you for protecting me," she turned back to Francisco, "Cisco, your brother has caused all of this trouble, and he told them that we are on the train. The FBI will soon be closing in on us, and when they do, they will be coming with their guns drawn, and people could be hurt. Ourselves and our friends could be hurt and jailed. We have to stop this now. If anyone becomes offended, then we will apologize later. Please…"

Justin looked out the window, "Emma's right. I might be just a dumb cowboy, but soon they will be closing in, and it won't be me who gets caught in the crossfire. It will be a train of Mexicans. Emma is trying to save your lives, but first, you need to stop concerning yourself with Roy and listen."

Chapter 22

After the train pulled onto the siding tracks in Granby, the track switch switched back over, and the rail lights started flashing red. From the cab, Emma saw a fast-moving freighter coming around the river bend. It roared past their train with a foot of separation, shaking the cab violently and causing her to grab the handlebar. "That was too close!" She said. Francisco nodded. He picked up the mic, switched the radio channel, and called Rachel at track dispatch. This is RMS 10 requesting track time for two hours from milepost 285 to Milepost 320 through Moffat, over…" 'Copy RMS 10; this is Rachel standby for your request for track time from milepost 285 to milepost 320 for two hours, standby… Roger, RMS 10, you are clear for two hours track time from Milepost 285 to Milepost 320 through Moffat Tunnel. Proceed as soon as this next train passes eastbound, copy?" Francisco cleared his throat, "I copy that, Rachel. Thank you. I am clear after the next eastbound for two hours of track time from milepost 285 to milepost 320 through Moffat."

Next, he switched channels, "OK, when the next train goes by, we are going back on the line. Make sure that you have your PPE for the tunnel, ten four. Let's have a grinder wheel party before that next one comes." 'Copy that.' He pushed a button on the console and left the cab with his nine-six-teenths inch wrench. The first grinding car on his side, he opened a cabinet door on the outside as the others did, grabbed some nuts and grinding wheels for his pocket. With the spark skirts raised, the men inspected all the grinding wheels. He and Chico worked from the front, walking towards the center, replacing worn wheels, as Diego and Luis returned from the last grinding car at the back and replaced them moving forward. They opened another cabinet and tossed in the worn wheels. "OK, back to our stations," he said.

Diego radioed as he reached the rear car, 'I think I hear it coming.'

Francisco said, "Copy that. Are we good on water?"

Diego said, 'Yes, sir.'

"Copy that. OK, be ready on fire watch." He held the gear lever in his right hand while his left was ready to release the airbrakes. The company man, Justin, shut the door and climbed into the left seat of the cab.

"We ready to roll?" he said as he looked out the window. The mid-day sun stood off to the western side. He looked at his watch, "I think we have enough time to get to Boulder Creek. Do we have enough water to grind to there?"

Francisco nodded and looked in his rear mirror, "Here they come." A large freighter train rushed by their side track. While traveling nearly a mile a minute, the freighter required two and a half minutes to pass their train. 'All clear back here,' said Chico.

"Copy that," said Francisco. "This is RMS 10 calling dispatch Rachel, over... 'this is Rachel; go ahead, RMS 10.' "We are clear of the switch now on the main line." 'Ten-four RMS 10, call me when you're clear of the tunnel.'

He pushed the throttle lever across two notches as they entered the main line at an easy twelve miles an hour, then lowered all ninety-six grinders and their spark skirts onto the tracks. The cab hummed and buzzed. Behind the firehoses, water shot down the tracks as they made their way closer to Moffat Tunnel. They followed the Colorado River as it wound through narrow canyons and over gorges, crossing bridges and the tracks seeking the most level way into the mountains. When the train neared road crossings, he pushed the raise button on his console, and as soon as the cab was passed, he hit it again, lowering the grinding carriages, but if not done correctly, it would damage or destroy many of their grinding motors.

The company man, Justin, said, "Hey, I'm sorry about that fight back there, but this is just way over my head."

Francisco looked at his gages and nodded.

"Never-the-less, we might have to grind that tunnel two or three times from the reports I saw. Do you have hours to work continuously, or shall we plan another day before our Denver stop?"

"We can make it work; we'll just grind through the night. We'll work together for a week after Miguel returns, but then I'm out."

"Do you mean you're quitting?"

"Going home to Del Rio, spend some time with family, and look for a job closer to home. Miguel will take over. I've been training him for a while for this."

"I am sorry to hear you're leaving. Miguel will do a good job, but I like you you're a good man, Cisco. Do you want me to talk with Harsco and work a better deal for you? Would you consider my earlier suggestion about coming to Union Pacific? We need good supervisors."

"No, I want to live a normal life with my family." He looked down at his phone. There were no messages from his family but one from Luis. He shifted in his chair to read the message. Chico just wanted to know if they were stopping for dinner.

The train followed the Fraser River south to Highway 40, along the winding river bank through Fraser, another big ski resort town nestled at the foot of giant mountain peaks just miles from Moffat and Winter Park. Francisco would need to raise and lower the carriages four times for the street crossings at the southern edge of town. The tracks moved away from the highway through residential roads before re-merging next to the highway after town.

He blew the horn two long blasts followed by a short one as he neared the first crossing. In the crossing, he blew one long blast at the next and would do the same. Justin pointed to his left, "Hey, Cisco, we have company." He pointed over to a police car with its lights and siren on.

Francisco blew another two long bursts with his horn, then a short for the next intersection, pulling up grinder carriages, blowing a long blast, and lowering them again. The train rolled through the residential condo area. He rang the bell and blew another two long blasts.

Diego and Chico radioed, 'Is this cop trying to stop the train? We are being followed now by two cop cars, an ambulance from the fire department, and a firetruck.'

Up ahead was another crossing, Kings Crossing Condos, so he blew the horn, raised the carriages, blew another long blast, lowered them, and continued. On Lions Gate Drive, the caravan of police and fire vehicles chased the train. The police cars stopped at Vasquez Creek and stood waving their arms. Francisco pushed the dynamic braking lever back, and the train slowed to a smooth stop before the officers. Francisco said, "Just stay where you are, and let's see what these officers want with us." He called over the radio, "I'm going to talk with these guys, so everyone else, just stay put, don't make a move. We don't need any accidents." He turned to Justin, "Jesus, the damned cops are here, probably to arrest all of us."

Justin said, "I tried to get you to have your mom call Roy and talk some sense into his head before anyone gets hurt or arrested. What do you want to do? It's too late to make any calls now, and we can't make a run for it. Hell, they have half of Colorado services out here now."

"I'm going to call my mom; those guys can wait." He grabbed his phone from its cradle, "Hello, Mom, have you talked with Roy today? Could you call him right now? Because he quit his job on the train and thinks he is coming into some money, and asks him if he told the hotline where they could find Emma… she is a cook on our train. Please, Mom, it's imperative… yes, right this moment, yes. I will tell you everything, but you might see it on the news. Whatever you hear, none of it is true. I love you and will be home next week. Call Roy." Next, he switched calls to Emma.

"Hi… I don't know why several police and fire units are stopping the train. Just stay back there… Justin and I will see what they want. If I don't come back, call my mom. I'll text her number. Got to go." He sent the number and put the phone and his wallet in his front pocket. "OK, let's go see what they want."

They climbed down from the cab, and in front stood four police officers blocking the tracks. Above them was a news helicopter. He rubbed his chin and said, "What seems to be the problem, officers." The police officers wore dark sunglasses with their state trooper hats tucked down onto their brows.

The officer radioed dispatch and said, "Sir, your train is on fire," he pointed underneath. Justin chuckled and shook his head. Francisco watched the firefighters set their hoses and start pumping water under the train.

Justin said, "Can you have them not do that, please."

"Sir, I must ask you to stand down so we can do our jobs here. This is a residential area, and the last thing we need is a fire at this time of year." The officer talked into his mic, 'You are clear; go ahead.'

Francisco said, "Well, actually, it's supposed to do that. We are a griding train, so we grind the rails. This is our inspector, Justin Case, from Union Pacific, and I'm Francisco Garcia from Harsco.

"Do you have some identification?" Francisco and Justin handed them their rail cards. The officer looked at them and said, "OK, just show your information to that officer, and we'll let you return to your grinding business. Man, we saw you guys hosing the flames down and figured we would help before it burned down the whole place. Next time, let us know ahead of time."

"I apologize for how it looks; we use three water tankers to keep the flames down and refill them daily."

"Dang, every day, that's a lot of water," the officer said. He shook hands, then waved to his crew, "All right, you're clear to proceed, be safe."

Francisco and Justin half chuckled as they climbed back up to the cab. Francisco flopped in his seat and wiped his forehead. "Geez, that was scary. What the…"

"Yeah, I've seen many different things, but I thought, oh geez, that's it, we're going to jail."

The door flung open. Emma ran up to the cab, "What just happened? What did they want? Did they try to arrest you?" She looked out the window at the blue news helicopter. Did you guys see them up there? They have the whole train on tape, so it won't be long before someone recognizes us."

Justin leaned forward, watched the helicopter, and said, "They didn't seem too interested since the train was not on fire, and there they go. I don't think that is a concern."

"Well, I do," said Francisco. He shook his head and checked his phone messages. "That was scary. When I went out there, all I could envision was being tasered or shot. This is a super white town, and I'm brown-skinned. You are pure white; of course, they will listen to you first, but I have seen too many times Latinos have been shot on the spot along with blacks."

"No, you were just being paranoid because they only came to put out the fire."

"We should call ahead to Winter Park. We don't need to take any more Colorado Roulette chances; that was just too close for me. I think I just aged ten years." He said to his phone, "The number to police Winter Park Colorado… call number." "Good afternoon, this is train RMS 10 on the mainline track from Harsco, and I am Francisco Garcia, the train's supervisor. I want to notify you that we are grinding the main line rails and will be entering Winter Park to grind your sidetrack. If you see sparks coming from our train, that is normal while grinding operations are active… Thank you." He shook his head, looked out the window, and said, "This time, I'm not taking any chances. From here until we leave Denver, it's nothing but residential areas or something like this with the ski resort towns."

Justin leaned back and put his boots up, 'OK, we have about four miles till the tunnel. Do you want to stop first for fuel or water?"

"Next time, but we need to hit the sidetrack first, then grind our first pass in Moffatt. So we should cross into the tunnel in about an hour if they give us track time from the spur."

Emma said, "Look at all this; it's so beautiful. Can I go out on the front?" she bounded down the steps, turned the corner, and went out the front door. When her hands clutched the railing, she looked down as the train moved forward, the railroad ties blurred as they slid past underneath. The fresh alpine air made her smile. After a deep breath, she leaned her torso on the rail to look across at the mountain peaks. Condos and shopping centers covered the road next to the tracks. Outside, tourists and enthusiasts walked along streets, shopped, hung out, and others rode mountain bikes. She pointed them out to the cab window. She pointed to a large eagle flapping its wings while crows henpecked it by dive-bombing it. The tracks continued to follow Highway 40 south along the Fraser River, past a campground, and then into the outskirts of Winter Park. The grinders rose as they crossed a street at the Timber House Ski Lodge and then Copper Creek. Around the corner, Emma saw the large ski mountain of Winter Park. The ski lifts started near the tracks. Up ahead, just before entering the tunnel, the tracks crossed an overhead bridge above the town and the river.

Welcome to Moffatt Tunnel the sign read. Emma opened the door and went back inside.

Francisco said, "Well, they gave us track time through the tunnel for an hour. Are you staying upfront with us?"

She said, "I probably need to start dinner, but is it too late to get back there?"

"No, you have some time if you hurry."

Justin said, "Don't you think that would be a bit risky since the tunnel is right there?"

Francisco shrugged and said, "The air isn't bad until we get into Moffat, so she's got time. Go, hurry, and don't stop. Radio when you're there. I'll slow down till you call."

"Don't go; please stay, Emma."

"I'll be fine. I'll call in a couple of minutes," she said. She kissed Justin's cheek and smiled. "Thanks for thinking of me like that." He leaned forward and watched her go out the front and around the side of the engine. "Well, at least stop before the tunnel; it's too risky for her to go by herself like that."

"Fine, but I think you're just being paranoid, amigo." He pulled the throttle lever back and applied the dynamic braking. Soon, the train stopped just before the tunnel entrance, and the whistle blew three long bursts.

The radio crackled, 'I'm back in the dining car, thanks, Cisco.'

Francisco let off the brakes and blew one long and short burst as they entered the tunnel. The walls were illuminated with yellow and orange flashes from the grinders.

Justin laughed with Francisco, "Yeah, bud… maybe it's been one of those days for both of us."

Francisco nodded and said, "At least in this tunnel, we are out of sight."

"Yeah, I agree, bud… hard to imagine how anything can go wrong between here and Denver."

Chapter 23

Emma watched from the dining car window as the train slipped into the tunnel. The train's grinding wheels and engine noise reverberated off the concrete walls, amplifying their noise levels. It was mesmerizing, like watching a campfire. Emma stood leaning on the dining table, looking out the window for minutes. The tunnel walls glowed from the shower of sparks. When she sat, she saw a text message from Martin.

'Hey, the police just left, and they asked about a train and if I knew where you were. Then they asked why I made that pic of us together at my parents' house. I should probably get an attorney. They sound real pissed off.' She texted him and hit send and received the message UNABLE TO SEND. She tried again and again with no different results. She picked up the radio mic.

"Hey, Francisco… do we have any cellular or Wi-Fi?"

'Negative Em, not inside here, we don't. It will be another half an hour till we get out the other side.'

She said, "Go to channel six," she pushed the selector, "Are you there?"

'Ten-four Em, what's up?'

"Martin said the police came to his parents' house and asked where I was, that they were looking for a train. I need to call him."

'Copy that. Well, don't use your phone. When we return to Winter Park, buy a new burner so they can't trace it. Do you need cash?'

"Ten-Four Cisco. How much longer will that take?"

'At least another hour and a half Em.'

"Alright, ten four." She went to her room, and the adrenaline wore off, then she was sleepy. She fell asleep as soon as she laid on her bunk.

The airbrakes set, and the dining car jolted to an abrupt stop. Emma looked out her window, and the train parked next to the ski lifts. She slipped on her shoes, slid the car door open, and ran to find Francisco. She asked Luis, and he pointed to the water tanker cars. She found him talking with Mike, the water hauler. "Do I have time to run into the Walmart?"

Francisco said, "Hey, Em, I tried calling you on the radio, but you must have been asleep." He handed her some cash, laughing as Mike told a story.

Emma said, "I'll be right back." She drove the pickup to the store and returned twenty minutes later. In the dining car, she called Martin's cell. After five rings, it went to voice mail. She tried again with the same results. Then, on the third try, he called. "Hell, there you are… I am doing good, and I don't know why my mom is spreading that story. It is false, and I am fine. What else do you know? Oh… what? Yes, I am on a train and have a job here. So, what if the crew is Mexican, black, white, or yellow? We all work hard, and I am doing a good job. I can stay on all summer for school money. When I get a replacement copy of my rail card ID, I will send it to you to prove I work here. We are so close to Denver that we will be there tomorrow… I have to call my mom and try to talk her out of this crap. Love ya, thanks, Martin."

She went to the fridge, grabbed a can of Pepsi, and called her mom. "Hi, Mom, it's your daughter… Pick up the phone… hello hello…" she put the phone down and rubbed her temples and eyes. The phone rang, "Hello, Mom…" She went to the dining car patio, leaned out, saw Francisco, and went inside. "Hi Mom… I'm sorry to disturb you this late. No, I didn't see the news… that's nice, and I am sure your voters will be happy. Mom, I know it's late, but it's important. Innocent lives are at stake because of this false— I know you are busy and must be tired… tomorrow? that will be too late. Mom, did you know that I have a job with the railroad? Please just stop this abduction claim before people… Mom…Mom?" she set her phone back down, leaned back, and exhaled before she went outside.

She said, "Cisco…I tried to call my mom, but I don't think she was listening." She paused as she watched Mike turn the pump motor off and close a valve on the back of his tanker.

He returned and said, "That reminds me of the time last summer we were grinding this spot coming around the bend, and suddenly there was another train stuck on the tracks. Chad was driving our train when he realized we were going to crash. He set the brakes, lowered the throttles, ran to the front door, and jumped off. We might have been going thirty when we came around the corner. The rest of us just braced. It was so strange; I could hear him screaming as he jumped off. He hit the gravel when he landed. We were doing maybe eight miles an hour by the time we hit the other train. It was a slow-motion crash; it shook us a little, then stopped. We got out and went back looking for Chad from Minnesota, and there he lay, all crumpled up. He was in the hospital for months and never the same in the head after that."

Emma asked, "Why did he do that?"

"Don't know, Emma, maybe his fight or flight instinct was hard-wired for flight cause when trouble was imminent, he tried to fly the coup. Yep, we all just walked back to him. None of us had a scratch, and he was all busted up trying to save himself."

Francisco asked, "What would you do in that situation, Emma?"

"I think I would totally freeze up, and I'd be too scared to move."

Francisco's radio squawked, 'All right, we are secure up here.' He said, "Copy that, all right, prepare to roll out, then I'll call for track time." He shook Mike's hand, "See you next time on the other side of the mountain. Drive safe."

"I'll be there this time, but I don't know how much longer I will do this. Might just sell it all and move to the mountains."

As they returned to the train, Emma asked, "Is he serious?"

"Nah, he says that all the time. Did you hear from your mom?" She followed him to the cab.

"Where is Justin?" she asked. Francisco shrugged, then called rail dispatch for more track time.

Dispatch cleared the train for another hour of track time, just enough to get the tunnel finished before the next freighter would pass. Emma texted Justin while Francisco prepared to roll out. "He's on his way," she looked out the window, "I see him." She waved and then ran down to the front platform. He ran up the steps, picking her off the ground as they embraced. After she kissed him, she said,

"You're late, now come on." The train bell rang, and then the platform swayed. Inside, he closed the door behind them. Hey Emma, today is Denver Day. Are you half as excited as I am, Darlin?"

"I'm all yours for the next few days," she giggled.

Francisco said, "Hey, we're about to go back over the bridge and into the tunnel. Are you staying up here, Emma?"

Justin gave his head a slight nod, no. Emma said, "I'm going back. How much longer will it be until we get to Golden?"

"Once we get out of the tunnel and that train passes us, we will run at sixty and be at the Denver yard in another half an hour."

Emma went out the door and saw the tunnel opening up ahead. She ran down the side of the engine, then down the side of the following engine, and across its patio to the first grinding car. Then, she went through its engine room around machinery and out the other door to the next grinding car. But as she went along the passageway past the next engine, her rear pocket caught on a valve handle for the hydraulics as the carriages were lowered. She was stuck. She pulled and twisted until her coveralls freed and went out that door. She climbed up the nine ladder rungs of the first water car at the catwalk on the top. She saw the tunnel was a quarter mile off. She had just minutes to get back inside. She ran to the other side and felt for her phone. She dug her hand into her back pocket, then the other back pocket and her front pockets. She screamed, turned, and ran back down the ladder. Not seeing her phone, she downclimbed and returned to the grinding car. She crawled on the floor, following her path back, moving her hands under equipment, and feeling for

246

her phone. At the front of that car, she stepped into the next grinding car, and by the hydraulic valves, she stopped. She felt underneath, and something moved. She lay down and saw her phone. She leaped up, turned, ran for the exit, and then grabbed the ladder rung of the first water tanker through the next grinding car. She looked back at the tunnel before climbing to the top, running across, down, and back up the next water car and the next as fast as she could run, like on the ridge of Provo Peak. The dining car was in front of her, just a few yards to go.

The train chugged into the tunnel, and she lay atop the final water car. She stopped moving; fear overwhelmed her mind. The train blew three long bursts while the grinders howled and screamed along with the large diesel engines revving up to maximum power inside the tunnel. She looked again, and the walls were right next to her. The ceiling was too low to stand upright. She moved her belly forward, her face covered in soot, and her vision blurred. Her eyes burned and blurred her vision, so she wiped them, making them sting worse. She put her arm in front, then pulled herself, then her left arm, like on the chain-link fence in the third grade. She grunted and cried, laying her head on the car's roof. Farther into the tunnel, the smell of burning metal mixed with rotten eggs and hydrogen sulfide gas. The right arm stabbed forward sharply, and then her palm grabbed the ladder rung. She was at the end of the last water car just a few feet from the front of her dining car. The next hand grabbed the rung and pulled her belly to the edge. The grinding noise and dust darkened the air. Inside the tunnel, the yellow train was soot black.

Unable to see, Emma turned her body around, her foot, feeling for the first rung, and slipped off it. Her body fell until her grip on the top stopped her fall. Her feet swung in the darkness, kicking at the ladder and just hoping a foot would land on top of a rung. Her grip loosened, her hands slipped, she kicked faster, and then a foot hit the top of a rung. She tried to pull her body back up as her arms shook violently. Emma was going to fall. She screamed as her hands let go. Emma screamed out from a sharp pain in her left arm as a flash of light flashed across her eyes. She lay on her left side with her head over the car's edge while sooty air blew over her face. Disoriented and unable to decipher what part of the platform she must have landed on, she froze while she awaited her senses to discern her position.

The whistle blew three more long bursts, and the grinders screeched and roared, showering a continuous river of sparks. After a minute, she saw the back of the water car and the patio rail. She did a stomach crunch, lifting her torso and shoulders off the deck enough for her hand to reach for the railing. When her hand reached for a rung, it slipped off, and she fell backward. Again, she tried to raise herself and reached using her good arm. Her hand grabbed the rail. She pulled herself back on her feet, looking across the abyss to the dining car's patio. She yelled and jumped across, as her right foot landed on the ledge and her hand grabbed the railing. Using her torso for leverage, she rolled over the railing and onto the platform, where she lay breathing hard.

Inside, she stood over the sink, washing her hands and face. She wiped her eyes and reached for the radio mic, 'Hey, I made it back. Sorry, I forgot to call you earlier.'

"We were worried about you. Are you alright, Em?"

"Uh huh… I'm tired and think I'll just go to bed for a bit." She put the mic back and reached into the bathroom cabinet for Advil. She swallowed three with water and went to sleep as the train reached the end of the tunnel. They switched to the siding track minutes before a two-mile-long freighter roared by. Low on fuel, Francisco planned to stop at the Union Pacific yard in Denver just a few minutes down the track. As they awaited approval for track time, they relaxed in the front cab while the men slept in the bunks.

Francisco said, "I think I'll grab something to eat. Can I get you anything?"

"Sure, how about one of those burritos if there's any leftover? Otherwise, a ham sandwich sounds good." Francisco turned to leave and stood looking down at the gauges, his seat out the window and over at Justin.

"You all right, Bud?"

"Si amigo," he looked at his watch, "Buenos dias." He left the cab, closing the front door behind him.

Chapter 24

Francisco looked out the window over the sink when a flash of brilliant light blinded his eyes. He put his hand up to block its burning brilliance. The ski run lights at Winter Park's ski lifts were illuminated after dark, even in the summer months. Emma slept Down the hall, and the men slept in the crew car. He made a cup of coffee and slid onto the bench with his cup. He looked at his watch and then down the hall. Emma usually was making breakfast at that time. His phone rang, so he read the caller ID, Justin.

"Hey, what's up? No, I haven't seen her yet. Usually, she's making breakfast by now, but the men just went to bed a little while ago for a quick nap while we wait for track time. OK, sounds good, thanks." He looked at his watch, lay on the bench, and propped his head up using his coat as a pillow. He yawned and fell asleep.

Outside, the horizon glowed with the faintest light towards the eastern horizon. Above, Venus, the morning star, shone its brilliance. In the stillness of the predawn, robins and doves cooed and sang their morning songs. Pine and fir trees scented the air with their perfume-like resins. Winter Park got its beauty sleep and recharged for another summer day of adventures.

The train engines droned with a steady vibration, blocking any outside noises. The crew tuned the train's white noise and vibration out, and that drone helped them sleep. Francisco snored when his phone rang and woke him; he scratched his neck and checked it, then laid his head back and yawned. He went to the bathroom and flipped the light switch. The sink was covered in soot and black mud. The cream-colored towels were blackened and strewn across the floor with a small trail of blood on top of them towards Emma's stateroom. He finished washing his face and knocked on her door. After four knocks, she called for him to enter.

He slid her door open and called out in the dark, "Em…" he said just above a whisper, "Em…?"

"Hey, Cisco, I don't feel very good."

"Was that your mess in the bathroom?"

"I lost my phone, and I went back to find it. I got scared… Cisco, I was really scared."

"What happened?"

"I don't know, it's all a t-t- ter…" He gave her a water bottle, and she swallowed and took a breath. He held her hand, feeling her head and hand trembling, "It was a terrible nightmare. I keep having these dreams that my head is dangling above the tracks, and I am on a rope that is being cut while my face is speeding into a rock wall. I think I fell while trying to climb down the water…"

"Don't talk, drink. Here, let me take a look. Can I turn your light on?"

She rolled over and reached for her night light, "Yes, my night lite, ouch… geez, that hurts." She rolled onto her back. He switched it on, giving the room a green LED color to her face from her froggy nightlight. Dark black streaks ran down her arm in the greenish light.

"You're bleeding, Em… we need to get this looked at, don't move." He pulled his phone from his front coverall pocket, cupped his hand over his mouth, and said, "Hey, get over here, to the dining car, immediately… thanks."

"Em, we are going to get you out of here. The emergency room is right around the corner."

He picked up her robe and helped her put it on as she sat on her bunk. Her face winced as her left arm went into the sleeve. His head turned when the back door slid open, and loud footsteps ran across the floor.

"Hey, Cisco," said Justin.

"Hey, we're in here. Could you help me get her to the hospital? Easy Em, you'll be fine. Let's get you up. Case, grab our pickup and meet us at the steps." Emma set one foot on the floor. He bent his knees, put it in her slipper, and then the next foot. "Can you stand?" She grabbed his hand, and he eased her to her feet.

"Ah, dang, that hurts. I'm so sorry. I didn't mean to make you worry."

"You're doing good, Em. Are you lightheaded?"

She nodded and shrugged, "I'm not sure 'cause it's so hazy."

Taking small steps and holding her upright, they crossed the dining car to the rear platform door. Again, he bent on his knees and lifted each foot over the little threshold to the car's patio to the railing. Emma leaned her torso over the railing as Francisco looked for their pickup, "He should have been here."

"Cisco… I'm tired. Can I just sit here just for a minute?" He turned and reached his arms as her body slumped backward, her hands letting go of the railing. He wrapped his arms under her arms, bending his knees, as he lowered her onto the patio deck. He pulled out his phone while holding on to her, leaning his nose to the screen, redialed Justin, and dropped his phone on her. "Shit, shit, shit. No, Emma, No." He put his ear next to her mouth and checked her pulse, "No, Emma, No." He clasped his fingers into a fist, then rolled onto his knees, his head facing her torso, and pumped her chest to perform CPR, "One and two and three and four and five… He rechecked her breath, then blew in her mouth with two quick breaths with her nostrils pinched off. "Come on, Em…"

The patio was illuminated with brilliant white light. From Francisco's periphery, flashing-colored lights of blue and red reflected across the yellow train car as the other night with the rioters. He turned and stared like a deer caught in a car's high beams. He saw Police and SWAT vehicles to his right and FBI and the US marshals vehicles on his left. Above, a helicopter circled, shining its spotlight across the train. From the brilliant light, radio voices crackled, 'We have a visual of the suspect. Prepare to close in Red Team. Francisco could not see which unit the radio came from. The light was too bright, "Step away from that girl, do it now, step away, put your hands against the wall with your legs apart. Stop, do it now, or we will shoot.'

He waved his arms and shook his head, "No… you're wrong. Look, she needs medical help. Help me hurry." He waved and waved, but no help approached. He leaned over her body and tried to give her two more breaths. The voice said, "Move away immediately."

He continued to give a second breath of life when a blinding flash came over his eyes, and his body twisted. The noise seemed slow, arriving in his ears long after the flash. It echoed and felt muffled as if his ears were in a laundry hamper with someone outside of it striking metal with a hammer. His shoulder felt warm, then hot. He looked at Emma's unmoving body. He struggled to call out but didn't even recognize his voice. As his lungs gurgled, his throat raspy, he tried to shout, "No…" His head spun; the lights flickered and then blurred. It seemed as though he were underwater in a pool. He was tired. His hand stayed on Emma's shoulder, and his head laid on the metal deck.

Chapter 25

Sweating and breathing hard, Justin tried to run forward to the dining car, "No, let me go. Can't you see she needs help?" Four officers held him pinned next to a large black SUV. Sirens wailed, adding more flashing lights that flooded the night's darkness. He saw an ambulance stop at the dining car. Several officers and firefighters opened the back doors, and one of the medics pulled a gurney. A second ambulance stopped next to the first. The men opened its back door and slid out of its gurney.

A female officer stood at the back door of the SUV. She said, "Please remain calm, sir. We have the situation in hand." She acknowledged her superior on the radio, then said, "Just as soon as we can verify your identity, we will release you, but for now, please remain calm, sir." She held his identification card to her flashlight as she read the info over her radio. He leaned forward with his head down, pulling at his hand restraints while sweat dripped on his lap. Ahead, over twenty officers with their weapons drawn ran to the crew car, and lights came on in the windows. He pulled at the large zip ties and winced as they dug into his wrists.

The radio said, 'He checks out, so go ahead and release him.' The lady officer nodded, "Ten-Four copy that." You're free to go as soon as we clear the scene. Do you have any personal possessions you need to retrieve?"

Justin looked at the scene of medics, officers, and federal agents wearing dark suits hovering at the dining car's steps. Medics transported a gurney off the patio, two on each side, carrying two more IVs. His eyes watched through the windshield as the ambulance closed the rear and front doors and drove back the way it arrived. He wiped tears and sweat on his shoulder and shook his head, saying it was all madness. The officers held the top of his head and sat him in the back seat.

After a moment, he said, "I need to get my phone and my wallet."

The female FBI agent said, "We are clear; go ahead and cut his restraints." Another officer said, "Lean forward, sir." Then, cut the restraints. Justin rubbed his sore wrists.

The lady officer said, "Here's your ID and wallet, so ensure everything is there before you exit the vehicle. We need to take you to the station and fill out a report. If you have any questions, here is my card."

"Officer, will you escort Mr. Case back to the train when it's clear?"

Justin exited the SUV as two extra-large SUVs drove off with the crew escorted by two police cars. The lady agent told the guard, "OK, we are clear. You can take him to get the rest of his personal things. Mr. Case, meet me when you finish, and we'll get your statement."

"Where did you take Emma? Why were there two ambulances?"

"Sir, meet me here when you have your things. Hurry, the train is being locked out."

The officer followed as he walked along the railroad ties. He paused at the dining car and then continued to the front engine. He leaped up the steps, opened the door, grabbed his gear bag from a locker, shut the door, and jumped down. The adrenaline seemed to give him wings. He and Emma had plans for a fun week off in Denver once the train finished the tunnel job and stopped. The night chill stung his arms, so he pulled a sweatshirt from Colorado State over his head and walked to the black SUV. "Can you take me to the hospital? I need to be there for Emma."

"Get in. Have you known her for long?" she asked.

He slid into the back seat as the officer took the passenger seat. "I met Emma when I picked up the train by Grand Junction. Have you ever been in love?"

The woman nodded as she turned the car back onto the road, "Of course I have."

"I fell in love first with her burritos, then that night she came to the front with dinner for us, Francisco Miguel, and myself. Here was this small fireball with these big bright eyes; she always smiled. I wonder if her personality will change after this. Her mom is a US Senator; she brought all this upon all these innocent people because she wanted Emma to be at her re-election speeches. Emma practically worshiped her mother."

"Don't be so sure. We have it on good intel that she was abducted and being held by them. I wouldn't shed a tear for any of them." When the SUV parked, he looked across to the emergency room doors. Above the hospital, morning illuminated the horizon with a dull grey as clouds thickened against the mountains.

"Thanks for the ride," he pulled her card from his pocket, "Miss. Chadwick. You're with the feds; you guys still have it all wrong."

He opened the door and said, "Treat the men well; after all, they all are innocent." He grabbed his bag and ran for the doors.

He stopped at the front counter, and the nurse behind the desk asked, "May I help you, sir?" She raised her finger, excuse me." She answered the phone. Justin wandered along the long counter to two other nurses; one turned his way.

"Excuse me, Emma Chase, a young woman was just brought in, so where can I find her?"

The nurse tapped the keyboard and typed, "I am sorry, sir, that information is classified. Are you a family member?"

"No, just the person that was just with her before you brought her in here…" He rubbed his scratched wrists and looked down the corridor. "Hey, at least tell me what state she is in. Give me something, please."

"Sorry, sir, that information is limited to the direct family."

"How about Francisco Garcia, possible gunshot wound? He would have arrived at the same time. Where can I find him?"

Again, the nurse shook her head, "We cannot release any information at this time… sorry, sir."

My name is Justin Case, and should either come to then please call me; I will be right here. Here is my number," he handed each a business card. "Call me, please. I am not leaving until I can see them." He flopped into a chair in the waiting area and looked at his phone. There were several messages from family and work. He listened to his voicemails, and his parents worried for him, then his boss. Next, his boss said to call him ASAP; one was from Harsco.

He leaned back and pulled his ballcap low to block the light. Even with his eyes closed, he saw the flashing lights from the scene. He closed his eyes tighter and rolled to the side; still, the lights flashed behind his eyelids, and sirens echoed in his ears.

The lobby hummed with whispering voices over the drone of the ventilation. Though it may have seemed an eternity, after a few minutes, Justin's body relaxed, his mind slowed, his breathing changed, and he fell into a shallow sleep. A change in the background noise woke him, and his phone rang. 'Hello, this is he… say that again… I'll be right there."

He jumped to the floor, grasped his phone, and ran back to the front counter, "Emma Chase, I'm here to see her; you just called." His tall frame hovered a foot above the woman.

"You're Justin? She looked at the screen and said, "Come with me, sir." They walked back to the elevators. She pushed the UP button, and when the doors closed behind them, she said, "Emma has regained consciousness, and she asked for you. We can't give you much time, please tell her you have to leave and will see her soon. I can give you five minutes." The elevator dinged as it passed the second floor. They stood in silence as it traveled up, then when it dinged the next time, the doors slid open, "This way, sir." He took a large breath as they went around the corner and down a long corridor to the Intensive Care unit. Ahead, he saw two police officers guarding a private room. The nurse told the one standing, "This is Mr. Case."

The officer said, "I'll need to see some ID, sir."

After checking and calling into a police supervisor, at last, they admitted Justin inside. He stepped through the wide doorway, and her bed lay across the floor in the center of the room. Emma lay under a monitor screen that displayed her body vitals; an IV hung above her arm, and a clear small tube for oxygen went into her nose. An EKG monitor showed her steady heart beating. Screens covered the windows. The room was darkened except for the light over the bed. She laid still until he broke the silence. He whispered, "Hey, Darlin." He held her hand, and it felt cold and waxy. He smiled when she turned her head and then kissed her head. "I can only stay for a minute; do you remember what happened on the train, honey?"

"No… I'm not sure, how is Francisco?'

"I don't know yet. Do you remember being with him in the dining car at all?"

"I didn't feel good, so Cisco was helping me, but I guess I must have fainted, and then I woke up here."

"Your mother is on her way out here. Emma, I must ask you something, but I don't know the right time. Tell me what you want."

"I just want to be happy. Ever since I came on the train, life was real, not a dress rehearsal for what's to come someday. It was the realest thing ever... I want a real life." Her head looked up at the ceiling. She asked him, "Are we in Denver?" The nurse stuck her head in the door and waved for him.

He nodded and said, "Almost, Darlin, we will be there soon. Get some rest. I will talk with the nurse and see you in a minute. If you need anything, press this button."

Back in the corridor, the nurse said, "You asked about a gunshot patient. Is his name Francisco Garcia?" He nodded, and she said, "Come with me, sir."

They walked around the corner back to the elevators; she pushed the button for UP. Inside the elevator, she said, "He is under arrest. It seems the feds, the state, and the local police all want him. What did he do?"

"Nothing. He was helping Emma when I went to get the truck to bring Emma here. When he brought her to the steps, the cops showed up and shot him. I tried to tell them they were mistaken and to help get Emma here, but they arrested me instead. Did they shoot him? Is Cisco going to make it?"

The elevator dinged with a soft chime. As the doors opened, she whispered, "I don't know, but he is lucky to be alive. This way, sir." Two guards stood at the doors when they opened. Again, he showed his ID and followed them to a room guarded by two more officers. The hospital had a prisoner wing on the top floor. The guard looked up his name on his clipboard, Justin? This way." Inside was a private waiting room. "He is in surgery, but you can wait here."

There were seats, a coffee maker, and a set of double doors to the surgery room. He looked through the observation window. Inside, several people draped in gowns wearing face shields leaned over Francisco. They watched a monitor screen while they worked to remove the bullet. "How much longer will Cisco be in there?"

The nurse said, "It depends on whether there are any complications. They should be moving him into post-op soon."

"Is he going to make it OK?"

The nurse shrugged and said, "I think so, but when he recuperates, they are taking him to jail. It will be a while before he comes to. I can call you then."

"Take good care of him. He's innocent. Call me when I can talk with him, please."

Back in the elevator, it chimed at the main floor and then slid open. The lobby was filled with cameras and reporters. He walked around the mob, looking for an empty seat, but there were none. Reporters filled the inside and outside filing reports. He turned the corner past the elevators, and down the corridor was an empty bench by the nurse's station. It was noon when he sat and looked at his phone messages. What could have happened to Emma back on the train? She was fine when she left the train engine. If only he could talk with Francisco, he might know the answer. He yawned and stretched, then asked the nurse why so many reporters were in the lobby. Unsatisfied and still needing answers, his head bobbed up and down several times before he slumped and fell asleep.

Chapter 26

That day, the Winter Park Medical Center parking lot and the resort next to its parking lots were full of reporters awaiting the scoop of the year when Senator Chase arrived to be with her daughter. Emma's near-fatal accident while attempting to escape her capture on a moving train will indeed become a sensational story. The political theater could not be grander. Every man and woman in the press salivated to get an interview with Emma and her mom for the greatest Colorado story in modern times. The police locked down Emma's hospital floor while she regained consciousness and recovered from her injuries. Meanwhile, the press waited downstairs, receiving updates from the hospital staff. If Justin had been awake and seen the spectacle, he would have called it a freak show circus, but he lay sleeping and dreaming, most likely of Denver.

When Emma awoke, she pressed the button on her lap. A nurse came to her bedside in the darkened room. "May I help you?"

"I'm thirsty…" said Emma's dry, weakened voice. She pointed to the curtain, "Could we open them."

The nurse opened the curtains but kept the blinds turned away from the light and said, "I'll just get the doctor."

When the nurse left, there was another knock at her door, "Miss Chase, I am Officer Grant of the Denver US Marshals office. I am here to review your witness statement and gather a few samples with your permission. Is now a good enough time to begin?"

"Not sure what you are referring to, but come in…" The officer entered with a tape recorder and another local police officer. They stopped at the bed foot.

"This is Officer Barrett from the county sheriff's office, and she will be assisting me today and be a witness to your statement. Is that OK with you? First, I want to administer a DNA test. This separates any of your DNA from your captures, so please swab your mouth with this."

Emma swabbed inside her mouth, "Wait, you said separate DNA from my captures…" She did the second sample, "But they never…"

Next, we would like to examine you and perform this test."

"Is that a rape test? No, of course, I won't do it." She drew her knees up and wrapped her arms across them while the officer asked her account of the last seven days since she left the auditorium at the Hyatt in SLC. Emma did her best to persuade both officers that there was no intercourse nor abduction and that, yes, she did get injured, but it was her fault. She should have left the phone and retrieved it later, and then she would have been fine.

Officer Grant asked, "Are you aware of the Stockholm Syndrome?"

"Of course, we studied its effects in pre-law. It's when the victim associates with their captures and becomes part of the gang, as with the bank robbers. I am Emma Chase, daughter of Elizabeth Reid Chase of Utah, but I am no criminal. I have a job with the railroad, and I was not abducted but hired to be a cook on RMS 10, a rail-grinding train working its way across America grinding the rails to prevent trains from going off the tracks. My supervisor is Francisco Garcia, of Del Rio, Texas. The same man you guys shot and tried to murder while he was saving my life. Now take your damned rape kit and get out." She pushed the button on her bedside. "Hello, nurses, get the doctor in here. I'm leaving."

"Miss Chase, these are serious charges against your colleagues, and unless you want all of them to rot in a federal prison for the rest of their lives, you will listen. Now sit down."

Emma's eyes froze on Officer Grant's eyes. Her knees lowered, and her head leaned against the pillow, "That's right, the nurse will be here with a doctor. You tell them you made a mistake and we have work to do here if you want to save your friends.

The door pushed opened three nurses and two doctors rushed in, "What is the meaning of this interrogation?" asked the senior doctor.

Emma said, "It's all right. I overreacted when I woke up. Sorry, but everything is fine.

"You two must leave. She is a very sick girl and needs rest, not this."

"Very well, doctor. Emma, should you have anything further to add to our conversation, call me." Officer Grant and Barrett each gave their cards and left.

The nurse wrote her vitals down, examined her eyes and mouth, and then took her pulse. The doctor pulled up a stool, "Hello Emma, I am Doctor Evans. You gave us all quite a scare this morning, so how are you feeling?"

"I feel fine. Do I need all this stuff hooked up to me, doc?"

He shrugged, "Is it uncomfortable?"

"Yes, it scares me. How is Francisco Garcia?"

The nurse said, "The gunshot patient doctor."

Emma said, "The police shot him while he was trying to save my life. I hope he sues them for millions. Is he going to be alright?"

The doctor nodded as he looked at his clipboard. "I think he will make it. They are transferring him today to Denver."

"He's innocent, treat him well."

The nurse said, "Your mother should be here any minute. She is most anxious to see you. She asked for updates every hour since you arrived."

"Mother? Coming here? God… now I get it. Hey, please do me a favor and send that cop back here. I need to talk with her some more. Mother…"

The doctor looked at her, "It's common for girls your age to desire their independence."

"But I am not, and my mother was always too busy with my older brothers and her career. Even my dad couldn't stand living with her anymore when the Marines retired him. I've tried to do my best at everything my whole life just once to hear her say, "Good job, Emma, I love you. And now I have a job, the first one in my life and the first time I've ever had to be responsible for helping others, and it was so great, doctor. I felt like I mattered and that I was finally appreciated. And now my mother says these terrible things on Facebook about them, and it's disgraceful."

The nurses looked at the senior doctor. Their lips tightened eye, lids pulled back. Emma looked at each of those eyes, yet the doctor shrugged it off and smiled at Emma, with a little nod with his eyes like hey, you got this girl. I believe your mom is what you say, but I can't, in my position, go against the powers that write my paychecks. She nodded back. The door knocked; Officer Barrett opened the door. "Is this a good time to complete our interview, Emma?"

"Yes, come in. Doctor Evans, I want you to stay as my witness if you don't mind."

The nurses closed the door behind them as they stepped past Officer Grant. She asked, "Emma will you submit to this rape test?"

"If it proves they are all innocent, then yes I do." She looked to the doctor, and he nodded.

He said, "If you want, I could give a quick pelvic examination to verify if there is any physical evidence of intercourse." Emma and the officers nodded. When he finished his examination, he handed the officers specimens for their kit, filled in their report, and signed it. Emma also signed the documents. The officers thanked them both for their cooperation and left them alone.

The doctor said, "Sorry, Miss Chase, but now that that's over, what can you recall from last night?"

Emma rolled her eyes and took a drink, "It's so blurry, let's see… I was coming back to the dining car, and we were on the other side of Moffatt Tunnel. They wanted me to stay in the engine. I wanted to make burritos for the crew. I made it to the dining car and realized I lost my phone. I needed to call my mom to get her to stop this nonsense of abduction crap. I went back over the water cars and into one of the grinding cars somewhere. Anyway, I found it. Then, on the way back, climbing over the top of the last water car, we went into the tunnel grinding. I froze, and it was hard to breathe. I was scared to death. It was loud, and then there was this terrible smell of rotten eggs. I had to crawl along the top of the tanker to the end, where there was a ladder down to the dining car. Somehow, I lost my grip. I must have hit my head when I fell. I washed in the bathroom and went to bed. I was very sleepy. Then Francisco found me and helped me with Justin to the patio, where Justin went to get the pickup truck. We waited, and I leaned over the rail. There were swirling bright lights and yelling, then I woke up here."

The doctor remained silent, his eyes on her eyes. She took another sip through her straw. "Humph, wow, Emma, that's incredible. You are very lucky to be alive. So many dangerous things could have happened. I'm so sorry about your friends, one of whom must be Justin, who is downstairs asleep. Would you like to see him?"

Emma smiled, "I love him. Do you believe in love at first sight?"

The doctor smiled again, "Yes, that happened with me and my wife. I knew she was the one for me the second I saw her. I just hoped that I was good enough to be the one for her. I still try my hardest every day. I'll send him up here."

The door again knocked, "Doctor. Her mom has arrived. Shall I bring her in?"

Emma squirmed, and her face wrinkled like a rabbit. Then, after a long exhale, she nodded yes.

In a soft voice, she said, "Doctor… thank you." Her hand reached out, and he took it in his, "The pleasure is all mine, Miss Chase."

The door tapped again, and Mrs. Chase stuck her head around the door jam, "Hello, Emma?"

Emma put her hand out to stop the doctor from leaving. She turned her head. "Hi, mom."

"What are you doing, Emma? We have a press conference downstairs, and you are not even dressed. Oh dear, now I am going to be late." She looked across to the doctor, "Excuse me, Hi, I am Mrs. Chase. Could it be possible that we get my daughter downstairs soon?" She smiled and stuck her hand out for his, and her eyes bore into him with gleaming little lights dancing in her eyes. Her Christian Dior blue floral print dress matched her sapphire blue eyes and gave her a taller appearance than her five-foot-three-inch frame. Her hair was reddish-brown, but it was not as dark as Emma's, yet they looked similar. But Emma's eyes were almond-shaped, while Mrs. Chase's were distinctly Nordic decent. Her voice was deeper and stronger than Emma's.

The doctor said, "That depends on the patient. Emma, are you ready for your interview with the world?"

"No. Would it be possible to have some privacy, please? I feel drained and not in control of myself at this time." She gave the doctor a little nod with her eyes, and he smiled and departed.

"Now Emma, what's this business with you not ready? We have to be back in Salt Lake, and I have a speech to give and a dinner to attend. Where are your clothes?"

"Right there, mom."

Her mom picked up her sooted coveralls and shouted, "Oh my God, this is so disgusting. Emma, how could you embarrass me like this? This is so humiliating. I will have to order some proper clothes. Good thing it's still early."

"Mom, we need to talk…"

"About what? That you ran off and did the most humiliating thing possible when you were left on your own? Your brothers and I are so embarrassed."

"That's just what we need to talk about, Mom. Why are you embarrassed of me? Why did you make up this phony abduction story and then rape?" Innocent me are going to prison because of you, Mom."

"I am for justice and truth; I believe in family and doing the right thing. Those animals all had their way with my daughter, and it's so disgusting."

"Mom, stop it; none of it is true, and you know that. Stop it… please. They are all innocent, and no amount of your telling lies will change the facts."

"You will not speak to your mother with that tone, young lady."

"Like dad used to say to you, 'Never let the facts get in the way of your bullshit.' Now I know what he meant. So, no wonder he couldn't stand you for the last years of his life. He drank himself to death practically to escape from you."

Mrs. Chase crossed her arms at the window, "You talk to me with respect, or you will truly regret this. Now get yourself together because when I come back, we are going downstairs, and you will be glad I am here to rescue your pitiful ass. Then we are returning home, and you will never set foot in Colorado or talk with those animals again."

Emma shook her head, wiped her tears, drew her knees back up, and wrapped her arms around the blanket that covered them. "Fine, Mom, but only if those men are set free with no charges."

Her mom turned from the window, "We will need one of them to stand trial, so which one will it be? I can get the case moved to Utah to control the events better. Do we have a deal?"

Emma nodded and wiped her eyes again. Her mom smiled, "Good, now stop acting like a spoiled little brat; your new clothes will be here soon. Be ready by…" She looked at her Dior watch, "By ten am." She left the room before Emma could take another breath, say another word, or have another thought. Like that, it was over. Emma was going home a failure and an embarrassment to her family. At least that's what her mom thought. After all, her mom held all the power and knew it.

Emma looked out the now open blinds. Outside was an overcast day. The mountaintops were hidden underneath a cloudy white blanket. She pushed the button next to her again, breathed, and said, "Nurse, please send the doctor back in?"

Chapter 27

Doctor Evans told the nurses he would retain Emma overnight for more observations and tests to Emma's relief. Alone with her thoughts and consciousness, Emma again began contemplating the new world she enjoyed. Alone with her, she daydreamed of Denver and saw herself as half of a relationship and becoming a vet. She imagined wearing a doctor's white lab coat, inspecting Fido on the table in her office, and then meeting Justin for lunch. How much time had passed with her lost in her thoughts? Looking out the window, she could not tell. A smile drew across her face, curving upwards.

Like a shattering mirror, the new clothes arrived along with her mother. Her entrance raked across Emma's soul, making her cringe. Her fists gripped her blanket, and her knuckles turned white. Her pulse quickened, and her blood pressure rose, changing her breathing and setting off alarms. Her mom seemed oblivious to the alarms from her obnoxious disturbance.

"What's this business of you staying another night? We need to leave in the hour, Jesus Christ, Emma! It's well after ten, and I have to be at the capitol to give a speech at three."

The doctor said, "Sorry, Mrs. Chase, but Emma became sick, and we had no choice but to hold her."

The mother shook her head, "We will see about that and what kind of doctor you think you are. I am friends with the board at Denver. It would be best if you thought twice about your ill-advised decision. Just look at her doctor. There's nothing wrong with her;

she is faking it. There is no reputable doctor that would fall for such sophomore antics." She left the room with her assistants.

Emma said, "She isn't kidding, you know."

"I've seen worse. I better let you get your rest; you have a visitor."

The door tapped, and the doctor said, "Come in, Mr. Case."

Justin stopped at her bedside, "Hi, Darlin."

She stretched her arms out, "Come here," she said.

They hugged, and he kissed her, then her head, as the doctor closed the door. He pulled a chair up to her bedside. "When I thought of vacation time with you, I thought of a place a little more romantic than this. Wow, Em… look at this. I saw your mother downstairs talking with reporters. She must really care about you the way she went on and on."

"Don't be fooled, Justin. Some people are much different behind closed doors."

"So, when do you leave? What's next for us? Denver?"

Emma shook her head, grabbed another tissue, and wiped her eyes. She reached for him again, and when they embraced, her chest heaved. He held her tight until her sobbing slowed. She shook her head when he looked at her, "No… I am so sorry, honey." she said. Her lower lip trembled.

She told him about the agreement with her mother to release the men and of the police interview regarding possible rape. "Honey, it's over, so now I must return to SLC and stay in law school. My own mother told me she and my brothers are disgusted with me. She brought new clothes when she saw my work coveralls. She said it was beyond disgusting."

"I guess that means no Denver for us. How about if I come out there instead?"

"—Perhaps, but not until we know everyone was released with no pending charges. Have you seen Cisco yet?"

"He was in surgery this morning, so I don't know when we can see him."

She pressed her button, "Sorry, nurse, we need to see Francisco Garcia. Can you take us to him, please? And will you please take this stuff off of me?"

After the nurse checked with the medical staff, she returned and removed the IV, along with Justin, and got Emma into a wheelchair. "Oh, wait, you must show the guard ID Emma." Justin grabbed it off the table and pushed the wheelchair, following the nurse back to the elevators. They went to the top floor and were permitted to the nurse's station down the hall.

Justin said, "We are here to see Francisco. How is he doing?"

"I will let the doctor know you are here; please have a seat."

After a long wait in the guarded waiting room, the doctor appeared in his surgical gown, holding a clipboard. He took off his cap and glasses. "So, you're Emma Chase. I have heard so much about you from Doctor Evans. He speaks highly of you and told me some of what happened. I commend you on your bravery. Usually, patients like that don't survive, and you have a strong will to live in you. Now Francisco, my patient, has been the same, and I would not have given him even odds of surviving when they brought him in this morning. I work out of the main Denver hospital and occasionally show up here, usually for celebrities who overdo it. I was here with my family on vacation when I received the emergency call. Francisco suffered from a gunshot wound near his heart. He has a collapsed lung and is not out of the woods yet. He lost a lot of blood, and it will take some time to build his strength back. Both of you are lucky to be here."

Justin said, "Is it OK for us to see him doc?"

The doctor smiled and said, "He is asleep this way, please."

They followed the doctor into a private room where two guards checked their IDs and took pictures for the record. The lead guard opened the door and stood at it. Inside, Francisco snored while the heart monitor beeped at slow, regular intervals. Emma looked across the bed, and his face had a short, bearded stubble. Also, his skin looked a greyish color. If not for the snoring, his motionless body with his head tilted to the side looked unalive. She took his hand and looked across to his monitored vitals. Yes, he was alive. Justin stood next to his head, holding her other hand.

The doctor said, "He should recover well, though he will have some limitations."

Emma whispered, "He didn't do anything except be good to me. No one kidnapped me. I tried to get my mom to stop that conspiracy, but she wouldn't listen, and Roy's lust for gold overcame him. He just wanted all the reward money."

The doctor asked, "Who is Roy?"

"He is Cisco's little brother, a trickster. He did this as revenge for me turning his advances away earlier, so when my mom put up the reward money, he figured he deserved all of it. They say good triumphs over evil, but that's a lie. Roy got his reward, my mom got her way, and this poor man lies here fighting for his life, and the crew is in prison because of this injustice."

Justin asked, "What happens next for Cisco?"

"They will take him to the detention hospital, where he will stay until he is convicted."

Emma leaned over Francisco; she caressed his face with her fingers and then kissed his

hand. The guard said, "Sorry folks, times up."

Emma stopped her wheelchair outside the door, "When do you take him to jail?"

"Tomorrow, Miss."

"He's innocent, and this is all just a waste of time. I will prove his innocence in court. Take extra good care of him till I get him home."

Justin pushed her back to the elevator. He said, "It's a madhouse in the lobby."

"Tell me about it. I've seen it for years—such a waste of time.

The door chimed on the second floor, and he pushed her to an exterior corridor with a view of the mountains. Together, they held hands and watched the birds. Later, he said, "Have you had lunch?"

"No, I wasn't hungry, what are you thinking?"

He smiled and said, "How about I get us a Smashburger and a shake?"

"That sounds real good, honey. Will you stay with me tonight?"

After he took her back to her room, he went out, passed the throngs of reporters unmolested, and returned with burgers and shakes. That night, they played cards, laughed, and told childhood stories. Since Emma had to return to SLC with her mom the next day, at least they would have one night, and Winter Park was as good as Denver in the scheme of things when you're young. They made promises to each other at night and fell asleep in each other's arms before the morning star rose.

The nurse knocked on the door. Justin climbed off the bed, turned the lock to open the door, and then moved it open an inch. "Sorry to disturb you, but you requested a personal wake-up call."

"Yes, thank you, nurse. Would it be possible to have breakfast sent up? Thank you."

After breakfast, Justin said, "Well, Em, today is the day. I'm sure your mom will be here soon to rescue you from your terrible ordeal." She held his hand. "When you get settled back home, I'll come for you. Have you called the office yet? Maybe they can hold your job?"

"My mom said no more of this. I have to go home, or they will stay in prison. I don't have any other choice."

Emma grabbed her phone and said, "Oh, look, here is a video of Roy getting the reward money, and there's my mom giving him a check." She shook her head. "It's terrible, Honey, terrible. How can bad people always win? She is the cause of all of this and Roy, well, he is just a despicable human, just like… My own mother."

"Don't give up, Emma, something will come up." He stood and leaned over and kissed her as the door knocked.

"That must be your mom, and I guess I should be leaving for now. Don't give up. I love you, Darlin."

He opened the door, and the lady said, "Hi, I'm Officer Grant, Federal Marshall's Office Denver. May I have a word with Emma, please?"

"Oh, we thought you were Mrs. Chase. Please come in."

Chapter 28

Justin said, "Sometimes fate comes knocking and letting her in is best. That's what my uncle taught me. I am Justin Case, and I have been with Emma on the train for the last several days."

Emma nodded to the officer, "Yes, and he can attest that I was never abducted or forced in any way."

The officer carried with her a briefcase. She said, "Hi, sorry to bother you, love birds, but I have your report, and I thought you might find it intriguing. First of all, the exam proved there was no prior intercourse. That will help with your request, and it should reduce the charges for the men considerably.

"But there should not be any charges. They are all innocent." Said, Justin.

"Well, certain powers disagree on that point, so there will be charges made, and unless the men can afford bail, they will remain incarcerated until their trial date. There is still a matter of assault. You were found unconscious on the train with one of the men attacking you."

Emma shook her head, "So if someone gives someone CPR, then that gives you the right to shoot them for trying to save the other person's life, really?"

Justin said, "Hey, I was there too; no one has asked me what happened yet. Remember, I was the one that went to get the pick-up when you stopped me at gunpoint? I remember you from that night, Officer Grant. That night, I tried to tell you what was happening and to help us, but you had other ideas. I hope Cisco sues the police and wins. I hope that you have to apologize for trying to kill him for being a good Samaritan."

"I appreciate your opinions, but for now, my business does not concern you or your opinions." She held her eyes on his, and he nodded to Emma.

"Darlin, I'll be out in the hall." He gave the lady one more look as he exited. He turned back to the officer and said, "Why do I get the feeling you are not going to go through with all this gibberish of trying Cisco?"

She watched until the door closed, and then she brought a folder from her case.

"Emma, here is your pelvic report and one from your DNA analysis. You might find this more than just interesting. And Justin is right with his last remark. Here, take it." She offered the folder. Emma looked down at it and moved her hand away. "Please, take it for Mr. Garcia."

The agent's phone rang, "One second, Hello… yes… yes… I am with the victim now… I can be there in an hour. Thank you."

She turned to Emma, "That was the district attorney, and apparently, she wants a meeting to review the evidence before formal charges are filed."

"What are they Looking at for time?"

"Worse case, up to twenty years each, but if the evidence is weak, maybe three years."

"What evidence do you have?"

"We have eyewitnesses from Green River that claim they knew you were being abducted, and there is another that claims you were abducted."

"Roy, just to collect the reward, asshole." Emma shook her head. "He was the only one who tried to make out with me, and he gets a nice reward for lying."

"Read this report, Emma, and I'm going to get coffee. Can I bring you back anything?"

"Why, what are you trying to tell me that's in here?"

Just read the report, and call me if you have any questions."

Emma tilted the bed higher and switched on her reading light. Her phone beeped, then left a message as she began to read the report. She flipped through the pages and then grabbed her phone. "Officer, I don't understand, so can you explain this? Thank you."

The door knocked, and Officer Grant entered. She and Emma talked for an hour. She pointed to the report and showed another report based on the DNA. Exhausted, Emma handed this second file back to agent Grant. Emma lay in silence when the door closed behind the officer. She looked across to the stooks where her new outfit lay draped. She lifted the blanket, pushed the stool away with her leg, and clutched the folders to her chest. For years, Emma dreamed of gaining her mom's adoration and approval. For years, she wanted to be just like her brothers. Now she lay in a hospital bed, just after her twenty-first birthday, in trouble with her mom and her only real friends going to prison. Their only crime was being friends with her. Her happiness never did matter. Only her self-image as a senator's daughter and her ability to behave accordingly mattered. Now she understood why.

Her door opened, and her mom said, "What are you doing? You should be dressed. Get up from there this instance, or I'll be late." She pointed to her assistants and the new clothes. "Get her dressed, I'll be back." She flew out the door, throwing it open.

Emma said, "STOP, get her back in here. I'm not going anywhere."

Her mom returned and crossed her arms, "Now what is it, you little impf? Haven't you caused enough trouble?"

Emma motioned for the others to leave the room, then she climbed from her bed and stood momentarily clutching the rail until she regained her balance. She slowly walked across her room to the window. Outside, the birds flew about, busy with their morning, and tourists unloaded bikes and gear from cars. Her mom stood in silence when Emma turned and smiled.

"Well, mom, you did it this time... I suppose you'll want a cigarette when we are finished having our little family chat. I doubt just one will do. No, you're going to need a whole pack of smokes." She opened one of the folders, "It says here no one assaulted me. Hell, the doctor did the exam and signed off on it with a federal agent as a witness, along with a police officer. So, what crime was committed? Abduction is your claim, though no one will admit to it except for some skank named Brittaney and Roy, who collected the reward profited from your false claims. It'll be a real embarrassment to the department when this goes to trial." Emma walked back across to the new clothes on the stool. She held them. "Designer this and designer that, ha, hate them would never select any of these to wear. Mom, what are you even doing here? Is your election campaign going that bad? Is the Democrat actually going to unseat you? Because never in my life were you ever there just for me."

"Stop this nonsense now. We have a deal unless you have forgotten. Keep this up, and I'll walk out that door, and those men will rot in prison for the rest of their lives. How could you hang out with a bunch of Mexicans, of all things?"

"You mean Mexicans, as in Eduardo Sanchez?" She kept her eyes on her mom. She watched as her mom swallowed.

She looked at Emma and said, "I don't know who you're talking about."

"Are you sure about that, Mom? I bet you can't wait to stick a cigarette in your mouth. Ooh, that urge is getting to your mind. I can see it. Right now, that's all you want. To smoke."

"Get on with it, Emma. What games are you playing?"

"Well, Eduardo is half Mexican and was in the US Marines. In fact, he was on the same base before I was born. He was later sent overseas to fight just like Dad. But, unlike Dad, he is back in the United States. How would you like to have a reunion with him, mom?"

One of the things that happened yesterday, along with that disgusting pelvic exam, was a DNA test so they could discern whose DNA was whose for the rape test. As it turned out, here are my DNA results. I am a quarter Mexican, your illegitimate love child from an affair twenty-one years ago with Mr. Random Dude. Mom! When were you going to tell me? Huh?"

"It's not true, there's a mistake, it's not—"

"It is true, you know it; there is no mistake. You lied to me my entire life. That's why I could never be as good as my half-brothers, and that's why you and your husband fought so much after I was born. He knew the truth and drank himself to death. No burglar assaulted him."

"Yes, he tried to protect his family but was stabbed by an illegal Mexican."

"No, Mom, that's your lies. He took a garden hose and hooked it to the tailpipe of the car, closed the garage doors, and ran the car till he died. Anything to get away from you. Now I understand why."

"No, you are a terrible daughter. How can you say such evil?"

"Mom, I'm not one of your adoring stupid fans that will suspend reality for your bullshit. Here is what's going to happen—"

"No, you will get dressed in those clothes immediately or else…"

"Or what? No, Mom, here is what will happen: I will take my reports to those reporters downstairs waiting to talk with me, and you will not only lose the election but will disgrace the family name and probably be banned from all holidays with the Chase family. You have 3 seconds to make a call and release my friends immediately with no charges and a full apology." She handed her mom the federal marshall's card and her phone.

Emma dialed Agent Grant and handed the phone to her mom. She said, "Release them quickly after they sign agreements never to speak to anyone for security reasons. Yes, that is correct. Immediately."

After her mom made the call, Emma said, "We are done, and I never want to see you again, you psychopathic witch. Now get OUT!"

Epilogue

Six months later, it was Christmas, and Emma sat at a table at a local Chile's restaurant in Denver. Her hair was cut shorter and shaped tinted midnight black; it curved inward, giving a soft, classic look to her rounded face and enhancing her dark eyes. Francisco stopped at the table, leaped up, and grabbed him in a big hug. She pulled him so tight he could not breathe.

She said, "Oh, I missed you so much. Come have a seat."

Francisco's short beard could not hide his big smile as he looked at her. The corners of his eyes sparkled like a boy with a magnificent secret. Emma was excited partly to see her old mentor and friend, but she also held a secret. They held hands at the table, and when the waitress arrived, they motioned for her to leave, not to interrupt their moment. As she left, they laughed with each other.

Emma said, "You first…"

"Ladies first…," said Francisco.

"Very well, so, how does it feel to be a multi-millionaire?"

"Well, after the lawyers got their share, it was only two and a half. Now tell me what's next for you, Emma Chase?"

"I am finishing vet school. Oh, and my name is no longer—"

From behind came a familiar voice over hers, "—That's Emma Case now,"

Emma stuck her ring finger on the table as Justin emerged from around the corner with two beer mugs and an iced tea.

Francisco stood up, stretched his hand, and said, "Congratulations."

Emma said, "Look, we are having our first baby." Her hands clasped her womb, and the sparkle in her eyes gleamed a little brighter. Francisco stared at her belly. "We are so happy, we decided on naming him after you. Will you be his Godfather?"

Francisco hugged Emma with one arm and continued to shake Justin's hand. Emma reached into her bag and pulled out a book, "Here is your book back for the next student of life. Thank you for so many, many, many great gifts. Come, let's all eat, I'm starved. Cisco, with all that money, surely you can buy."

"Oh, I have another one along the way, and I was accepted to USC film school starting next semester."

"So, the family has kept you very busy these days. I read another book recently, and I think it may be by the same mystery author," she set another book out. "Have you read this one yet?"

Francisco picked it up and flipped through the pages, "How was it? Did you find it too boring?"

Justin chuckled, "No, Emma couldn't put it down. Who would have thought a story about boredom could be so fascinating." He waved for the waitress and said, "You have some explaining to do; either you quoted this author, or he has stolen your quotes."

Emma paused took a drink of water with Cisco watching, After swallowing she asked, "Have you seen Roy lately?"

Francisco nodded and said, "Not long ago I visited him. H is doing good. These days he has become a sort of chess champion. What about you?"

"Not since the trial. Why Cisco? I don't get it. Him, my mom, why are some people like that?"

He said, "I don't know Emma, but I think deep down they want to be loved and are just scared of rejection."

Emma shook her head then lifted it with a grin. She dug into her purse and laid a card on the table. "Look Cisco, we were invited to the Chase Christmas party, which was amazing. We were back in upstate New York with the Chase family. You are not going to believe what my Christmas gift was. A ranch in Colorado just outside of Denver."

Francisco choked on his water. He tapped his chest and coughed. Then he said, "But, wait… didn't you discover who your real father was?"

"It's strange how people will react when you have power, so I guess maybe there was a bit of guilt for all those years of doting over my brothers, or maybe it's for my silence. I want to think maybe they are proud of me in their own way. No matter, I am proud of me."

Justin said, "The last few months have brought many good changes, and look at Emma. She's like a new person."

"I feel washed and clean, like I have been given a new me since that day we met."

Fransisco nodded, "All those years you were waiting for life to start needing you mom's approval. You broke away from your mom, saved the crew and saved my life. To do that takes a real good person Emma. I believe that one could say that what changed is now you're self-empowerment, so now you have the power to be the real you. Welcome to your own world."

THE END